To Pat,

Happy reading

Pursuing Happiness
...one more time

from Mary Lou

A novel

Mary Lou Peters Schram

authorHOUSE®

AuthorHouse™
1663 Liberty Drive, Suite 200
Bloomington, IN 47403
www.authorhouse.com
Phone: 1-800-839-8640

First published by AuthorHouse   3/16/2009

ISBN: 978-1-4389-5482-0 (sc)

Library of Congress Control Number: 2009901347

Printed in the United States of America
Bloomington, Indiana

This book is printed on acid-free paper.

Previous Novels by Mary Lou Peters Schram

"Stranger in the Dark" - Berkeley Books (now out of print)

"KLIK" - iUniverse, 2004

"Taddy and Her Husbands" - iUniverse, 2007

For lovely Ingrid
who was with us too short a time

Chapter One

Marion told Bridget this. Later on, when she could talk about it.

When it happened, she hardly knew what to do. One moment she was standing staring down at him as his color slowly faded. The next she was at the nurse's station signing something, maybe the bill. Almost the very next moment she was standing at the front entrance, outside the double doors that 'whooshed' importantly when anyone entered behind her. She was alone. It had all been so sudden she hadn't had time to call anyone to join her there.

She had driven here, she knew that, but couldn't remember where she had parked her car. After some minutes, she turned and went back inside and asked to use the phone on the Volunteers' desk.

The sign overhead said 'INFORMATION', but that was a misnomer. Even when someone came to the desk with a question, the volunteers, a bevy of pigeons in white hair and pink uniforms, were usually too busy talking to each other to give out any answers.

They hardly looked at Marion. They gestured toward the phone and went back to their twitter.

Marion called Alice, her sister. She apologized because Alice was at work, and gave her the news. Alice's voice came over the phone in a screech of alarm.

"Of course, I'll come, but I don't know how soon." She would meet Marion at the house, as soon as she could get someone to relieve her. She couldn't just leave Dr. Felder with no one to help him.

"Why did he go and do that? Isn't that just like Jeb? I'll get there as soon as I can, but it may not be till afternoon."

Marion wondered what she was supposed to do till then. She guessed that she was becoming invisible. She went back outside and walked up and down the parking lot till she found her car.

She drove the old Tercel home and put it in the garage beside Jeb's Navigator. How would she deal with two cars? The sun was shining but inside the house was cold. They had left at 4 a.m. without turning on the heat. She was cold and limp, feeling as if she hadn't enough force to even punch the light switch.

"It's not fair," she said out loud.

She wandered through her house, touching objects, trying to banish their strangeness, bring back their familiarity. Jeb's blue plaid shirt was hanging on a kitchen chair. He had had it on the day before and she had never put it away. She picked it up and then put it down again. The coffee was still plugged in. When they got up at Jeb's insistence that something was wrong, she had made the coffee automatically, then they had left for the hospital without drinking any.

At the nurse's station, they had asked her what funeral home did she want to use and could they do an autopsy? She had never thought about those things, had no opinions, was afraid to say yes or no. Jeb had always made the decisions.

She unplugged the coffee, having a struggle to get the plug out of the socket. Nothing was going to be like it had been or act as it should.

She leaned against the patio doors and looked out. Leaning there, her forehead against the cool glass, she was nearly felled with loneliness. To have only herself in the house didn't give it enough energy to operate. She could visualize lights going out and clocks quitting, all because there was only her there. She had a moment of cold anger. He had promised her more than this. How did he think she was going to cope?

She wanted to hear his voice. It might still be on the answering machine. He left messages for her from time to time, calling on his cell phone, which he had no other purpose for since he retired, saying he was going to be late or wanting to know what to buy at the store. She went to the telephone alcove and pressed the button for messages.

The machine flew into action, rewound, then beeped and the spectral voice said 'no messages'. Jeb, of course, had erased the messages. She went back to the glass doors, looking at the deep green lawn behind the house. Surely he was right out there – or else in the garage - and would come through those doors in a minute. She listened for him but could hear nothing except the distant sound of a phone ringing in the house next door.

Her elbows were cold. Her head ached. Deep inside, she felt hollow, as if she had caved in so there was nothing inside her to keep her back bone and chest apart. That feeling of hollowness frightened her and only minutes later, a sob came that was so deep she bent over double with it.

Oh God, this couldn't be happening.

Finally she got the box of tissues out of the downstairs lavatory and took them and lay down on the living room couch and just kept crying. There seemed to be nothing else she could do. Nothing would change anything anyway, the future was closed off, everything had ended right here.

When Alice finally arrived at something after four, she rang the bell then bustled in without waiting for a response. She was flurried, her hair tossed around this way and that. Her rubber-soled shoes squeaked as she walked. "I couldn't get away. I'm so sorry. We had a ton of patients and I couldn't get anybody to come in."

Marion sat up on the couch where she had been dozing and Alice sat down beside her and they embraced awkwardly, their full bosoms butting. Embraces didn't come easily to them, and Alice was clearly scared of Marion's condition, leaning back to look at her critically.

"You look a sight. Did you faint?"

"I don't know."

 "How could he die? He wasn't even sick."

"I don't know. Heart, I guess."

"Did you eat anything?"

"No."

Alice went to look in the refrigerator. "There's not much here."

"I don't want anything."

"You have to eat."

"Not now."

Alice fished a pillbox from her purse and extracted a pill. Without explaining it, she got a glass of water and gave it to Marion who obediently swallowed it.

3

Alice was taking charge which is what Marion had been waiting for all these hours. Alice was good at that and now that her children were grown, she hardly ever had a crisis to get her teeth into.

"Go to bed."

"Should I really?"

"Yes." Alice was an RN and therefore to be obeyed. Marion climbed the stairs, already convinced that she would sleep.

*   *   *

The rest, Bridget knew from her own experience. Right away Alice had sat down and started calling Marion and Jeb's three children as well as Marion and Alice's two brothers, and a couple of Marion's friends who lived nearby, including Bridget.

It was not an easy job. The same things had to be said over and over, at least twice to each person she talked to. People had trouble taking it in all at once. "No, nobody knows what was wrong with him. It just came on suddenly. No, no funeral arrangements have been made yet. Yes, Marion seems to be bearing up but is lying down right now."

Bridget arrived first. She was wearing orange silk, not the best choice for the occasion, but she hadn't wanted to waste time changing.

Alice was much relieved to have someone to share her burden with.

"Do you think I should call the hospital? I feel like an idiot with no more information than this."

"Ask Marion," Bridget said.

Alice thought that was a good idea; she went upstairs to get better instructions but found Marion fast asleep.

When she came down, she said to Bridget, "I never liked him. I wish she hadn't married him. He had no imagination at all and he was a very fussy eater. Now see how it's ended. They're both only sixty five; they should have had some retirement years."

Bridget nodded, taking off her jacket. "I didn't really know him but Marion always seemed happy enough. And the children turned out all right, didn't they? They all seem to have jobs."

"Yes, they're okay. But Jeb was no brain, to tell the truth, and he made some unfortunate decisions about his pension. They should have retired with a lot more. It was Marion who made everything work. She would have made anyone happy, no matter whom she married."

Alice took off her glasses to wipe her eyes. "Our mother was like that, just got busy cooking and cleaning and saw to it that everyone else was happy and never thought much at all about herself or what she wanted. Not too many of those around any more."

"What can I do?" Bridget asked.

"Do you know anything about funeral homes?"

Bridget nodded vigorously. She felt herself expanding with the opportunity to offer something of use. It was what she had come for.

"I know all about funeral homes. I talked to every one of them when Eve Saintsbury died. There's only one good one, unless you're Catholic."

"Good, you can do it again. We're not Catholic. You call and I will concentrate on getting dinner."

In spite of the pill, which had only been a Tylenol, Marion woke up after a while and came downstairs to see what was happening. Her hair was flattened and her blouse wrinkled from lying down. It was five thirty and Bridget was sitting at the diningroom table with the cordless phone and the phone book while Alice was in the kitchen.

Bridget didn't say anything but got up and put her arms around Marion who clung to her warmth.

"Dear, I'm so sorry."

"Did you get all the children?"

"Alice did."

Alice came forward from the kitchen. "They want to know what to do, when to come. Should I tell them to come tomorrow?"

"I don't know. You decide." Marion was still clinging to Bridget who was patting her on the back rather awkwardly. When Bridget disengaged herself, Marion stood there helplessly until Alice came to take her by the arm and lead her to the couch.

"Are you hungry?" Alice asked, sniffling a little and tucking in her blouse. Her tops were always pulling up too far and blousing out. "I'll make you some lunch – I know you never got lunch. Did you get breakfast? - then I'll start dinner for whoever is going to be here by dinnertime."

"No, no breakfast. They brought me some coffee."

Marion backed up and lay down on the couch again.

"Go in the freezer. There's spaghetti sauce already made, and a turkey breast that has to be defrosted before it's cooked."

"I've already made a meatloaf with that hamburger you had, but I haven't put it in the oven yet. Bro and Letitia will be here about nine. Probably they won't eat on the way. They'll stay here overnight. You know Letitia, she likes to be in the middle of everything."

"Is Addie coming? I'd like to see Addie."

Alice nodded, agreeing with the need for a daughter. "She's going to try to get here by tomorrow night."

Marion started to cry again, but she was prepared with a wad of tissues in her hand. "What will we do with all of them?"

"I'll sleep on the couch, Bro and Letitia can have the spare bedroom, and Addie can go over to my house."

"Someone can stay with me," Bridget said. "Marion, I've been calling the funeral homes and I have all the information written down. You just have to make a choice."

"I don't know anything about funeral homes. Why did he have to die now, just before we were to go to Alaska?"

"Do you want him to be cremated or buried in the ground? If you want him buried, you'll need a plot. You don't have one, do you?"

"No."

"Maybe he better be cremated."

"That doesn't sound very nice." Marion's face sagged. "I don't think Jeb would like being cremated."

Alice and Bridget exchanged glances.

Bridget said, "Dear, you were a good wife to him. You had a good marriage. That's all you have to think about now. Don't worry about these other things. Be happy that he didn't suffer, didn't know what was happening. Did he?"

Marion was curled on the couch again, her head on a pillow. "I don't know. He was frightened. Because it came on so sudden and we didn't know what it was. You know Jeb. He always got mad if he wasn't in charge."

Alice nodded. "Men are all like that. It's good when they don't linger because they can't handle it."

"If you decided on the crematorium, they have the service right there, in place of a funeral parlor," Bridget said, wanting some results from all her efforts.

Alice said, "I think I'll call Reverend Schroeder and let him help you with these decisions."

"All right. If you want to."

"I'll do it," Bridget said.

Alice stood up, shaking out Marion's apron which she had put on. "Maybe I should defrost the turkey breast also. We have to have enough food. You know Bro's appetite."

Marion began to cry again, soundlessly, mopping her eyes with the tissue wadded up in her hand.

Bridget was amazed. She had never thought of Marion as a crier.

"I'm sure you can get your money back from Alaska," she offered. "I'll make that call tomorrow."

The Reverend Schroeder was away until Friday. Bridget was at a standstill again.

"What do you think?" she asked Alice.

"I think we should wait and let Bro make the decision about cremation or burial," Alice decided and Marion had nothing to say.

When the turkey breast was in the microwave and the meatloaf in the oven, Alice came back into the living room. Traces of old tears showed on her face.

Bridget was sitting restlessly at the diningtable. "Poor Alice," she said.

Alice shook her head. "This is all too familiar. It's only been five years. That's what I got for marrying an older man."

Bridget silently pointed at Marion whose eyes were closed.

Alice nodded. "Marion, do you have any pills?" she whispered.

The eyes flew open. "What kind?"

"Something to calm you down. I think you should take a shower and then a pill and another nap while Bridget and I talk about what else has to be done. Do we wait for Reverend Schroeder?"

Marion went obediently upstairs again with Alice. They found an aspirin with codeine, leftover from Jeb's gum surgery. Alice got her into a nightie and under the covers. "We'll take care of everything. You just sleep and you'll feel better in the morning."

"I'm afraid I'll have bad dreams."

"No, you won't. Lie down and I'll bring you a glass of wine. On top of that pill, you won't know a thing."

7

Bro and Letitia arrived at eight thirty because they had broken the speed limit the whole way. Along with Bridget who was still waiting for more to do, Bro and Letitia ate meatloaf and turkey both; then Alice settled them in the spare bedroom. Before they went to bed, cremation was decided on and an appointment made. Bridget called the Reverend Schroeder at Tahoe and notified him that he was needed back here. She also called all the neighbors she thought were worthy and told the likely time of the service.

It was nine thirty when Alice had the dinner dishes cleared, and the dishwasher loaded and running. She was now trying to remember where the spare blankets were for her makeshift bed. She had found some sheets and laid them on the sofa but couldn't find any blankets. She looked about to come undone.

Bridget decided it was time for her to go. "Just call me tomorrow when you want me," she said. "Here, I'll do those sheets for you. I can run home and get a blanket if you need one."

"There's the throw. That will be enough. Do you think she's doing all right?"

"We'll see tomorrow. We can always take her in to the doctor's and get something stronger."

"She's never been a pill-taker."

"She's never been a widow before. Pills are important."

"I should know," Alice sighed.

"I've never been a widow," Bridget confessed. "I always got divorced. I guess that's easier."

"Well, definitely easier than the death of someone you lived with most of your life. I don't know how we stand it."

Bridget patted her shoulder, thinking every family should have a nurse like Alice. "You are very good for her."

"She can't expect me to be here all the time," Alice complained, already worn out with caretaking. "My vacation is next week, and I'm going to Atlanta to see my son's family. I've been waiting for that all year."

Bridget nodded. "Of course you need to go. Someone will be here."

Chapter Two

Jessie Slater came home from the office at 5:30 and dropped into her favorite chair, kicked off her shoes and closed her eyes. Her shoulders hurt from leaning over a computer as did her ear from being pressed to the phone; also her eyes burned. All this even though she hadn't gotten into the office till 9:30 and had left at 4:30, not a long day.

The computer and the phone were bad enough but what had finished her off was the traffic; her commute was twenty miles through Marin County where every year a few thousand more cars traveled north to open fields and hillsides. Unfortunately for them, the pristine land retreated as more and more houses were built, which put more and more cars on the road the next year.

Her Volvo was showing its age by vibrating at high speeds until she had turned off at the exit for Route 37.

4PWB802. Why was she remembering that? That license plate on a black BMW that had been ahead of her much of the trip had worked its way into her consciousness because she had had a spurt of fear. Maybe she was driving too close and the BMW would brake, then she would have to brake and the car following her too closely would crash into her rear end. She could almost feel the impact ahead of time. Of course, she could claim, rightly, that it was all the fault of the BMW who would, by the time the highway patrol came, be out of sight, maybe even parked at home and its owner enjoying his cocktail while he looked over the job his gardener had done that day.

All this fantasy had etched the license plate into her memory although her mind was sometimes like a sieve at work, unable to remember the addresses of houses she needed to see.

She tried to turn her mind to quiet, comforting thoughts. It still looked like mid-day outside. The May sunshine streaming through the slats of her white shutters was still brilliant and beautiful as if informing her that there was still time for this day to be rescued, to produce some form of happiness. Happiness. It was not too late for that.

She closed her eyes and then opened one to see the clock on the mantel. It was a 19th century shelf clock made in Connecticut that chimed the hours; she thought it added gravitas and history to her living room. The trouble was that it had to be wound every night and there were nights when she swore she was going to sell it instead. Last night she must have wound it because it was ticking away and now said 5:45.

Time to stand up and get busy. She continued to sit.

Edgar was due at 6:30 for cocktails and they had a dinner reservation at 7:15, the time he always insisted on for dinner. She had planned on leaving the office earlier, allowing time for a nap and a shower to restore her, but some new listings had appeared and she had been busy at her computer (still not as skillful at it as the young realtors were) trying to read all the details.

Also she had lost a client - the Philbys - who she had counted on selling a house to in the next few months; they had gone over to another agent for reasons unknown. Were her skills leaving her or had the market turned against her? She wasn't as quick on her feet as the younger ones. Where did they learn the tricks they came up with? She had made a reasonable living for a many years. Now though, the business had gotten more cutthroat as the prices of housing, and therefore the size of commissions went up.

There were other things she knew she had lost with the years. Like her ability to laugh at herself, and the pleasure she used to take in finding a house that delighted a client. Was this her penalty for staying in the business too long?

The clock ticked again, and the graceful hand moved up a notch. She closed her eyes hoping that would help the burning sensation. She was aware of smells - the roses on the coffee table - this morning's coffee, and sounds - a whining at the door which she had been ignoring. The dogs were still in the yard but of course they knew she was home. They wanted to be indoors with her.

The whining had turned to a scratching. She got up and walked swiftly to the French doors to the garden. Scratching was forbidden; they would scrape the paint off the door. She opened it and was engulfed in 200 pounds of Afghan - Tiburon and Belvedere, or Tibby and Belvy. Tibby was a light blonde male and Belvy a dark grey female, both neutered of course, and they were the height that allowed them to rest their chins on the dining table or, if you were sitting on the couch, your shoulder.

"WHAT DO YOU THINK YOU'RE DOING?" she shouted at them. (It was lucky there was a garage and a wall of bushes, sound barriers, between Jessie and her nearest neighbor.)

They dropped to the floor and looked up pleadingly.

"YOU THINK YOU HAVE A RIGHT TO BE INSIDE, BUT YOU DON'T. NOT TILL I WANT YOU. DO YOU UNDERSTAND THAT?"

Two pairs of dark eyes lowered at the scolding and the skin on their noses quivered, accepting the criticism.

"YOU THINK LIFE IS NOTHING BUT A BOWL OF KIBBLE, DON'T YOU? AND THERE IS NOTHING ELSE I HAVE TO DO BUT TAKE CARE OF YOU. WELL, THAT'S NOT TRUE." Her voice lowered its volume and pitch, and now became reasonable. "If I want to be home for a while without paying attention to you, I'm entitled to it."

The dogs noticed the change in tone and their heads came up eagerly.

"PAY ATTENTION!"

Their heads went down obediently, but not as low as they had been, and their eyes stayed on her, waiting out her mood. When someone went out to choose a dog, she should be careful not to get one with too much intelligence. Living with even a dumb dog required constant alertness; an intelligent one was three times that much trouble.

In her stockinged feet, Jessie limped back to her chair, the calves of her legs aching from the high heels she had worn. Edgar would arrive promptly; he always did. Why had she said yes? She didn't even like eating dinner anymore. It made her groggy but unable to sleep until it was digested. She did better on a big lunch and only yogurt or salad for dinner but if she tried limiting herself to one appetizer, Edgar would be upset.

"That's why I take you out to dinner," he would say. "So you can eat a proper meal."

When she was at the office, the fact that she had a date that night made her life more interesting, her work more bearable. She might even drop some hint of it to her co-workers. But once she was home, the anticipation of it tended to fade.

Some days the memory of long years of unhappiness pressed on her, and were not appeased by her current pleasant life. She had stayed in an unhappy marriage for years and years, not knowing what else to do. Now women knew better. A wife could walk away. Many doors were open. The younger women saw this but Jessie had come very late to this understanding.

The dogs were still hovering nearby, their minds on dinner.

"Kiss kiss," Jessie said.

Two snouts were pushed into her face and she put a hand on each head and talked nonsense to them. When she had run down, they made a quick trip to the kitchen to see if anything had appeared magically in their bowls. When these were found empty, the two hurried back, a moving tide of need advancing through the room. Being more or less trained, they then sat primly in front of her and whined again. They had been rescue dogs. Jessie had been persuaded by the woman in charge of Afghan Rescue to take the pair just for a month, but she had found their devotion too rewarding to give up. That had been five years ago.

"All right. All right." She heaved herself to her feet. Dogs served the same function children did, they kept you active, burning off calories even when what you wanted was rest.

After feeding them, she hurried to change her clothes and then went into the bathroom to repair her make-up. She nodded at herself in the bathroom mirror, pleased with her reflection. She was still the best-looking woman in her office, and probably the best looking one in Shady Acres too. Yes, she had come a long way but too bad she hadn't worked out how to accomplish that when she was thirty and desperately unhappy. It was almost as if everyone really needed to live twice; the first time to find out how to do it; the second time to put it into practice.

Surveying herself, she decided to remove the brown mascara and in its place, add green plus some false eyelashes and see if that would freshen the tired look. She was in the middle of this intricate task when the doorbell rang. She ignored it and a minute later could hear the door opening, Edgar's privilege after years of friendship.

"Hello there!" he called out.

"I'm in the bathroom."

Instead of coming to her, she could hear him go to the kitchen and open the freezer for two frosted glasses. He would be making their martinis. She added the bright green to her eyelids cautiously; the magazines always recommended stronger color for evenings. Yes, it helped some. She could hear the shaking of ice in the martini pitcher. When was it she had stopped liking martinis? But that never stopped Edgar, a creature of many habits.

He believed habits were good for one, they were what kept the world going around; it was restful to mankind to do the same thing over and over. One could forget about daily tasks, let the cerebral cortex take over, save one's mental efforts for something more important.

"Come and get it!"

When she went out to the living room, he had the martinis on the coffee table and was standing at the French doors looking at her garden, his trim grey self an appropriate note in her handsome living room.

A good looking man, an intelligent man, interesting to talk to. It was only after some time that it became apparent he was chockful of unfortunate ideas. He had retired ten years ago and his wife had promptly died. No longer working and then wifeless, he was doubly bereft, he had neither enough to do nor any feminine encouragement. Someone told Jessie that he had been a star at the university. That increased her interest; never having gone to college herself, she had been flattered by his attention. She had offered her sympathy and he had been in her life ever since.

Almost like the dogs.

He turned and smiled at her. He had a pointed chin and grey-white hair cut to a quarter of an inch. Thin and fit, with that air of command that most men seemed to lose when they retired. Really, every other woman in Shady Acres envied her.

"Well, don't you look exceptionally nice!"

"Thank you." Jessie sank to the sofa and accepted the drink. She had put on flat shoes to rest her back, and white slacks, and a bright green silk blouse, which, with the eye shadow, had brightened her look. Now if only the drink would take away the ache in her shoulders.

"You're tired, aren't you?" He had taken a chair close by and was peering into her face.

"A little."

"It's that job. Jessie, why are you working at your age?"

She sighed. She was not going to say she actually needed the money. "Money is nice."

He snorted. "You have your social security; you have your husband's pension. You have investments. I don't believe you need to work. I think you just don't know how to tell them you're quitting."

"What is it people do when they retire except get lazy and fat?"

Since this was obviously not true of Edgar, he didn't know how to reply so she chose to amend. "Can we please not have this discussion right now?"

That was hard for him. She could see him struggling with all the things he usually said and wanted to say again. Jessie should stay home, get plenty of rest and exercise and then be ready for all the activities he was always planning. She could do some volunteer work if she got bored. She would be much happier, not to mention healthier, and they would have a better time together. They could take short car trips to the mountains or down the coast.

"When can we have this discussion?"

"It seems to me we've had it a lot." She usually didn't say things that sharply. She raised her eyes to his, pleadingly.

"Okay," he said after a minute. "Shall we go to Avignon?"

"Fine." Didn't they always?

At Avignon, Jessie ordered mussels. It was an appetizer, but almost a dinner, so it satisfied Edgar that she was really eating. She passed up the bread and finally agreed to a small salad and one glass of wine. It all sat heavily on her stomach and her shoulders were no less tired than they had been at home.

"You could take up gourmet cooking," he said halfway through the meal.

"Why don't *you* take up gourmet cooking?" Jessie smiled.

He shook his head in surprise. "You're really not feeling well, are you?"

The sympathy unnerved her. She looked away. "Oh, not too bad."

But if she said she felt fine, he would want to spend the night and she was just too tired for all that.

He stole a look at her. After a minute, he accepted what she was not saying, and looked away, disappointed, his sharp chin turning downward a little. He began talking about his day in the college library. He was researching in preparation for writing a book about what had happened to their California town during the Civil War. He had been looking up sources and taking notes for several years now but didn't seem ready to get to the writing part.

At the end of the evening, he escorted her properly to her door and stopped there.

"I guess I won't come in," he said, testing the waters.

"Not tonight. Maybe Sunday."

He nodded, accepting it but disappointed. He squared up his shoulders and gave her a quick kiss on the cheek.

Once he was gone and she had shed her clothes for a nightie, Jessie sat up in her bed with cream on her face and a romance novel, and then turned on the television so she wouldn't have to read it. News, blah, blah, blah. Music from the sixties, a reprise for all the old folks. A sitcom with a gay character, now all the rage. It occurred to her that with all these elderly men in Shady Acres, most of them past sex, it was almost like having a raft of gay characters.

At least Edgar wasn't entirely past sex, although he relied more on her activities than his own. She turned the TV off and leaned back on the pillows and listened to the silence.

Or rather the silence punctuated by the sound of Belvy licking herself.

"Stop that."

Of course what the dog did was come to the bed and rest her chin on the covers, begging with her eyes for a pet. Jessie obliged, stroking her head. She had had to take them out when she came back from dinner but had cheated on their expedition, taking them only a few blocks on leashes because she was too tired to go farther. She usually tried to run them for half an hour in the morning. They deserved some attention; they never told her to quit working.

"All right, there you are. Now lie down."

Belvy retreated to her cushion in the corner and lay down but Tibby got up and came for his share. After she gave him pets, Jessie waved him away and thought tiredly about Edgar. Where was all the excitement, the warmth and satisfaction that was supposed to come with having a man in your life? She hadn't found that. Did other women make all that up?

She wouldn't dare quit work if Edgar was around to organize her life. She wasn't going to quit anyway. If she quit, she wouldn't have quite enough to live comfortably. Also, the need to go out to a job kept her on her toes, kept her paying attention to how she dressed and how she looked, kept her mind focused. She didn't want to let herself go slack, let herself get old.

She might find an office that would let her work part-time but that would leave her more vulnerable to the plans of Edgar Santee, former history professor, lover of tennis matches, martinis and trips to Hawaii, all things he had started doing in his twenties. She felt only irritation when she thought of him. Was there something wrong with her? But to be fair to herself, the things they did together had very little to do with her, with what she was interested in or felt like doing. Also she suspected that, in spite of his efforts to prove the contrary, he was never really interested in her opinions. She was, perhaps, mostly a reflection for him – The Woman in His Life. And yet that wasn't entirely fair. He was always eager to see her, was certainly well mannered, liked meeting new people and would talk on any subject anyone brought up.

What would her life be like without him? She instantly pictured evenings during which she spread out her art materials on the walnut dining table and started new drawings, (she had had fantasies in high school of being an artist), or rented all the tearjerker movies she wouldn't want anyone to know she watched. Wouldn't it be sheer fun to be alone and unencumbered by a man? Not everything came too late.

Twenty years ago she would have found that incredible. A woman needed a man in her life. That was a known fact. She would regret it if she did anything to end her relationship with Edgar, wouldn't she?

Who else would there be to tell her she looked wonderful and take her out for an evening?

Chapter Three

It was Bridget, sometime friend and, as she put it, "onetime May Queen", who pointed Jessie in a new direction.

Saturday was the only morning that Jessie had off this week. She was quietly drinking her coffee, savoring the silence, admiring her house. It had taken fifteen years after her only child left home and several years after her divorce was final before she finally put together a home just the way she wanted it. She had bought this house when it was in bad condition, and room by room had torn it out and started again until she was pleased.

The French doors to the patio were open even though it was still chilly; like a true Californian she could not bear to close the day out. The sun spread voluptuously across her shoulders and the dining room table while Jessie read yesterday's newspaper and waited till 9:30 when she could have her half piece of toast and half a banana.

There was no keeping Bridget out when she had decided to pay a visit. Her arrival was announced by a short toot of horn from the driveway and then she was in plain sight through the glass of the kitchen door, knocking and waving at the same time.

"Damn!" Jessie said.

There was not much she could do. Bridget seemed to like Jessie a lot more than Jessie cared for Bridget. Now she was looking directly at her.

After an earlier visit of the May Queen, during which Jessie had complained mildly about the fickleness of her clients, she heard Bridget had told a neighbor Jessie was having trouble keeping clients. In response, Jessie had called Bridget up and roundly scolded her. Didn't Bridget see that sort of rumor might cost Jessie future sales? Bridget had felt wounded and stayed away for some weeks, but just a few days ago had showed up again and Jessie found she was no longer angry.

She opened the door. "Good morning." If there was any news Jessie wanted broadcast to the neighborhood, here was her chance.

Jessie was a tall, handsome woman with a model's slenderness. Although at the moment, she was wearing an old Japanese silk robe, she was usually impeccably well-dressed even by Marin County real estate standards. It was only after a third or fourth look that one began to realize she was no longer young.

The May Queen was shorter than Jessie and wider, weighing perhaps forty more pounds. Her once-red hair now was expensively streaked with red; her mauve pants and matching shirt had been featured in Saks Fifth Avenue window on Post Street in San Francisco.. She wore a straw hat to protect her still-pretty face, and dark glasses with purple frames. She reminded Jessie of a bubbling fountain, her thoughts usually popping upward too fast to be clearly expressed, like a small engine tossing off ideas with each toot.

She waggled a white sack under Jessie's nose. "Look, I brought some pastry from Artisan. Croissants."

"How lovely," Jessie's said flatly. If she ate any pastry, she would have to forego lunch altogether. Bridget was already plump and didn't seem to care.

"There's no more coffee."

"Don't worry about it. I'll make it. Where do you keep the coffee?"

"Never mind. I'll do it."

Undismayed, Bridget opened an upper cupboard and took out a plate. When she laid out the pastry, Jessie saw two almond croissants, worth probably 400 calories each.

"How have you been? Haven't seen you for weeks."

"I'm fine."

"I saw Edgar yesterday and he told me you two were going out last night."

Jessie was startled. "How did he happen to tell you that?"

"Well, we talk now and then. We used to be married."

Jessie seldom showed surprise but this time she blinked twice and turned her large pale eyes on her neighbor. "When was that?"

"Oh, forty years ago." Bridget was a little embarrassed, almost apologetic. "I don't usually tell anyone. It was my first marriage and he was so attractive, and I was afraid no one would marry me. You know how we were then! So we were married right after I graduated. That's when he was teaching at the state college."

Edgar had never spoken Bridget's name. The thought of the two, Bridget and Edgar together, was almost impossible to imagine and yet it was funny too. Wasn't anyone what they seemed? It was easy to forget that all these people in Shady Acres, the adults of the Adult Community, had once been other than they were now.

"That's amazing. All the time I've known him, he has never mentioned your name. And I thought he had always taught at the University."

"He wasn't that happy when I moved here. Thought I was still after him or something." Bridget grinned. "I guess he was hired at the University after he wrote that book which was so popular."

"What book? How long were you married?"

"Five years. It seemed like an eternity."

At this, Jessie looked into the wide, merry face and nodded in sympathy.

Bridget was pleased at this sign of acceptance. "You see how he is now, but then he was even bossier. I can't remember the name of the book."

Jessie busied herself pouring coffee into a filter while she tried to deal with this information. You could only say they had been divorced for thirty five years so both had probably changed totally.

"And are you still friends?"

Bridget had seated herself at the table and was hungrily eyeing the croissants while she waited for the coffee. Her pale grey purse was snakeskin as were her low-heeled pumps. Another reason to dislike her

- she spent a fortune on good clothes though many of them would have looked better on Jessie's spare figure.

"Well, not exactly friends. He mostly avoids me but I always speak and so he has to answer. He's always interesting to talk to, don't you think, if you don't stretch it out too much. And he's kept fit, hasn't he?"

"He rides his bicycle several miles every morning."

"Have you been dating him a long time?"

"Yes. Probably not as long as it seems."

Bridget looked at her with sympathy. "I know. It's a good thing he was married to what was her name? – Alison - for such a long time. Not a lot of people could put up with him."

Jessie made a face and plugged in the coffee. "I'm glad to hear you say that. I thought it was just me. What is it about him that is so irritating?"

"I was so young. It took me all of five years to get irritated but yes. He is so self-absorbed. And so rigid. But maybe you could change him. Jessie, why don't you marry him? Then you could quit working."

"You just said he was impossible to live with. Anyway, I don't want to marry anyone. And I like working."

"How could you like working? Sometimes you go in seven days a week."

"Not usually." Only when Jessie had a hot client, which, unfortunately, she didn't right now. "And I have no interest in marrying Edgar. Nor does he have any interest in marrying me. It's a friendship." She was calculating how soon she could edge the woman out the door.

"I envy you that job. Not that I would want it, but that you got good enough to make a living at it. That must be very rewarding."

Jessie looked at the May Queen with new interest. "It is, I guess. Sometimes I forget that in the day-to-day."

"Like anything else."

Jessie had brought napkins and plates to the table and now arranged them. "What have you been up to this week?"

Bridget made a pouting face. She was really quite pretty but had a wardrobe of exaggerated facial expressions. "Lawyers, nothing but lawyers. Then they want to be paid for confusing me."

Jessie murmured something comforting. It was her realtor manner. And she did feel sorry for anyone who had to pay lawyers, though not so sorry for someone like Bridget who had received shares in a number of successful businesses as a divorce settlement.

"What is it this time?"

"It's the eyewear business. One of the partners wants out so I may either have to buy him out or sell to him. It's very worrying. One of these days, I'm going to sell everything and buy an annuity and never have to go through this again."

"Really?" The coffee was ready and Jessie got up to pour it. The croissants still rested on the plate Bridget had gotten for them. Was Jessie really going to eat a croissant and ruin her diet for the day? Maybe she could eat just a little from the end. And then what? Throw it away after Bridget was gone?

Bridget had got up to look through the French doors at the garden. "Oh, your silver roses look beautiful. Would you give me a slip?"

"You can't start roses with a slip." Jessie was sure they had had this conversation before, and as before, Bridget seemed satisfied. Probably she didn't garden at all but had someone do it for her. She came back to the table to settle into her croissant.

"Delicious," Jessie said reluctantly, after a nibble.

Bridget smiled. She had really been uneasy when she arrived, not sure of her welcome. But the Edgar revelation along with the croissants seemed to have made Jessie friendly enough. "Yes, these are the best in town. And just made this morning. So, when will you quit working? When you're sixty-five?"

That was the question. Someday Jessie would just not be able to do some part of the work anymore, whether it was reading the contracts or all the driving. Maybe at that point, she would have a convenient heart attack and die. The gloominess of the thought faded in the brightness of the day. It was the first croissant Jessie had had in maybe five years. It bathed her mouth in butter and her mood went up in spite of Bridget.

"Never, as far as I'm concerned." She was not going to get pulled into a discussion of her age.

"But won't they make you quit? When you reach some birthday or other?"

"No. I'm not an employee. As long as I can do satisfactory work, it's to their advantage to have me around." She didn't add, as long as she kept producing.

"You're probably great at it, the way you are great at decorating, and that terrific party you threw last year."

The praise warmed Jessie. "I've always been good enough to make a good living. But that's getting harder and harder. The young women getting into the business seem to have been born knowing so much more than I do."

"It's the computer. I haven't worked in offices that much but I can tell you all these people under forty five must have been born knowing how to work the Internet. It's amazing, isn't it?"

"Why is that? I'll bet their parents didn't have computers, or teach them all that."

Bridget shook her head. "My second husband and I used to talk about this. They didn't even learn it at school; they learned it from each other. It was in the air they breathed."

"Does every generation grow up knowing more than their parents?"

"That would be weird, wouldn't it? I don't know. When my children were home there were too many other things to query them about."

Jessie nodded, though it was hard to remember Naomi, her only child, who had followed a man to the East Coast several years ago and hardly ever seemed able to get away for a visit.

Bridget changed the subject to Marjorie who was feeding the ducks again and was about to be fined by the Association. The Association had taken advice from a Wildlife Center that the illicit feedings disrupted the ducks' natural cycle, it made the males stay in heat all year round while the females were not. As a result, the males were constantly attacking the females and there were fewer of the females every year. No one was allowed to feed the ducks in Shady Acres.

"What is the matter with her, anyway?"

Jessie shook her head. It was not a subject that interested her very much. "Maybe she's just doesn't like a lot of rules."

Shady Acres had a homeowners association whose CC&Rs, or rule book, was so many pages that few people read the whole thing.

"I hear they're going to fine her two hundred dollars. It must be the motherly instinct; she can't stand to see anyone hungry and not feed them."

Jessie nodded. "Maybe."

"You and I have a motherly instinct but we don't transfer it to ducks."

Jessie knew she transferred it to dogs but she wasn't going to admit it.

Bridget was eating her croissant slowly. She cut off a small piece with a knife and then put it into her mouth and chewed slowly. The instant it was swallowed she cut off another one. Hers was nearly finished. Jessie still had half a croissant left and considered giving it to Bridget. Only it was very good.

"You'll never guess who just died!"

Jessie sighed. She wasn't in the mood for another neighbor's death, although since they lived in a community where everyone had to be over fifty five and a fair number were over eighty, deaths were a regular part of the news.

"Who?"

"Jeb Frewalter."

Jessie caught her breath. "I just saw him last week and he looked fine."

"I know. I saw him only three days ago. He got up the other morning saying he didn't feel well. They so seldom saw doctors, Marion didn't know one to call. She took him into Emergency, thinking they would send him home fast enough. Instead, they started giving him tests. But before they found out anything, it was too late. In a few hours, he was dead."

"What was it?"

"She didn't say. She's hardly able to talk. They were supposed to go to Alaska next week. Had been planning that trip for years."

Jessie picked up the coffee cups and took them over to the sink. She didn't want any more of this subject.

"He's just retired. I think he was only sixty five. It must have been a stroke. But he was right there in the hospital. You'd think they could do a better job than that." Bridget looked indignant. "Is that what I can expect from the hospital when I get sick?"

"They have good doctors. You don't have to worry about that."

"I give money to that hospital every year. They'd better take better care of me than that!"

"Have they scheduled a funeral? Should I send flowers somewhere?"

"They took him to Moriarty. We can call there and find out when the service is scheduled. Would you like for me to pick you up?"

Jessie felt trapped. "All right. Unless I'm at work. Then I'll come back to town and go directly."

"I keep forgetting you might be at work. It's been so long since I was. And that was only to help Norm out at his office occasionally. Doesn't it interfere with your life?"

"Bridget, I keep trying to tell you, I like working."

Bridget shook her red-streaked curls. "I can't believe that."

"Well, it's true. And because this is my only morning off, I have to go to the market and take the dogs in for their baths." Jessie stood, indicating their chat was over.

Bridget quickly gathered her purse, wiped crumbs from her mouth. "I'll go and let you get started on your day. But Jessie…"

"What?"

"Phyllis wanted me to ask you if you knew that dating service. You know, the one down in San Rafael… What's it called?"

Jessie hesitated, knowing it well, but not wanting to admit it. "Togetherness. Are they still in business?"

"Oh, I think so. A month ago they had all these ads on the radio. What do you think?"

"Tell her to go in and talk to them."

"Did you ever do that?"

"No," Jessie lied, "But I know women who did and they thought it was all right."

"They met nice men, the right age?"

"Yes. Some. But that's all I know about it. Are you interested?"

"No. I think I've had all the men in my life I can take. I tried marriage three times, and I had this long affair a couple of years ago. I've sworn off men."

"I'm thinking of doing that myself." Jessie grinned.

"Yes, I think Edgar alone could cure one."

After Bridget left and before she could have second thoughts, Jessie swept the second half of her croissant into the garbage disposal. She was suddenly lighthearted. Not everything came too late. She would get her marketing done for the week and then she would call Togetherness and make an appointment. She would get new pictures taken; the ones they had would be ten years old now, which was not permitted by Togetherness; they believed in honesty. Should she have her hair done first?

After that, maybe on Thursday or Friday, she would have her last date with Edgar.

Chapter Four

After this friendly hour with Jessie, Bridget felt herself blooming. Ever since she had seen Jessie's slender figure, stylish wardrobe and impeccable house and learned that she made a living in a tough business, Bridget had wanted to have her as a friend. However, her efforts in that direction, which had been rather awkward, had not met with encouragement. Now maybe at last they were on a good footing.

Leaving Jessie's house, she had nothing special to do. She drove away slowly, trying to decide where to go. She had been in Shady Acres only a year, and making friends had been difficult.

After her last divorce, Bridget had decided she would never marry again and, rather impetuously, had embarked on a long affair with a handsome but difficult young tennis pro. What monumental anxiety that had brought her! (Did she look too old to his friends? Was the way she dressed too old? Should she take up sailing and wear shorts? Should she lend him money?) The women she met then, other older women with younger men, mostly wanted to be friends with her so they could compare her affair with theirs. Would hers last longer than theirs?

When Bridget and the tennis pro broke up, she never saw those women again and quickly gained forty five pounds.

She decided then and there to spend more of her time with women. She remembered the days in high school and college when her friends were warm and unpretentious and excited about the blossoming possibilities of their lives. She wanted that again. That was why she had moved to Shady Acres.

After dropping off some drycleaning and checking her post office box, Bridget bought more pastry and went to see Phyllis to tell her about Jessie and Edgar as well as Jeb's upcoming funeral.

Phyllis's small house always smelled like cookies, and her coffee was excellent. Everything was polished and clean and worked well though, unlike Bridget, Phyllis had no household help. Unfortunately, Phyllis always went just that bit too far - blue in the toilets and doilies under the coffee cups, but Bridget had had a ton of aunts back in Pennsylvania who did the same so the association was pleasant.

"Come in, come in," Phyllis said in a cheerful manner as she waved from her doorway and pushed the buzzer to unlock her gate. She was the only citizen of Shady Acres Bridget had met who had a lock and buzzer on the gate to her patio.

Phyllis's once-blonde hair color had been replaced at some time in the past with the bottle variety, home-applied, which tended to be streaky, and sometimes grey at the roots. Phyllis dressed oddly too. Today she was wearing another one of her faded and washed-out sweat suits. And she was deeply suspicious of new ideas. But she was lively and warm, liked Bridget, and sometimes had interesting things to say. Bridget had found Phyllis a willing repository of confidences.

Also she felt sorry for her. Bridget had become friends with Phyllis after hearing her history.

"It shouldn't happen to anyone!" she had said one time to Marion.

"What?"

"Her life. The things that happened to her."

When Phyllis was thirty years old, she had found herself in a logging town in Northern Oregon, a single mother supporting a young daughter. She had come across the continent for a particular job with the school system so she hadn't known ahead of time what the town was like. It didn't take long to find out that in this town people saw it as an aberration of nature for a thirty-year-old woman to live without a man. She must have a husband or at least a lover to protect her.

Phyllis wasn't there a week before she was besieged by determined men and teased, gossiped about and accused by the women until she thought she would go crazy. For a good (though divorced) Catholic girl, there seemed no choice but to marry one of the many men clamoring for her attention. There didn't seem to be a lot of difference among them so she picked the least objectionable one and was married in a Lutheran church six months after she got to town.

They were still married twenty-two years later. They had moved to California for a better choice of jobs when he developed cancer of the esophagus, and then cancer of the stomach, all of which required surgeries and radiation and chemotherapy, plus nursing home stays. Their small retirement fund was soon exhausted, and they began to borrow against their house. Phyllis went back to work. Then finally when hope was gone and money in short supply, she had to give up her job and stay home to watch him die. Still he lingered. Born from covered-wagon stock, he was unwilling to quit the game.

When he died after nearly four years of illness, Phyllis owned only a small fraction of her house, an eight-year-old Toyota, a pair of hunting dogs with gastritis, and enough bills that even her creditors recommended she declare bankruptcy. Her daughter had long ago gone to Los Angeles to a separate life.

She spent the day after the funeral on her brass bed with her striped tabby and several pots of tea. She was past crying. She had to think.

Enough time had been spent on Al; now what was to happen to Phyllis? She was fifty-five, and her salary as a bookkeeper would never pay off her debts. Among all the women she'd known, it had always taken a man to get them out of financial problems, and she couldn't see that the world had changed much in spite of a few years of women's lib. What difference did that make? Men had all the money just as they always had.

She had picked the wrong man all those years ago in Oregon. She had chosen Al for his nice smile and agreeable manner but he had no savvy when it came to making or hanging onto money. That's what it takes to survive in the world.

She made an unhappy face. "He wasn't that much fun to talk to either!"

She would have to find another one.

"But where do I find one?" She didn't know a single unmarried man!

"There aren't any loose men our age. That's what they all said to me, but I refused to believe it. I said, more men than women get born. I read that in a magazine. They're somewhere, but where?"

No one knew. Her friends had mostly been married for years. So Phyllis had put a leash on the tabby cat and walked it slowly around the block, waiting patiently while it lay down, spreading its soft striped flesh on a comfy patch of green and began to wash its face. No men appeared at that moment. The streets were empty.

"She shook the leash but couldn't get the cat to stand up. She had to pick her up. Nothing for it, she was going to have to get a dog if she wanted to walk something.

"Poor Phyllis," Bridget had breathed in great sympathy. "What did you do?"

"I spent hours thinking. I had never thought so hard in my life. Until it finally occurred to me that the place to find men was on the job. That's where men and women meet conveniently. But not my job. I worked in the back room of an insurance company where I saw the same four women week after week. I needed a job where I met new people every day."

"How wise of you," Bridget said to Phyllis.

"Of course she should have started using night cream and moisturizer right then since she hadn't started earlier," Bridget said to Marion.

Instead Phyllis went for the Help Wanted section of the newspaper and only three weeks later, she was introduced to her new duties. She was now a 'front desk girl' for an auto parts store.

It was usually cold there; even in summer the air conditioning was cranked all the way up; and, because of stacks of tires in each corner, it smelled of rubber till Phyllis suspected she also smelled of rubber. The floors were vinyl, highly polished, and people's shoes squeaked as they crossed the room to her counter. There were huge windows which made the light so bright she took to wearing her sunglasses. But she had been right about one thing; all day long men came through the door, often ill-tempered because something had broken, or else trying to figure out how to finagle their mechanic into installing the part without charge. Phyllis ignored their various moods and joked and teased until she could win a smile from almost all of them. Her new boss was delighted with her.

"Wasn't that smart of her?" Bridget asked Marion.

There was a catch though. Ninety-five percent of the customers were under forty. Phyllis needed a man who was sixty.

"Why? Because men always want to marry someone at least five years younger! Didn't you ever wonder about this?"

"Yes," Bridget agreed. She had finally decided that the five years was an experience advantage a man liked to have, plus, of course, a five-year younger woman was bound to be better looking than one the same age.

"Sixty was a little scary." Phyllis went on with her story. Like Al, he also might develop cancer at any moment. "However, there was nothing I could do about that. I was almost fifty-six and the years never ran backwards."

After hearing about her quest, Bridget began dropping in on Phyllis to see how it was going. At this time, Bridget was still gaining weight and, looking at herself in the mirror every day, was amazed she wasn't upset about the spreading that was transforming her body. Why did she have to keep the weight she had been in college, she asked herself. And she still had a pretty face in spite of her climbing dress size. While she professed not to be worried, she wondered whether she could ever go back to her previous size. What if she decided she also wanted to meet a man? Bridget began to call Phyllis frequently, even when she was at work, to hear of her progress.

"Better call me at home," Phyllis said finally. "My boss is beginning to notice."

Phyllis had been keeping a little tally under the corner of her desk pad, and she could tell Bridget that the odds were not good. The first week she kept track, it went something like this: Under 20 - 15; Under 30 - 26; Under 45 - 33; Over 55 - 2. One of those two surely didn't count - he was a cranky seventy-five-year old who was all of five feet tall and let out such a blast of profanity that she backed up clear to the wall. The other one, who wasn't all that good looking anyway, paid her no attention.

After three months of this, Phyllis began to be discouraged. This was a job where she was on her feet almost all day, therefore much more tiring than her previous bookkeeping job. And she had to cheer up the customers. If she wasn't feeling cheery herself, that took a lot of energy.

Maybe all the older men were on the golf course where she would never be able to reach them.

It wasn't too many days after this unhappy reflection that Phyllis was standing by a frozen food case in Safeway one evening when a voice asked her, "Can you recommend any of these?" and she turned to see an attractive man across the aisle by the frozen dinners.

"Any of what?" Phyllis rushed toward him.

"Chicken, I suppose." He was a handsome man, rather tall, slender, with such an expression of kindness she was immediately won over.

Phyllis gazed raptly into his face. He flustered a little at this attention. "Our housekeeper has quit and my wife is an invalid. I'm not very good at this."

Of course, a wife! There was no truly handsome man on the face of the earth who escaped wifeliness; even a widower never lasted for more than a month.

Phyllis shook her head. "They're really not too good. I would recommend you get one of those hot barbecued chickens at the front of the store."

"Those are all right, are they? I've never tried one. And what about the rest of the dinner?"

Where had the man been all his long life? She put a hand on his arm affectionately and led him along the aisle. "Here, take some frozen peas, just dump them in some hot water for a few minutes. And here, you can microwave these potatoes. You have a microwave?"

He nodded. "I learned to use that for the housekeeper's nights out."

They secured the peas and the potatoes but Phyllis stayed with him. She abandoned her cart and followed him to the checkout stand. She wanted never to let him out of her sight at all. "You know, they have a really good take-out menu at the Chinese restaurant across the street."

"That's what I did the last two nights," he admitted. "But my wife complained that I was being a spendthrift."

Then why hadn't she given him some guidance about buying food? It sounded almost wicked. Phyllis expected a wife would see to the meal even if she had to do it by proxy.

"Has your wife been an invalid for a long time?"

"Years and years." He sighed. "But we've always had good help till now."

"Good help is so hard to find." Phyllis had never tried to hire household help but had heard other people say this.

"By the time I tucked him – Sam Wheeler was his name -into his car with all the things he might need for the evening and morning meals, we had become fast friends," Phyllis told Bridget by phone. "I gave him my phone number so he could call anytime he was fixing dinner and had questions. I told him I was a skilled bookkeeper in case he ever needed one of those." She had smiled with as much charm as she could muster at 7:00 in the evening after a work day and had promised to help with the hiring of a housekeeper.

Phyllis went to work the next morning with a new hopefulness. She was more cheerful and helpful than ever and her boss congratulated her on her attitude.

"I had given Sam my phone number with the idea that he would call me the next day or soon after about the housekeeper but he didn't. After a week of waiting and wondering, I pulled out the telephone book and looked to see if he was listed. Sure enough. There was an S. Wheeler with no address."

"That was lucky, wasn't it?" Bridget said.

A woman answered. Of course. Or maybe he had already gotten the housekeeper.

"Is Sam there?" Phyllis had asked with her best stage helpfulness.

"Who's this?" Must be the wife. Sounded too unpleasant to be really sick.

"You must be Mrs. Wheeler. Sam told me you are looking for a housekeeper. Have you found one yet?"

"No." Some drop in hostility. "Are you a housekeeper?"

"No, no. This is Phyllis. Just a friend. I have someone for him to call."

"Well, you'll have to talk to him. He takes care of all that. Not very well either. And he's not here. I'll tell him you called."

"I went back to work with a headache and growled at the next man who came in the door. But I was not going to give up. I went home that evening and spent two hours on the phone searching for housekeepers."

A few days later, Phyllis reported to Bridget: "He called."

"What did he say?"

"He was very grateful for all the information I could give him on housekeepers. We've become fast friends. He even came into the store."

For two weeks, Phyllis spent her lunch hours interviewing housekeepers and finally found one who was perfect. She was also grateful and eager to help Phyllis whenever Phyllis called Sam's house.

Phyllis became that household's best friend. A few months later, she had to search all over again for a practical nurse because the wife really was sick. And after that, she found someone to wash their windows and even an attorney. If Gretel, the wife, had hoped that Sam would come forth as a competent household manager once she took to her bed, she must have suffered deep pangs of disappointment - there were a thousand tasks he had no idea about. Even Gretel got somewhat friendly when Phyllis phoned.

"Phyllis, you are a wonder," Bridget said.

Phyllis helped Sam put together his papers for the tax accountant and in turn, Sam helped her find a cheap, secondhand car.

"I've never had a woman friend like you before," he confessed.

"I'll get my reward in heaven, I suppose," Phyllis said tiredly to herself when she put together her own tax papers, "just when I can't use it."

And then Gretel died. Phyllis couldn't feel any triumph, at least not at first, because Sam was so broken up. One might have thought the wife had been an angel rather than the bad-tempered tormentor Phyllis knew her to be.

"I don't know what I'll do without her," he said over and over.

Phyllis arranged the funeral and the burial. She wrote out the announcement cards and called the three children several different times because the time of the funeral had to be changed more than once to accommodate their various commitments.

During this period, she visited Sam's house for the first time and walked slowly around admiring the paintings, the grand piano, the Oriental rugs. Gretel had had a taste for heavy European furniture that Phyllis didn't care for, but she thought she could die happy in this house. It made it hard to go back to her own cracker box.

Ten days after the funeral, Sam arrived outside the auto parts store at five o'clock just as she was leaving for the day. His hair was tousled and his shirt missing a collar button. Phyllis thought the housekeeper needed straightening out. How could she let him go out like that?

Still he looked wonderful, with his high cheek bones and a kind of fierce cheerfulness he had adopted.

"I couldn't wait any longer," he apologized.

Awkwardly, he pulled something out of his pocket and it turned out to be an old-fashioned gold ring set with small sapphires. Phyllis thought she might swoon right there in the parking lot.

"Let's go somewhere."

"All right. We'll go to Duffy's and have a glass of wine. You will accept, won't you?"

She managed a smile and touched his arm. "I have to think about this."

Over cabernet, she said: "What are your children going to say?"

"It's not their life. It's my life. Besides they are all back East. None of them stayed around to see how I was going to make out on my own."

That was true. They clearly were not devastated by their mother's death, and not overly worried about their father although they seemed affectionate with him. They had busy lives; they had done their duty and come for the funeral. With evident relief, they had all packed their bags, selected one or two valuable items from the house, and hurried off to the airport.

Phyllis had been holding herself back, afraid to make a mistake, wanting to savor the moment or some such reason, but now it came bursting forth.

"Yes, yes, yes," I said.

"I only thought I was happy when I was twenty-something. It took getting to fifty-six to know what happiness really was," she told Bridget.

Six weeks after their wedding, Sam was diagnosed with cancer of the pancreas and he died in another five months.

"So she didn't get the house?" Marion had asked.

"Well, you know, the children had to be satisfied first. But he left her enough money for a new house. You've seen it. She owns it free and clear. And she got the piano and some of the rugs, but she didn't get Sam for very long. So that's why she's cranky sometimes."

And she never started using night cream so now her skin is ruined, Bridget thought but didn't say.

*   *   *   *

Bridget was gazing at the ruined skin across the table and was grateful her mother had been a famous complainer and fault finder. She had told Bridget at twenty five to start using moisterizer with sun block and night creams. Bridget, who had beautiful skin at that time, had been indignant, had loudly denounced this interference, but then she had done as she was told. And look, her skin was still fresh and unwrinkled!

It was very odd that she and Phyllis had become friends. It had happened only because Bridget was new to Shady Acres and Phyllis found her standing looking nonplussed at her garbage can.

"What's the matter?"

"They came but it's still full."

"You have to put it on the other side of the street."

"Why?"

Phyllis nodded sagely. "I know it sounds silly but those new big garbage trucks don't have room to turn around so they come down the street, empty the garbage with that arm that picks up the can and then they back up to get out. They would have to make another trip, backing down, to get any cans on this side. Well, you know they're not going to do that."

"There are tricks to all trades, aren't there? Anyway, thank you."

Then Phyllis had asked what Bridget had paid for her house. She, Phyllis, had walked through it when it was for sale, and thought it was a good house. Bridget, who really didn't like talking about what she paid for things, told her because she was grateful for the garbage information. And Phyllis told her what she had paid for hers. Considerably less, but she was pleased about that. Finally, after such friendliness, Bridget suggested they have coffee, and they became friends.

The better she got to know Phyllis, the more Bridget was amazed at her. Phyllis was the person for whom the term 'single-minded' had been invented. The United States might go to war, there might be hurricanes and floods across the country, or the first murder in twenty years in town, but Phyllis went on thinking only about her problem of the week. It might be how she was going to afford new drapes for her living room, or why the price of coffee kept going up, or her cat's fleas. Whatever it was, she worried at it till either she solved it or decided it wasn't going to be solved and gave up.

The subject of Jeb Frewalter's funeral brought up the fact that Phyllis's next door neighbor had committed suicide a few months back. Phyllis was highly indignant at this.

"People should have known that was going to happen, but nobody thought a thing about him. His wife just died a few months ago and the poor man couldn't cook for himself, he couldn't see well enough to go anywhere, he didn't even know how to find his programs on television."

"Did you talk to him?"

"Yes, I did. I told him to go into a home. I even told him I would help him find one, but he scorned me. Said he could take care of himself. I suppose part of it is on my head. But I've watched two husbands die; I just didn't want to do it again for someone who couldn't even be polite."

Bridget sighed. "Probably dying was what he wanted all along. Poor old guy."

"Men just aren't any good without a woman to do things for them."

Bridget wasn't going to argue with that.

Phyllis looked at Bridget's fingernails. "I hear those fake nails are bad for your real nails. They just rot away underneath all that glue."

"These aren't fake nails. They're my real ones. I just had them done."

"Huh. Well, they look fake."

Bridget guessed that was a compliment. She held out her nails and admired their length, their Candy Apple Red, the way they matched her lipstick.

"And what is that Jessie up to now?" Phyllis asked. She was too intimidated by Jessie to attempt friendship with her. She took a bite of the cream horn (Bridget had made another purchase at the bakery). Unlike Jessie, Phyllis had no objection to pastry, was diving into hers while the coffee was still perking. She could afford to. Phyllis had somehow remained thin. Probably born skinny. Only genes were sure to keep you thin for life.

"She is trying to tell me she likes to work, doesn't want to quit. I can't believe a word of it. Edgar probably made it clear he won't marry her."

"Maybe he won't. You know, sometimes I wish I was back in the auto parts store."

"I don't know," Bridget reflected. "He married me." She cast her mind back to that exciting long-ago time when she had been 21 and had shocked her family by marrying her professor. "She's still very attractive. For her age."

"What is her age?"

"I'm not sure. Except she's over 60, I'm sure of that. You know, I think she's going to start looking for another man. It's just a feeling I got."

"Where does she look?"

"I don't know." But Bridget was remembering her own remark about Togetherness and the sudden look of interest in Jessie's eyes.

"You don't think she uses the Personals, do you?"

Bridget shook her head. She had watched friends try the Personal ads in the newspaper and find them a trial to the ego. Most of the men wouldn't meet without first receiving a recent photograph. And they wanted the woman's age and weight even before that. Jessie wouldn't put herself through that. But Jessie didn't have any worries in the weight department.

"Maybe she'll use a dating service."

"They cost a lot of money, don't they?" In spite of having received the house virtually free, Phyllis still lived on a shoestring, having given up the auto parts job.

"Relatively," Bridget said. Money was not her problem. If she wanted to spend a considerable amount of money to meet a group of men who turned her down because of her weight, she could do that, but it sounded like a way of seeking out misery.

When it was a distant possibility, she could daydream about just the right man going with her to all the events she liked, admiring her wit, offering assistance with her car and her VCR. But when she had gotten to the door of Togetherness, she had lost her nerve. She remembered the ugly and protracted arguments during her affair with the tennis pro. It must have been the relief at being done with that affair that had caused her to gain all this weight. Hadn't she thought, looking in the mirror: there, I never have to go through all that misery again?

"I think she's through with Edgar!"

"He's so attractive," Phylllis murmured.

"And intelligent." Bridget agreed. "But not so easy to get along with. "So what are you going to do, Phyllis? Are you going to try to meet someone?"

Phyllis hedged, looked away. "I'm not getting any younger. I might."

"Not me!" Bridget said. Saying it out loud to Phyllis was a great relief. Her spirits began to come up. Enjoying the single state suddenly sounded very rewarding. There were a lot of other interesting things to do in the world that did not involve having a man in your life. If she offered a trip to Paris, her daughter might jump at it.

Think what fun that could be!

Chapter Five

Jessie stood in her patio, her nose as near as possible to the yellow rose bush while one hand massaged her chest. She had sought out the roses as if they might have a balm for her, but they remained isolated in their beauty, sending out no message. She hoped it was only her metaphoric heart which hurt, not her real one because it hurt very badly. Last night when she told him their affair was over, Edgar had cried.

Who would have thought it? Dry as a bone Edgar! She rubbed harder, avoiding her breasts, moving her fingers across her sternum as if the pain might be located nearby, just under the skin.

He had come close to begging.

She sniffed the roses harder, the smell tickled her nostrils but wouldn't reach her brain. If he cared for her, why hadn't he shown it? She hadn't said this to him while her eyes filled with matching tears. She was next to changing her mind, taking it all back. If Edgar had only said the right thing just then, she might have but he had probably been too distraught to notice her vulnerability. Or perhaps the tears would not have indicated surrender to him.

He had waited for her to change her pronouncement, but Jessie had turned half away from him, unable to say anymore. Finally, with the tears still on his face, he had reached blindly for his pocket but hadn't found a handkerchief. Tears were obviously a novelty to him.

"I'm in love with you, don't you know?" he had said.

Jessie had stood up and rushed to the nearest bathroom, dabbed at her own eyes, and hurried back with two tissues. He used them, neatly wiping his face, then handed them back politely as if she might have some other use for them. He buttoned his jacket. He had thought they were going to dinner and so was wearing a sports jacket and a dress shirt. Would she ever meet another man who put on a jacket willingly? Standing up, he peered down toward her face, waiting for the edict to be lifted. Jessie could not bear the anxious hopefulness in his eyes and so turned her face away.

With that, Edgar nodded his acceptance and walked out of the house, not bothering to close the door as if he had not enough energy for that.

After she had closed the door behind him, Jessie had stood silently, listening for ghosts in her empty house. Was that what she wanted? Only faint traces of people who were gone, only ghosts, no real people? But this house was very new. There were hardly any ghosts here.

An hour later, she had erupted into a whirlwind of housecleaning. Her eyes still welling up, she had scrubbed down her kitchen even though the cleaning woman was coming tomorrow. When had she last scrubbed out the sink? She couldn't remember, and couldn't find the scouring powder so did it with liquid soap which hardly worked.

Finally she gave the activity up and took a large whiskey to bed with her, and then fell into a heavy sleep by eight o'clock. Now, the morning after, the memory of his tears was as fresh as if he still stood there. Regret poured through her body like scalding hot coffee. She could never go back, never change what she had done. She hadn't stopped to think how he might feel. How thoughtless, how egotistical of her!

There weren't so many men who would fall in love with one when one was seventy three!

Maybe she should call him, at least apologize. But the thought made her shudder. She couldn't face his sorrow, or maybe by now, his anger.

She had a new date tonight. It had better be good. He had called on the phone yesterday, only two days after she got her picture to Togetherness. His name was John Roger Twining. On the phone, he was twenty times as energetic as Edgar. Energetic with a Texas accent.

41

She had begun to quiver right then, thinking what it would be like to face that energy in bed. Fate is with me, she thought.

Well, this John Roger had better be fantastic, that was all she had to say, for what he was costing her in wear and tear!

How long had she been staring at the yellow roses? She knew suddenly that she had to hurry even though she had gotten out of bed at six A.M., yawning a little because it always seemed so early though she did it nearly every day. When her bare feet touched the floor the memory of last night facing Edgar had overpowered her. This searing pain had rushed in. Now she had to ignore it somehow. She had an appointment in the office with a prospective buyer and she needed time to prepare.

After a tiny breakfast of fruit, and a shower, she looked through her closet, pushing hangers here and there while she thought about what the temperature would be by mid-day and would her feet swell if she wore the high-heeled brown sandals.

All right, she would chance it, only take another pair of shoes with her in the car in case she needed to change. She pulled out a summer outfit of white blouse, brown skirt and checked jacket. She would wear a pin, maybe a gold one.

She took one tablet each from the long array of medicines and herbal remedies on the counter and swallowed them one at a time. She heated the curlers and examined her face with a magnifying glass for stray hairs that might have appeared in the night. She put a moisterizer on her face, her elbows and her hands, and put the now-warm curlers in her hair. She opened the box of eye mascara and selected a chocolate brown to match the brown checked jacket. She put deodorizer under her arms and Vagisil on her private parts.

She looked over the bruises on her left thigh and upper arm, she had acquired two days ago tripping over something in the garage. They would probably be with her for a couple of weeks, that being one of the penalties of aging, but at least they would be covered by her office clothes. John Roger Twining would have to wait that long before she took off her clothes for him.

Now she sat on a high stool to put on make-up. Every now and then, she had to stand and lean closer to the mirror to see if she had it on evenly, even though she had already put in her contact lenses.

Over the make-up went the rouge and the eyebrow pencil, put on very broadly now that her eyebrows had aged out to almost nothing. At one time, they had been too thick, or so she had thought. Never pluck your eyebrows. They're never right after that.

She used the hand mirror to examine the rouge carefully because she tended to get it heavier on the left side where the window brought in less daylight. No, it seemed to be all right today. She needed to get one of those mirrors she had seen pictured which hung out from your neck and had both a magnifying glass and a light bulb on them.

Had there really been a time when all she did was brush her hair and put on some lipstick?

The hot rollers were making her head hot. If she wasn't careful, she would perspire and have to start the make-up all over again. She took out the rollers, carefully unwinding each still-hot curl and laying it against her neck so as not to straighten it. Then she applied the eye make-up, first the pencil around the edges of the eye inside the lashes, then the line of blue on the lid to bring out the blue of her eyes, (not as blue as they had once been), and finally the brown shadow blending up toward the eyebrow.

She examined the results with satisfaction. For once both eyes were alike, a difficult task. She carefully combed out the curls and noticed they didn't have as much body as she liked. She was going to have to change shampoo and conditioner again.

She went back to the bedroom and selected a pair of pale off-white pantyhose, sighing a bit because they had a healthy Control Top, which would be plenty uncomfortable by the end of the day. Once upon a time, she had put stockings on while standing first on one foot, then the other. No longer. She sat down on the bed and rolled a stocking all the way down to put it over her right foot, and pulled the stocking up carefully letting some stocking slide through her fingers but keeping the tension on. She remembered when stockings all had seams up the back. Seams which did make the legs look narrower but which, if you were at all active, would soon twist this way and that and show a meandering line up the leg. Every time the manufacturers tried to bring back stockings with seams, most women refused to buy.

Her left foot was always harder to get into the shoe because she had had surgery on it many years ago and it was slightly crooked. She ran a hand over it to see if it was tender anywhere, then she pulled up that stocking. She selected a half-slip that was the right length for this skirt and put it on. Then the skirt and the blouse which slid on effortlessly and buttoned at front and side. She needed to do her nails. She had them done professionally once a week but one had chipped yesterday when she was cutting roses, and she would have to do that nail over and probably the polish wouldn't match. She dipped the imperfect one into polish remover while she examined her hair. Should she back-comb and spray or let it alone? It looked a little limp but too much spray would make it sag more after several hours. Did her teeth look all right?

She made a face at the mirror, designed to expose her teeth. She had knocked a tiny chip off the bottom of a front one and the irregularity showed. Did people notice it? No stray traces of lipstick had gotten on her teeth. She looked at her watch, which was still lying on the bathroom counter. Only one more hour before she had to leave. And the hardest part yet to do.

After she had removed the nail polish, Jessie used the emeryboard, and put on two coats of new polish, and then hurried out to her desk. She took out her appointment book and began a new page in a spiral notebook.

Client name - Helen and Peter Raskin. Address. Met where and when. What did they want? What were they selling? Put their house on the market when? Did they have any nibbles? Children? No. How many bedrooms? How much could they put on a down payment? All the details she had gotten in their first meeting were in her purse notebook. She carefully transcribed these onto her new page and added new questions. Then she outlined how their meeting should go. What should she say when? Earrings. She had forgotten earrings.

What she did these days, now that she had begun to distrust her memory, was to put everything in this notebook and then open it out on the half-opened center drawer of her desk. The notes would be right in front of her but the clients wouldn't be able to see them.

When she had finished a careful outline of strategy, she turned to her company rule book and reviewed the things she could and couldn't say, could or couldn't do. Although she had been with this company for fourteen years and a realtor for twenty five, she read and then recited these out loud.

Then to the properties she knew about that she thought they might be interested in. She had printed these off the MLS last night. These days, it was a seller's market. As soon as the Raskin's put their house on the market, it would sell. The question was, how long before they could find a house they liked and successfully bid on it. And since the houses had all gone wildly up in price, the transactions had gotten more complicated.

It had been so much easier to be a realtor twenty five years ago. There were plenty of houses. Sometimes you had to show an unreasonable number of them to fussy clients, but there was always something to buy, and the other realtors were not so cutthroat as they were now.

Jessie went back to the bathroom for the earrings and the long mirror to make sure her skirt covered her slip. What she saw looking back at her - a polished blond woman perfectly put together - reassured her. Then she took her purse and dumped it out on the bed and put everything carefully back in so she would know what was there.

Finally she took her Leaving Card from her desk and checked it over. It said: Dogs outside. Water in their dishes. (That was done.) Turn down furnace. (It hadn't been on because the night had been mild.) Take keys. (She had just seen them in her purse.) Answering machine on. (Yes.) Extra shoes. (Those she had forgotten; she went and got them.) Map. Money.

She had forgotten the map, too. She went back to her office and pulled out one of the dozen she had printed out that showed Central Marin with her office prominently displayed. Belvy gave a howl that said Jessie was not supposed to go away again and lock them in the garden.

"Quiet," Jessie called curtly and shooed both dogs through the French doors and into the garden.

Finally, she went to the garage with her briefcase, purse, and the extra shoes and walked around the car looking at the tires.

How long had it been now that she had felt her boundaries shrinking, that she could no longer trust to her memory or her foresight and had to prepare for every eventuality? It was very tiring and left so little time for other things she liked to do.

But tonight she had something to look forward to. John Roger! And, if he didn't work out, he was a forerunner, a signal that there would be others.

Chapter Six

It was a week after the funeral. For a brief moment that event had united them all. Almost all the neighbors had come, even Jessie, looking elegant. The flowers were splendid. It was spring and most of them had been gathered from gardens rather than purchased. Marion had kept her tears silent though she could be seen angrily muttering. At Alice? At one of the children? At Jeb?.

In the eulogy, Jeb had been celebrated as wiser, more intelligent and more compassionate than anyone other than the pastor could remember. Bridget saw his neighbors look at each other wonderingly. Maybe they should have gotten to know him better.

Bridget thought happily she had been right to tell then to wait for The Reverend Schroeder.

She had ordered coffee and cake and little sandwiches for back at the house after the funeral. Alice served and nearly everyone who had gone to the funeral came back afterwards, even those whose names Marion had trouble remembering. The Reverend Schroeder, with grey curls and a round pink face, glowing with the success of his remarks, had eaten a great deal of coconut cake. All the small grandchildren had been banished to an upstairs room and given the cat to dress in doll clothes or chase around. For a moment, Marion had looked to be surrounded by friendship and caring.

Now, all that was over. Children and grandchildren had gone home. Alice had flown off to Atlanta for her one week a year vacation. Marion felt abandoned.

"I've been up since five," Marion said over the phone to Bridget. "I'm drinking leftover coffee."

Bridget tsked-tsked.

"What are you supposed to do if you don't have a husband to cook for or worry over?"

"You will get used to it."

"It just proves there is something fundamentally wrong with me."

"What?"

"That he left me."

"Oh, Marion, don't say that."

"You remember you told me you would help me look at the money." Marion sobbed and Bridget ached for her.

"Of course, I will."

"All right, let's do it."

"You mean now?"

At the funeral, Marion had refused this effort. "There's not that much to look at. His pension from the company stopped already. I don't get that. Just Social Security."

Now on the phone she said: "Can you come over this morning?"

"Now?"

"I need to know what it is."

"Yes, of course you do. How about forty-five minutes? Is that all right?"

"That's fine."

Bridget was forced into rushing around. Why had she said forty five minutes? She fed the cat, made the bed, watered the indoor plants and put away the dishes from the dishwasher. Then she lay down on the floor and did her stretching exercises. No time to read the morning paper that was still on the sidewalk outside.

While she exercised and wondered about the news, she also thought over what she should wear for the day. Someday she would institute a system, say hang all her everyday outfits in a certain order and then every morning start from the front end and work her way down the closet, a new outfit each day. That way she wouldn't have to make any decisions, just wear what was next in line. Then in the evening as she took her clothes off, she would either put them in the laundry or hang them at the other end of the rod so that they would take their proper place in line. Every time she was reminded of this plan, she would become enthusiastic, but then think it would require hours to organize and would necessitate dozens of decisions.

It was not just her clothes that needed organizing, it was also the rest of her life. There were all sorts of boring and depressing activities she had been asked to join in on such as volunteering at the hospital and or delivering for Meals on Wheels. To these, she had said no. What she had done in the past were the boards; these, which were beloved by so many women, involved going to a monthly meeting for at least a year to plan one fundraising event that climaxed in an evening which necessitated having a man to go to the event with.

Also, before the event, it was necessary to pledge some large sum of money. Bridget had become increasingly resentful at the repetitive nature of boards and so had quit them all.

Leaning at a forty five degree angle against the wall and then pushing away, (she forgot what this position was supposed to do for her body but she did it religiously anyway), she reminded herself again that she needed to keep up her appearance. After all, she had been Queen of the May Dance her freshman year at Birmingham South.

Bridget could feel again her heart in her mouth as it had been during that exciting time. The Committee had been stymied by a tie vote between Bridget and Mary Alice McCue; they had brought in the faculty advisor to break the tie and he had voted for Mary Alice. Bridget had cried all night - what had she done wrong? Where was it that Mary Alice showed herself to be a superior Queen of the May? And then Mary Alice had developed chicken pox and had to be hospitalized, and the Committee met again and gave the crown to Bridget. No doubt Mary Alice had had her own night of crying because Bridget went to see her the next day to commiserate and Mary Alice had been very unfriendly.

So Bridget had been chosen, her picture in the paper, a nearby modeling agency even coming out to take a look at her. And because her picture had been in the paper, Edgar, her history professor, had stopped her in the hallway to congratulate her. She could remember exactly the moment when Cupid had struck her with an arrow.

The two of them were standing in the center of the second floor hallway outside the History Department while students eddied around them; Bridget looked into his sparkling grey eyes with their thick dark lashes, and the direction of her life had changed.

Being Queen of the May Dance had determined her life, at least the first part of it. She had been really pretty, she could tell now by getting out old pictures. However, at the time, she hadn't liked her looks, her round cheeks and small nose and glossy red- brown hair. She had thought they were childish and common; she had wanted high cheekbones, green eyes, pale skin and hair 'black as a raven's wing.' The Elizabeth Taylor look.

Edgar had been a mistake, of course. She lay on her back and brought her knees up to her chest. He intimidated her thoroughly and deliberately and it took years to get over that. But how could she have known, when she was nineteen and he was so handsome and she was so envied? There might be some women who knew what they were doing when they were nineteen. But Bridget, along with all the friends she talked to, hadn't had a clue.

She climbed to her feet and shook herself out and wondered if she would have time to buy pastry.

So here she was at sixty two, well-off, healthy, full of energy, but with not enough to do. She needed to find something to be absorbed in, and get that glow she had seen on other women who had found their niche.

She threw everything in her purse that she might need over the day. It would be interesting to find out the details on how the Frewalters had lived and handled money. And she would get a chance to practice her expertise; she thought she was something of a wizard with money. Of course, dealing with someone else's life was always easier than dealing with your own.

Just as she was about to leave the house, she called Marion again. "Dear, I have some minestrone I made last night. Can I bring you some?"

"Well, that's very nice. I could have that for lunch. Phyllis made some cabbage rolls but cabbage gives me gas. And Hillary Kahn came down with matzoh ball soup, which was very nice of her. I hardly know her. And she was very sweet about Jeb. He used to play poker with her husband now and then but I don't know what's in matzoh balls so I'm afraid to eat them."

"I think it's just a kind of grain, like corn meal maybe. Anyway, it's very good."

Marion sighed. "That's a relief. You can take it home with you. I can't stand to see food go to waste."

Bridget arrived and unbagged the two croissants she had rushed out to buy. Marion had the coffee made.

It was evident that Marion had given up her weekly appointment with the hairdresser, her dark brown hair was not only long, but rather frizzy and its tell-tale white roots were beginning to show.

"How nice and long your hair is getting," Bridget praised.

"I think I'm going to let it grow out," Marion said shamefacedly. "Since I can't afford to have it done every week."

What other changes was she in for? It was really unfair the way women were left as widows.

"How do you feel, Marion?"

Marion regarded the question at length. "I don't really know how I feel," she said finally. "Everything is so strange. Most of the time I don't know what to do next. If I'd known he was going to die, I would have done everything differently."

"Differently how?"

"Well, I thought he was always going to be around, so there were things I didn't bother to learn. Like the budget, or how to take pictures, or when the car needed oil. Now I don't know how to do any of those things."

"You can learn now. You can make new habits."

"I suppose so." Marion always seemed perfectly willing to consider any and all suggestions, but as far as Bridget could see, she never followed any of them.

"I got everything out."

'Everything' consisted mostly of the bank statements and Jeb's monthly budget in a worn cloth-covered three-ring binder. Opened, it revealed months and months of expenditures carefully filled out in Jeb's neat handwriting. Beside it was a stack of bills, unopened.

"This is everything? Don't you have investments?"

"No. Everything's there," Marion amended. "The savings accounts come to me; there's hardly anything in them. The Social Security has been changed over. They've already talked to me. So that's all I get, his Social Security but not mine and a little bit of money every month from a bond."

Bridget picked up the small binder and looked over the budget. Jeb's pension had been nearly four thousand dollars a month, not a bad sum. No wonder he had a nearly new SUV! "Maybe we should start with a whole new notebook. Have you got another one? If not, I brought one."

"Do you think we need to?"

"Yes. And let's do income first."

With a sigh, Marion put down on the table her new statement from the Social Security Administration. "That's all of it."

"And the bond?"

"Sixty-five dollars a month." Not to sound complaining, she amended. "It's not that bad. I can manage. We have the house free and clear and the cars are paid for."

How could anyone live on their Social Security? Bridget crumpled her croissant. For once, she didn't want to finish it. She was going to stop buying them. All that butter!

"He didn't tell me his pension would stop. He should have told me that."

"He didn't have life insurance?"

"No. Just an IRA which we cashed in for the Alaska trip."

Bridget began to regret her offer. She couldn't perform any magic if there wasn't any money. "Did you get the money back from the Alaska trip?"

"Alice called. It's on the way. They were very nice about it. They didn't even deduct the three hundred dollars they could have. Alice said she'd put it in a CD for me."

Bridget shook her head. "The trouble with a CD is that every time it comes due, you have to decide on another one. Why don't you put it in another bond?"

Marion thought that over. The sag at her jowls had become more pronounced as they talked, and her shoulders slumped. Bridget wanted to shake her to get her motor started.

"I don't really know how to do that. Jeb always handled the money."

"Marion, you have to stop thinking about what Jeb would do. Think about what you want to do, about your own life and all the exciting things there are in the world that you might do." This was the advice Bridget had gotten when she divorced. It should apply to death as well.

Marion seemed to have become more dispirited during the time Bridget was there. "I can't think of anything I want to do."

"First, let's look at your monthly bills and write them down and see how much they are."

"I wonder where his poker winnings are."

Bridget was intrigued. "Poker? You mean he actually made money at poker?" She had never had a husband who gambled.

"That's what he said. I always figured it was his entertainment so I didn't ask about it. He didn't like the idea of taking household money for poker so it was always separate money and he didn't write it down anywhere. One time he won big and we went away for a weekend to Reno on that money."

They looked at each other as the thought of hidden treasure came over them. "Where would it be?"

Marion blinked, an expression of hope on her face. "We could look in his sock drawer."

"His sock drawer? Do you mean you haven't looked in there yet?"

After some hesitation because Marion was still of the opinion that it was Jeb's business, not hers, she led Bridget upstairs to examine the sock drawer. They found what must have been his poker stash. A tin can of change – several hundred pennies, nickels and dimes, no quarters. And a roll of one dollar bills, twenty-nine of them. And a lot of tiny scrawls of figures on an old shirt board that seemed to be Jeb's record of wins and losses. On the most recent date, there was the figure "+ $3.91". Bridget looked crestfallen. She had had a spasm of hope that there would be hundreds there. "I think you can forget about this."

"I guess so."

They went downstairs to the table and reality, the stack of bills. There was the Association fee, the PG&E, the water, the garbage, telephone, car and house insurance, and a small credit card bill. Marion admitted she hadn't paid attention to any of them in the past. Now she looked at Bridget as if expecting some magical alternatives.

Bridget handed them back. "You open them and write them all down and add them up" She had brought along her pocket calculator, and handed it to Marion.

Marion, looking aggrieved, slit the envelopes, opened the bills and laboriously entered each figure on lined paper. The calculator seemed to give her problems. When she was adding the column of figures, she had to go back and start over each time.

"I'm not really good at this," she murmured.

"You will get good at it. But there's no rush...you have all morning."

"This has to be wrong." Marion frowned and started entering the figures again.

Bridget stifled a smile. There weren't that many figures. She could almost have added them in her head. "Now add up your income for the month."

"That's easy enough. There are only two figures. Ohhh..."

"What's the matter?"

Marion shook her head vigorously. A long lock of dark, unhappy hair shook loose and fell over her face. Her nose twitched and she started the odd familiar crying that was beginning to irritate Bridget. A nearly soundless, whooping sob with her mouth open and her eyes closed.

"WHAT'S THE MATTER?"

"Look...look at it."

Bridget changed her glasses from the sunglasses with the purple frames which she loved to the bifocals that allowed her to read. Then she walked around the table and leaned over Marion whose tears were beginning to make her careful list of expenses run blue rivulets down the page.

"What?"

"Don't you see!" The expenses were $264 more a month than her income.

"What am I going to do?"

Bridget had a strong feeling they were wrong. She would do it herself. That's what she should have done originally. She took the stack of bills and listed each figure neatly in the new tablet she had brought; then she added them up on the pocket calculator. Marion had been wrong.

The total exceeded the total of Social Security and the bond by about thirty dollars but that was before she had allowed anything for food or gas or newspapers so the $264 would probably be close.

"I knew it was going to be bad."

Bridget walked across to the kitchen and fortified herself with a second cup of coffee. This was much worse than she had imagined. She hated being the bearer of bad news.

"Marion, why don't you sell this house? You've made lots of money on it. You could buy a mobile and put most of that money in bonds and have a good income."

Marion's face contorted in anger. "My house? I can't do that. My flowers and everything. I've been here ten years. A mobile? With all those trashy people? You can't make me do that!"

"That's only one suggestion. Some perfectly nice people live in mobiles. Didn't Jeb ever tell you his pension was going to stop? What did he think would happen to you?"

"You're blaming Jeb? The sweetest man…" Marion had to go in search of the Kleenex box.

I am blaming Jeb, Bridget thought. Marion had returned with the whole roll of toilet paper and was wiping her wet and sagging face.

"You must have some other money."

Marion could not seem to recover. "It's all right there," she said resentfully. Tears continued to seep from her eyes. She held a wet tissue in each hand and used them alternately to mop at her face. Her hair was now standing out at all angles as if begging to be cared for.

Bridget began reaching for straws. "Now we have to look at each expense and see what you don't need."

"How can I do that? Everyone has to pay taxes, car insurance, the electric bill."

"Well, yes, of course. But your car insurance, for instance, that will come down with only one driver instead of two."

This was too much for Marion. She left the table and went to lie down on the couch where there was already a roll of toilet paper waiting for her. "I'm going to have to give up my house, go into a home for the aged."

Bridget secretly thought that Marion couldn't afford a retirement home. Those things were getting quite pricey. What did people do for more income when they had no investments to move around?

"Don't worry, I'll think of something."

"I can't do anything more now," Marion said between sobs.

And so less than an hour after they had started, the session on money ended. After some minutes given over to comforting, Bridget gave up for the day and went home, almost as limp as Marion, desperate for the silent comfort of her own house.

As she drove home, she thought - I may have to give her a CD. Just something that pays her two or three hundred a month. Otherwise, she's going to starve. Maybe I could pretend to find it in Jeb's papers.

The next morning was sunny and things looked better. After coffee and reflection, she decided to put off the money worries for the day and coax Marion out for a drive to a new nursery in the next town. There was a big yard at the Frewalters; she could get Marion to buy some flowers and plant them. That was supposed to cure anyone.

But at the nursery, while Bridget was falling in love with a delicious smelling chocolate cosmos, all Marion did was wander the aisle and looked doubtfully at everything. "Jeb always did the garden. I don't know how I'll do it without him. All I do is water. He knew just when to feed everything, and when to plant."

"Well, spring is almost over so we're past most of the planting time," said Bridget who had a gardener to do all that. "But I thought you would find something new that you wanted and you could just take it back and stick it in the ground and see how it did?"

"I don't think I should try anything like that."

"Why not?"

"It doesn't seem fair."

It will all work out, Bridget thought. Somehow. It's only been a little while. In another month, she'll perk up.

Chapter Seven

Bridget sighed when her phone rang; she had just gotten to the Horoscope in the morning paper. Not that she believed all that nonsense but she liked the feeling it gave her about life, that new possibilities were constantly appearing and fate waited just around the corner with mysterious strangers bringing events heretofore unimaginable.

Not so exciting this time. It was her brother Ian.

"Very well and how are you?" Ian treated the fifty miles between them as a major matter except for two or three times a year when he called and wanted to take her out to dinner.

"Love to," she said, and they hung up shortly after setting a day and time.

She began to think of all the negatives of having dinner with Ian. For one thing, he was likely to get stomach pains before the end of the evening because he never remembered all the things that bothered his digestion. And he usually had some new idea for her to invest money in. At least once he would complain that she never came to see him.

Still he was a good looking man, and his foibles didn't show on first meeting so she always made sure they went to dinner someplace where they would be seen.

This time she took him to the Red Chimneys, a restaurant which had been created out of an 1890s mansion.

"I think we've been here before," he said, looking up at the white brick front.

"Probably. There are only so many restaurants here. I try to give you the full range."

"I can't remember if it's any good."

At one time, the house, which did indeed have three red chimneys, had been set in the middle of a whole city block of lawn; now the areas along the streets had been sold for small shops, cutting back the lawns until there was only a narrow strip of grass on each side of the house and a sidewalk that came in from one corner. It must have been a handsome home back then; it still had old-fashioned flowered wallpaper, polished mahogany floors, a fireplace in every room, mirrors above the mantels, pale pink tablecloths, and Queen Anne chairs with striped satin seats.

It was the optimum hour to see and be seen, if not the optimum day of the week, it being Wednesday. Bridget's eyes were shiny from the vodka and tonic they had had at home, and her cheeks glowed with rouge in a shade called pomegranate. The restaurant was filling up and, sure enough, there was someone she knew waiting in line for the hostess. Bridget nodded happily, hoping that if she was seen having a good time, someone who knew her would decide that she was just the person to invite to some splendid event.

"You'll like it here," she promised Ian, deciding that she would have the seared salmon.

"We did come here before. This is where I had the fish almost raw."

Bridget pretended she hadn't heard but her desire for the salmon evaporated. She searched over the patrons for other acquaintances. Just when the hostess was leading them to a table, Bridget looked across into a side room and saw Jessie deep in conversation with someone who couldn't be seen.

It was no surprise to run into Jessie here. This was one of her favorite restaurants and it was not at all unlikely she would take a new date here. She had even been known to eat alone here. Something Bridget would never do. But who was the date?

"Well, that's interesting," Bridget said, stopping and waving while she craned her neck trying to see Jessie's companion. This forced the hostess to stop in the room ahead of them and wait, her forehead frowning impatience while her mouth still stretched in a smile.

"What's interesting?" Ian asked, from behind her.

"Shush. I'll tell you later."

They were seated at a table tucked around two corners from the room Jessie was in. Bridget shook out her napkin in chagrin. When it was in her lap, she straightened and unstraightened the silverware. She was in a fever of unknowing. Who was Jessie with? Had she made up with Edgar? But she had seen the man's hands and those didn't look like Edgar's.

She could give Edgar a call right now on her cell phone. Of course he would be angry with her. But he had been angry with her ever since the divorce. Probably angry originally because it had meant he would no longer be the primary factor in her life. Then they had lost touch when Bridget started seeing Norm, and Edgar had lost interest in the details of her life. Or so he claimed, though Bridget had trouble believing it because he had cried at the divorce proceedings.

If she heard the phone ringing in the next room, she would know it was Edgar's phone and she could just hang up when he answered. But would she hear it over all these conversations going on around her? And what if he had one of those phones where he could see what number was calling him? She really didn't want to upset him.

She debated all these questions alternately smiling and frowning, till Ian gave up on her and turned to the menu, reading it with great concentration. Seeing the crease between his eyebrows, Bridget remembered that he was her younger brother, and deserved some sisterliness. He didn't look in the pink of health though he was in his mid-fifties and had never had a serious illness. His face was too white in the candlelight and his eyes were puffy. He didn't eat right. She might have to order for him if he wanted to get the roast pork because it had disagreed with him terribly the last time they ate together.

"You order the wine," she said when the waiter came.

He smiled. He liked to show off his wine knowledge, and Bridget made up her mind to be happy with whatever he ordered. She tried to think of some subject to talk to him about but her mind was mostly occupied with Jessie. How confident Jessie was, how sure of what she wanted in life. She had called the Mayor about potholes in the street in front of her house and, amazingly, the potholes had been fixed.

Jessie was willing to go out and find a new man in spite of her age, braving the possibility of being laughed at!

Ian had decided and informed the waiter of his wine choice. "So what's the bee in your bonnet, Bridie?"

"Just a friend of mine," she snapped, thinking it was none of his business. Then she smiled to make up for it. She tried to tell herself that it was not Ian's fault she was always snappish with him. It had something to do with their childhood though she wasn't quite sure what. Their other sister, Lorraine, always said they should have given Ian a name with more letters in it, maybe then he wouldn't be so half not there.

"Well, I'm not going to call him," she announced, to Ian's bewilderment. She might think she had learned something and be wrong. All she had to do was go to Jessie's table as they left.

Maybe she should call Mimi who lived next door to Jessie and ask what she had observed about a new man. She reached in her purse and pulled out her cell phone.

Ian was bewildered. "What are you doing now?"

Bridget liked whipping out her cell phone in the presence of other people. She hardly ever got to use it. It had happened to her more than once, that she invested in the newest toys and then had no way to use them. She had been the first person she knew to get a computer and, later, a cordless phone.

"Nothing," she said and put it away again. Mimi would think she was nuts if she called her out of the blue to inquire about Jessie. If she didn't find out tonight, she could drop in on Jessie tomorrow and ask who tonight's man was.

"Okay, okay. Didn't mean to disturb your highness."

Bridget held her fire. It was no use getting mad at Ian's idiosyncrasies. He wouldn't change; would only get mad and stay away.

"How is Constance?" she asked. Constance was his cat and Ian always had plenty to say about her.

"Got to get to the vet this week and don't know how I'll have time. Maybe you could do it for me, Bridie?"

"Come fifty miles to take a cat to the vet?"

"She could really be sick and I can't take the time off this week. You could do some shopping while you're in the city."

"All right. If you never again call me Bridie!"

This should keep him happy for the rest of the evening. She had promised herself to do one good deed a week; this one should count for two weeks. But maybe he would get home and find Constance not as sick as he had thought.

"You'll do it? That's great. Thank you."

Bridget ordered the seared salmon for herself, after all, and the roast chicken for Ian and these plates were just being served when a white-haired man appeared grinning beside their table.

"Jessie says to say hello!"

"You must be...who?"

"Yep, you've got it. I'm John Roger." He was a stubby man, who looked practical as a hammer, with a thick shock of white hair, and a face turning pink from alcohol. He had on a starched but far from new white shirt, and navy sport coat but was wearing some threadbare jeans, and was stomping around as if he was wearing spurs. If you were critical you might describe him as an old cowboy.

Bridget was warm with delight. Jessie had cared enough about her to send John Roger over to talk. "Well, tell her to get over here!"

He shook his head. His blue eyes had a dancing Irish look. "Our dinner is arriving right now. Why don't you come see us for a glass of wine at five tomorrow!"

Bridget squeezed his hand in thanks. She looked down and sure enough, cowboy boots. "All right, I'll be there."

Wasn't that was nice of Jessie, inviting Bridget to get acquainted with the new man! She must be very confident, not afraid to introduce him to other women. Well, she was safe with Bridget because Bridget had sworn off men.

Later, when Bridget and Ian were leaving Red Chimneys, she walked them through several rooms until she spotted Jessie and John Roger still at a table, holding hands around two coffee cups, looking moony. Bridget abandoned Ian and went over to say goodby, or hello and goodby.

John Roger stood up politely.

Jessie was glowing. Bridget looked at her straight nose and well-applied eye shadow, her unwrinkled face, her perfect blond bob and her fresh manicure. She was beautifully dressed in a long black skirt and a white satin blouse with a big circle of jade on a cord as her only jewelry. Only her neck gave away some age…well, necks were always impossible and best ignored.

"Lucky you," Bridget whispered in her ear.

"Yes," Jessie said softly.

"I'll see you tomorrow."

"Good."

*   *   *

The next morning, Bridget went to see Phyllis to tell her about John Roger.

They sat in Phyllis's dining room drinking coffee while her huge tabby cat snoozed on the brocade couch. The California sun was so strong it was opening the poppies in the garden outside the sliding doors, almost while they watched.

Although Phyllis's house and its appointments could not match Bridget's own, Bridget always found visiting Phyllis a treat because Phyllis had an innate housewifeliness, something practically lost since the sixties. Her garden, even just that part you could see from the window, was always gorgeous. And there was the baby grand piano, there in her living room, that had come from her second husband. Bridget had grown up with a piano in the house and a sister who liked to play so that, although Bridget had never learned to play, seeing a piano always made her feel as if music was just hidden under the keyboard, about to flow forth.

Phyllis was indignant at the news of John Roger. "It's only been a week since she broke up with Edgar. She must get them from the Personals."

"I don't know. She won't say."

Years ago, Bridget would never have thought that she would peruse the personals herself, but yes, she had. Not that she was going to admit to it, or do it again. After her last break-up, she had felt so lousy that Madge, a friend at that time had talked her into trying Personals Plus, the dating agency. And then after a few dates from Personals Plus which were not very successful, she began reading the newspaper personals ads. All of this was mostly on a theoretical basis, allowing Bridget to consider which man she might want to meet and daydream a little. She was too tentative to initiate any contacts, and she never put an ad of her own in though she wrote several, trying them out, wondering if she could write one as enticing as some she saw. But what was the use? Any reasonable-sounding man over fifty was already inundated with women. Either that or he was a serial killer and had been bumping them off.

"She must have another source. You said he was definitely over sixty. There aren't that many ads from men over sixty in the Personals."

Bridget grinned. How did Phyllis know? "There aren't that many men over sixty. But apparently there are some."

Phyllis nodded sagely. "All those heart attacks. I hear that's changing though. The men are not dying so fast as our father's generation did. What I think it is, a lot of the men are just not interested anymore."

Bridget agreed, but the idea turned her indignant. "Can you believe that? I remember when I went in fear of being raped every time I stepped out the door. There was always a man hanging around trying to get me into a conversation so he could impress me enough to go out with him. Even the postman."

Phyllis brightened at the thought. "Those were the days, weren't they?"

*   *   *

Bridget went to Jessie's at cocktail time.

John Roger opened the door. He looked somewhat older than he had looked in the restaurant. His greeting was warm. He sounded as if he had really been looking forward to talking to her again.

"Well, hello there. Jessie, you've got a friend here."

He ushered Bridget in energetically. Now that she was standing beside him, Bridget saw he had shrunk some, was quite short, maybe only five six. When Jessie stood beside him, she was four or five inches taller.

Jessie was wearing the smock she always put on for housework, and she carried a glass jar of nails and screws. Some task must be going on.

"I'll pour you a glass of wine. Then you have to give us a minute. He's just fixing the latch on the shower door."

Bridget took the wine and then followed Jessie back to the bathroom where John Roger had gone ahead to work on the door. She thought if any man ever came to her house for a drink and stayed to fix anything, she would lock him in the bathroom until he agreed to marry her.

Jessie was not entirely pleased to have Bridget looking over her shoulder. "Sit down. We'll be right there."

"But this is so interesting."

John Roger had tools spread all over the bathroom floor and the latch out of the door while he fiddled with it. He was whistling instead of swearing which was what most of Bridget's husbands used to do when they had to fix something.

There was a whine from somewhere in the house.

"Bridget, would you go and let Belvy into the patio?"

Which one was Belvy? Probably the one who was whining. "Oh, all right."

When the other two joined her in the living room, where Bridget was sniffing the vase of roses which had a lovely scent although they were beginning to drop petals, they were in a mild argument over the patio gate.

"You need a whole new gate!" he said.

"But they're terribly expensive. Can't you just put new hinges on?"

"The posts are shot as well as the gate. That's the problem. New hinges won't stay on because the wood is rotted. I'll put new posts in if you'll buy them as well as the gate."

Jessie beamed. "Would you? That would be wonderful! Isn't that wonderful, Bridget?"

"It sure is."

"Woman, if you want your guests to stay, you have to pour them some wine!"

"She has some."

"But I don't."

Bridget stayed until nearly 7:00 when John Roger pleaded hunger. At that point Bridget suggested they all repair to the Portuguese Hotel for dinner. The other two agreed.

Over dinner, there was some general conversation but when Jessie and John Roger addressed each other there was a note of excitement in everything they said, no matter how mundane. Bridget did not feel left out, but instead, felt bathed in their delight with each other.

John Roger told Jessie why the hot water in her shower came out so slowly, minerals had caked in the galvanized pipe over the years and narrowed the opening. That was why people preferred copper pipes.

He would have to take the pipe out and replace it. Jessie protested that that would mean tearing off the tile all down the wall.

"Woman, that's the only way to cure it."

Jessie gave him a long look, as if trying to divine how much of that was deliberate obfuscation. "Sometimes I hate being a woman and not knowing all those things."

He looked a bit sympathetic. "I'll lend you a book of you don't believe me."

"What would doing that cost?" Bridget asked to help Jessie out.

"Not a lot if I do the work!"

"Now let's stop this," Jessie said. "Or Bridget will think we don't talk about anything else."

"No, no. I like hearing all this. I'm learning something."

"Okay, I'll lend you the book." He said this with a droll look so the women laughed with him and the conflict was over.

Bridget called Jessie the next day. "What a nice man. Where did you find him?"

Jessie was a little evasive though pleased with the question. "Isn't he wonderful? We liked each other right from the start."

"Did you put an ad in somewhere?"

Jessie began talking about their plans to make a vegetable garden in the patio.

After that, Bridget joined them for a glass of wine several times a week and watched in fascination as their relationship grew. It would not take much to encourage a mild crush on John Roger. He told a good story and was full of enthusiasms.

He seemed to like Bridget almost as much as Jessie. "If you need anything done around the house, I'll do it," he promised Bridget, but she knew better than to accept this when the price might be Jessie's friendship.

Phyllis still hadn't given up on the subject. "Where do you suppose she found him?"

Bridget remembered Togetherness but wasn't going to mention it. "Friends of friends I guess."

"Not on your life."

Chapter Eight

Bridget was polishing her silver candelabras, not her favorite job. In fact, she was groaning and complaining under her breath as she held them under the faucet to get another layer of black off. Why couldn't the cleaning woman polish the silver? Somehow or other Maria Theresa, the house cleaner who was wonderful in so many other ways, had managed to circumvent Bridget on that task. Her grasp of English deteriorated, she looked helplessly at the proffered silver polish and - well, you can guess the rest! The one time Bridget insisted she do it, Maria Theresa had let the polish harden on the silver till it was murder to get off and Bridget was alarmed for the – in that case, a sugar bowl – and said she would do it herself. Which meant that the silver hardly ever got polished.

Today was different. Bridget had set out to spend the whole day detailing her house the way she had her car detailed. Jessie was coming

She threw out an arrangement of dried flowers that had seen better days, sorted through the magazines which had piled up unread in the magazine basket, replaced the partly used candles in the candelabra, put a high shine on the antique walnut coffee table. She had been planning to go to Annie Lamantia's funeral but decided against it. She was nervous about having Jessie here for the first time Anyway, you could get too much of funerals. Annie had been a good friend years ago but Bridget hadn't seen her for at least two, or maybe three, years. Probably no one would remark on her absence.

For the last few weeks, Bridget had spent two to three evenings a week having wine with Jessie and John Roger. Their friendship had blossomed because John Roger made it clear he liked having Bridget there. He had asked several times if didn't she have a man friend she could invite along and make a foursome but Bridget had shaken her head, and Jessie had told him to stop being nosy.

Maybe it suggested that she didn't think there would ever be a man friend for Bridget. Did Jessie really like her or was it just John Roger who wanted to have a second woman around so that there would be two people to laugh at his jokes?

The time the three spent together was never dull. There were all their assorted pasts to discuss, as well as the decisions that been shaped along the way.

"It's only a Wednesday," Bridget said once, when she was handed a glass.

They looked at her. "What does that mean?"

"Can't you remember a time when you only partied on the weekends?"

"You mean back in the dim days before I retired. That's too far in the past. I can't remember it at all." John Roger grinned, pleased at boasting about his age rather than bemoaning it.

Jessie raised her eyebrows. "You aren't retired now. You spend a couple of hours a day talking to people about property."

"A couple of hours. There were periods when I worked ten hours a day. But I usually went drinking afterwards. So your analysis is wrong, Red."

He had taken to calling Bridget Red, though her red hair was long gone except for the red highlights put in the streaks.

"And I'm not retired," Jessie put in. "The difference is that I work weekends as much as during the week. And as for partying on the weekends when I was young, we never seemed to get out that much."

"Didn't you? I did. I always insisted on going somewhere on Saturday night. What else is it for?" Bridget replied, remembering many interesting evenings.

"Your trouble, Jessie, is that you'll never quit. You see that, don't you, Red? When she's ninety five and feeling poorly, she will call up and tell them she's coming in late."

Bridget always went to Jessie's defense. "She's great, isn't she? I couldn't put in the hours she puts in."

And I'm younger, Bridget thought suddenly, though how much younger it was hard to know. How old was Jessie? Bridget had never gotten even a hint out of her. She was always so perfectly turned out, so perfectly made-up and dressed, but there was something a little fragile in her manner, like a suggestion of a fear of falling or failing at some physical task. Something Bridget had trouble relating too. That's how she knew she was younger. But did it matter? They were all getting older while they sat there, but they were all in good health.

"Don't be too sure I'll never quit," Jessie warned John Roger.

He laughed in response as if he had finally gotten the retort he had been fishing for.

Bridget was amazed. "Would you, Jessie? You wouldn't do it for Edgar."

Jessie only smiled. That evening Bridget had relaxed into the pleasure of being with them more than any other time. It was one of their best evenings so far.

John Roger always played host, opening the wine and then pouring more the minute any glass became half full, and Jessie watched him with pleasure, obviously enjoying the playful air he did it with though she never drank more than two glasses.

"Let's think up a fantasy job," Bridget suggested. 'What job would still be worth having when you were ninety?"

"Buying art!" Jessie said.

"No, buying race horses," John Roger said. "I've had that fantasy all my life. Your turn, Red!"

"Decorating a new house."

"Yes, yes," Jessie said.

"Oh, you women! That doesn't sound like fun to me."

"Did you ever decorate a house, or have you always had a woman to do it?"

"I'm not going to tell you about the women who've been in my life."

Jessie laughed. "How about how many…would you tell me that?"

"No way." He looked serious. "I will tell you something that is different…none of them ever had a real career the way you do, something they were good at. I haven't seen that before. I admire that."

"That's a nice compliment. Thank you."

Bridget watched the looks that passed between them. Something was going on here, deeper and more complex than she had expected. She was watching them pass new stages in their relationship. She also found John Roger to be more than she had expected. She had thought she was comfortable with him because he was too old for her; she couldn't imagine being interested in him, therefore she found him just perfect for friendship. But getting to know him, she wondered about this.

He had made a small fortune buying land and subdividing it, and he also talked knowledgeably about investing. Bridget found this of greater interest than Jessie did and wanted to query him at length on this subject but didn't because Jessie wouldn't enjoy it. Anyway, John Roger was a great find as a friend.

At the end of that evening, Bridget had invited the two of them to drink wine at her house. How could she go on accepting their hospitality if they wouldn't come to her house?

John Roger had looked at Jessie, and Jessie who never showed any signs that drinking wine made her more convivial, hesitated.

Then Jessie nodded. "That would be delightful."

Bridget was proud of her house and all the things she had collected in her travels but she seldom invited anyone in. Most of the houses in Shady Acres were about the same size, there were two bedrooms ones and three bedroom ones, and some with a separate diningroom or family room but they had all been built by one builder and originally priced pretty much the same. However, over the years they had begun to vary as various owners had put more or less money into them. Some sprouted extra rooms, and had added a lot of tiling and kitchens out of decorating magazines, hardwood floors, skylights, extended patios with elaborate gardens. Bridget had purchased a house that had already been extensively done over. The realtor who sold it to her had told her it was the most expensive house in Shady Acres. She filled it with her great-aunt's eighteenth century furniture and her collections of blown glass and New Guinea carvings.

Much of her furniture was mahogany in the Chinese version of Queen Anne. The rugs were Persians of high quality. When she had come back from London the year before, she immediately had a painter come in to do the living room over. She wanted a white ceiling, white woodwork and red walls like those she had seen in England. The painter pointed out that, this being a house built in the sixties, there was not much woodwork. Therefore, Bridget had a carpenter come first and add trim around the windows and doors, and crown molding, and a more extensive fireplace mantel so they would have something more elaborate to paint white.

When she was finished with this project, she had had a party for the neighbors as she would have done in San Francisco. Instead of being admiring of the house's transformation, the guests were critical, even caustic. It took Bridget a long sleepless night to realize they were envious. Since then, she had seldom invited anyone else in.

Now she thought she would like to show off the red room to Jessie. Jessie was too sure of herself to be envious and she would have a proper appreciation of Bridget's things, having been in so many expensive houses.

Bridget hesitated, furniture oil-soaked rag in hand, wondering if maybe she had been wrong to invite them. If Jessie thought Bridget was showing off that she was wealthier, she might lose the friendship. With the thought came a sharp piercing pain in her intestines.

She stood up carefully. She had been on her knees, oiling some chair legs that Maria Theresa never remembered to do. If she had to go into Emergency, that would solve her problem, only not in a good way. She carefully sat on a chair, trying to relax all her muscles and have them tell her what was wrong.

She watched the way the sunshine came through the open upper shutters and shone on the bountiful rubber tree beside the window. She was no green thumb but she had managed to buy several large plants for indoors. When any one of them looked slightly ill, she called in the nurseryman for immediate consultation and with this care, they had thrived.

At the end of these pleasant thoughts, she found that the pain was gone and was probably just something her body was trying out in anticipation of some trouble in the future. She gave up oiling the chairs.

Jessie and John Roger arrived fifteen minutes late, just as Bridget was becoming anxious. Bridget threw open the door in delight, and then nearly closed it again.

With Jessie and John Roger were the two enormous dogs.

Jessie was smiling brightly. "I hope you don't mind that we brought Tibby and Belvy with us. They've been alone all day and get so lonely."

"No, of course not," Bridget managed to get out. She knew the black hearts of those dogs. She had seen their snouts sweep casually across a table of hors d'oeuvres and scarf down everything, leaving the plates clean, though slobbery.

"If you mind, you go right ahead and say so," said John Roger, frowning. "I didn't think it was a good idea."

"Your trouble is you don't like dogs." Jessie sailed into the house, dropped the leashes and gave Bridget a kiss, enveloping her in a sweet perfume. "But I knew Bridget wouldn't mind. And they are so adorable, and never any trouble."

Bridget led them into the living room, preceded by the two dogs who were ranging ahead, quartering the ground, checking for small game. Bridget thought how lucky it was she no longer had the parrot who by now would probably have swooped down on one canine head or the other and started a war.

Jessie looked over the chairs admiringly and picked out a pale tan suede one that complimented her pale brown outfit. John Roger wandered the room examining the paintings with an occasional grunt, until he settled for the leather couch. Tibby and Belvy were sweeping their tails here and there and Bridget thought it likely they would sweep the coffee table clean of the small expensive sculptures.

"SIT!" Jessie yelled, and the dogs dropped where they were but then stood up and wandered another step or two before collapsing to the floor again.

Bridget went to get the tray with the wine and glasses. It took great courage to go to the kitchen leaving her precious things. What would happen before she returned? She had some small figurines from Africa made of paper mache', fur and feathers. Would the dogs think these were dead animals and chew them up? She tried to remember if she had ever had those appraised.

When she arrived back in the living room, the dogs were stretched out to full length in front of the fireplace while Jessie and John Roger were having a low-voiced discussion, perhaps even an argument as they both seemed very intense.

Bridget screamed. It was only her respect for a twenty eight dollar bottle of wine and three crystal wineglasses that kept the tray steady. Even respect could not get her across the room to set it down on a table. John Roger rushed to her to rescue the tray.

"What's the matter?" Jessie asked.

Bridget still couldn't speak. She pointed. Was it Tibby or Belvy who was chewing thoughtfully on something made of dark wood, the same color as Bridget's New Guinea carvings.

"What's he got?" John Roger had the tray safely on a side table.

He focused on the darker of the two dogs and advanced on him.

"Oh Belvy, what are you doing?" Jessie moaned, standing up.

"Damn dog!" John Roger had one hand inside Belvy's mouth and with the other he swatted the dog hard on the head. The dog yelped and let go.

"You've hurt her!"

"Jessie, will you stop worrying about the damn dog and see what it's done."

Bridget had recovered from her shock and was moving fearfully toward her object, whatever it might turn out to be.

John Roger had it in hand and held it out to her, sadly.

Jessie had swatted the dog again herself and was now stroking its head in apology. No wonder they acted like kings of the universe. "Bridget, I am so sorry. Whatever it is, I will buy you another one. What is it?"

What John Roger was holding out looked nothing like a New Guinea carving or an African animal. It had been chewed beyond recognition. What was left was about seven inches long and three inches thick with one rough bark-like side. Bridget took it gently in her hand and turned it over and over. She wanted to ask how could you ignore the dogs long enough for this much to be chewed away. But she didn't.

Instead, she started walking around the room with it, trying to see which of her beloved objects was missing. She wished the two would go away, taking those beasts with them, and let her mourn alone.

"What was it?" John Roger echoed.

She completed a circuit of the room. Nothing was missing. She turned the slobbery stick over in her hand. Oh! That's what it was. She started to giggle and sob at the same time.

"It's a stick. See! They must have brought it in from the yard." She held it out.

Jessie was on her feet and took it.

"That's their own stick from our patio. I didn't know they had it." She put her arm around Bridget and began to gently rub her back.

John Roger held it in his hands and turned it over. "I'll be damned. One of them must have brought it all the way in his mouth. And we didn't notice a thing."

Amid general relief, Bridget got John Roger to open the bottle of wine, and pour. John Roger was still sending angry glances at the dogs who showed little guilt at all the scolding although the light one had her paws over her nose.

Jessie was probably the most relieved. "Bridget, I was so worried. You do know that I would replace anything they damaged. I've had all sorts of experiences with these dogs, believe me. But I never had that happen before."

"Not half as worried as I was." After another pull at her wine, Bridget finally smiled though she was limp with the rapid changes of emotion.

When they had run out of comments on the dogs and reduced the bottle to one-third, Jessie and John Roger sat side by side on Bridget's couch and laid out plans for their future. Jessie would move to John Roger's place when Jessie's daughter could come back from the East Coast for a visit. Before that they were going to take a gourmet trip through Tuscany. Then they would buy a piece of land at the shore and build a house. They would bring John Roger's boat up from Mexico and move it to Clear Lake.

"Oh, oh," Bridget exclaimed in delight, but was really downcast. Jessie would move away and their friendship would be over.

"When is all this happening?"

"We're still working on that. I've started looking at land by the shore. It's hard to find a piece of oceanfront. That might take a while."

"I will put out feelers in the office," Jessie said.

Bridget looked from one to the other. She noticed the word 'marriage', had not been said. Equally interesting, the fact of Jessie's job, of those long Sundays when she drove couples from one end of the county to the other, or sat two Open Houses back to back and then drove new prospective buyers around, or those weekday mornings when she left at 7 a.m. to get to her office by 9, none of these facts were mentioned. Was Jessie really going to quit?

Instead of mentioning this or her regret, she offered: "Maybe you could put your boat in Lake Berryessa. It's much closer than Clear Lake."

They discussed the pros and cons of Lake Berryessa versus Clear Lake, as well as a scandal at the local hospital till the last inch of wine was only a memory, and the need for dinner drove the guests out.

Chapter Nine

Don Dorfman moved to Shady Acres from Oakland primarily because of the cost of housing. His retirement came a couple of years earlier than he had expected - his company bought him out of his job so they could eliminate it. That gave him thirty thousand extra dollars. The timing was good too because he and his wife had divorced the year before. Now he didn't have to split the thirty thousand with her. Timing was everything, his envious brother told him.

Don and his wife hadn't owned their house very long so, after the real estate fee, half the equity didn't produce another down payment for a house in Oakland. No problem to his wife who had moved back to Kansas where she had sisters. Houses were cheap in Kansas.

With his half and the thirty thousand, Don went hunting for a house he could afford. That was what you did when you retired, wasn't it? You bought a house somewhere away from the city where it was safe and green.

After driving to all the small towns within reach of Oakland and reading their real estate ads, he found Shady Acres where some of the houses were relatively cheap. Here, he found he could just manage to buy the smallest house available.

The night after he moved in, he felt a wave of confusion. He dug out the Canadian Club and poured a substantial drink. With that in hand, he stumbled through the stacks of boxes wondering what to do first. The moving men had put most of the furniture in place but none of it looked right. It wasn't homey. But when he looked it over, he couldn't see how to do it differently.

Maybe it would look better after he had got rid of the boxes. He needed to unpack the dishes and his clothes. There were tools and cleaning supplies, and a heap of things his wife should have taken but didn't want. He had reduced most of those categories by heavy donations to the Goodwill but it still made for a substantial number of boxes. All that unpacking might take days. He wasn't used to setting up a household.

He gave up on that, left it for tomorrow. Before he got any more tired, he was going to find the box that held his bedding, and make his bed. Next problem: there were no curtains on the windows.

He poured another Canadian Club and made the bed and sat down on it with the overhead light on because the lamps were all still packed away. Could anyone see him? He couldn't remember what was outside this window on the back of the house.

All right, you bought a house, then what did you do?

His retirement plans had always included Mary Margaret. Without her - and her bossiness - he wasn't quite sure what he was supposed to do. Also, in the past, when looking for new friends, he had always described himself by his job. Now what the hell did he say to people?

When the drink was finished, he lay down on the bed. Then he realized he couldn't go to bed now because he was hungry. He got up and went out to the nearest restaurant he had seen when he was house hunting, and had a hamburger. He came back through the dark unfamiliar streets wondering if he could find the house again. The houses in this development looked so much alike. Finally he saw the right corner and was grateful he had left the porch light on.

He parked the car at the curb and hurried inside, thinking he might have another drink. But he was too tired for that. He got into bed, leaving the lights off while he undressed because of the absence of curtains, and hoping that he would drop into sleep immediately. Instead, he stared at the ceiling for a long time. Moving was very disorienting. Retiring, even more so.

At least he had bought a house, which counted for a lot. But he didn't much like getting the smallest house. Were all his neighbors going to look down on him? Maybe they wouldn't know what he paid. Looked like a nice community, and it was a pretty place, with the healthy lawn out front and the front door painted dark red. He was good with a hammer and saw. Probably just with a little effort, he could make the place even spiffier than it was. That cheered him.

The divorce had been a thing he had never anticipated; it was all Mary Margaret's idea, though he had to admit she was right. Right or not, he had hated all the recriminations it unleashed. The next blow was the money spent on lawyers, then her insistence on the best of their family photos and all the newest furniture. Most of their friends decided he was the bad one; if Mary Margaret didn't want him anymore, he must have been running around chasing other women. They were convinced of this even though they had known him for years. It was a relief to get away from all that and into a totally new life.

He fell asleep on that happier note and slept straight through the night.

The next day he got to work. He found the hardware store and bought some paint and rented a power hose. It was a one-story house of stucco, not a hard job at all. He called his son, Martin, to come help him but Martin had tickets to the Giants game. He promised he would come help paint when Don started on the interior. Don cut back the bushes and hosed off the stucco, fumbling some with the hose because the power was stronger than he remembered. He had selected a light cream color to get rid of the muddy brown. However, after the first few strokes of the roller, he saw it was going to take two coats to cover the darker color.

It had been a while since he had painted. He should have picked a color closer to the brown. Also, he should have covered the bushes which were becoming speckled with paint. He remedied this, a little late, by taking the sheets off his bed and spreading them as far as they would go. He would buy some new sheets after he was done.

It took two days just to finish the first coat, but it looked good. Maybe he could just do some touch-up and skip the second coat. He was cleaning his brushes and rollers in the kitchen sink when someone knocked at the front door.

This was a little old lady with white hair. Shady Acres seemed to be mostly populated by these.

"You know you're not allowed to paint the house white," she said crisply.

"It's not white; it's cream."

"Just the same, it's white enough not to be allowed."

"Nobody's telling me what color to paint my house."

He scowled at her fiercely and closed the door in her face. Old nosy! Then he had to open it again a few minutes later because his open can of paint was out there. The old nosy was gone. Before he picked up the can of paint, he walked down to the sidewalk to look back at the house and admire his work. Clean and bright, a good choice and an excellent job! Even the sheets were not ruined but showed only occasional drips of paint.

That afternoon, when Don was easing his sore muscles with a beer and the final minutes of the Giants game on television, a man came to the door. He was a tall, elderly, rather fussy type, maybe with a little palsy in his hands. It was an adult community which meant everyone had to be over 55. But this one was possibly over 80. Don hoped they weren't all going to be like this.

"Good morning," the man began with a friendly air. "We haven't met yet but I can tell you your house color is going to fail. Sorry to be the bearer of bad news. Only earth colors allowed. If you'd come to us first, the way we ask you to, you would have been saved the work of doing it over. I'm from the Association, so I know. I'm a neighborhood captain. "

The beer and the sore muscles had something to do with Don's reaction. "I don't know what kind of place you're running here, but this is America. Nobody tells me what color to paint my house."

"But we can. It's in the CC&Rs."

Don had got up quite a head of steam by now. "Get off my porch before I knock you down."

Of course, it wasn't a porch, just a wide concrete step, what they called the stoop. The man looked frightened and backed away and Don slammed the door. Damn busybodys. Just when he thought he might like the place.

To distract himself, he went out shopping. He bought a pair of secondhand livingroom couches that would fill the front room nicely, and a secondhand dining table, chairs, and sideboard. While he was waiting for these to be delivered, he walked through his house and admired it. The threat against it had made it more valuable, more vulnerable, more his.

The carpet was fine. All he had to do was paint the downstairs rooms. Not that they were bad but he thought they needed brightening up. Then he had to put the kitchen together.

After the new furniture was delivered and he had moved it around till he was satisfied, he thought maybe he didn't need new paint indoors. It looked pretty good the way it was. Then he got busy on some small stuff. Having been a telephone repairman he knew how to hook up his satellite dish, his phone, and Internet connection, and repair the oven that had come with the house. As these things got done, he was more and more content.

He had to do something about curtains but here his determination crumbled; he had never bought curtains, didn't even know where to buy them. There was shrubbery hiding most of the living room windows. He hung a sheet over the rod in the bedroom. That would have to do for now. The second bedroom was empty anyway. And who ever heard of kitchen curtains?

He was cooking his breakfast the morning after he finished these jobs, just thinking it was time to go out and meet some neighbors when he saw a woman out in front pausing by his front walk. There was something odd about the way she moved and he went to the window and saw that she held a leash attached to her dog, a sorry looking oddball. The oddball that was just squatting on Don's front yard, that handsome carpet of intense green which had been mowed only yesterday by the Association gardener.

Don went dashing out. "Get that dog off my lawn!"

The woman glared at him. Clearly she was a bottle blonde, too old for that color hair to be natural, neatly dressed in red and navy, with bright red lipstick. "Be quiet until she's done, please."

Who cared whether a dog was interrupted? "I don't want her doing that on my lawn. Get her off there!"

The woman did not move while the full turds fell from the dog. When there were no more, the dog bounced happily away, relieved of her burden. The woman moved toward the turds with a plastic bag in her hand which was not meaningful to Don.

"Get off my lawn!"

"I was going to pick them up." The woman looked surprised; also indignant.

"You think that's going to make up for letting your dog shit on my lawn? And what about all the pee?"

"All right, if you don't want me to." She moved down the sidewalk pulled by the dog.

When she got to the corner, she turned back and gave Don a look that said she thought he was totally mad. He reciprocated by glaring.

It wasn't five minutes till there was another one. Don left the egg frying in the skillet while he ran outside. This time it was a really old lady, who tottered some in her gym shoes, and a small old dog of indeterminate breed.

"Get out of here! Get your dog off my lawn."

She might totter but she was not intimidated. "Violet likes it here. This is one of her regular spots. We come here every day."

"Not any more."

"I don't know what's the matter with you!" The woman shook her head.

"Come on, Violet." She pulled the dog away.

Half an hour later another dog, this one a white poodle leading a gray-haired lady, came by. This dog was bigger, older, wore a disdainful look, and he sniffed over Don's yard as he looked for the perfect spot to dump his load. Don ran outside.

"You get that dog off my lawn."

The woman was startled; she backed away. "I was going to pick it up." She waved her plastic bag at him.

"Get out of here."

The egg was ruined, the skillet would be hell to clean out, and the phone quit ringing just as Don got to it. He decided to go out for breakfast.

*   *   *

Phyllis walked her new dog, Pudgie, every morning at 8:30. As can be guessed from the name, Pudgie was not a beauty. When Phyllis arrived at the idea she needed a dog to walk rather than a cat, she decided to do the community and environmentally responsible thing and adopt an unwanted dog. Pudgie was from Dog Rescue, rather small, shorthaired, of mixed breed with a boxer face and a terrier body. He (a neutered he) was also given to biting and so had been determined unadoptable, which was what had appealed to Phyllis. What a good thing she was doing for the world, and for Pudgie.

However, it was not yet a successful marriage. Phyllis and Pudgie had their ups and downs, but Phyllis tried sincerely to make the relationship work and only occasionally was she reduced to threatening Pudgie that she would turn him into the pound and its lethal ways.

This morning was a good morning. She had Bridget's latest information about Jessie to think over and Pudgie had accepted his leash without snarling and seemed happy enough making a round of interesting smells. Phyllis had been able to persuade Pudgie to take a slightly different route so that she could go past the house on the corner of Shady and Alms where someone new had just moved in. This had been of general interest recently because, as everyone knew by now, the new owner had painted the exterior without getting permission on the color from the Association.

Phyllis was now the fifth lady with dog who had stopped at Don's lawn this morning. By this time he was on the phone to the Sheriff's Department, but was so indignant it was hard for him to get his words out. Without letting the sheriff off the hook, he came charging out of the house, waving his cordless phone and yelling at the top of his voice.

Phyllis screamed in fright, but Pudgie was made of sterner stuff. He made a dash for Don, pulling as hard as he could on his leash, barking loudly, wanting to attack Don with all of his seventeen pounds.

Seeing this ferocity, Don backed away toward the house. "You'll be sorry!" he yelled.

Phyllis trotted hastily back to her own house as fast as Pudgie could go.

"Can you believe that?" Phyllis said to Bridget by phone. "Can you believe him saying 'get that dog off my lawn'?"

"When," Bridget continued for her. "Guess what! It's not his lawn."

That was true. All the grass belonged to the Association to the glee of the residents because the Association had to water and mow all of it.

"Well, he probably knows that by now. Someone will have called the Office."

"I did. Right away. I didn't want to leave the man in ignorance."

But when Phyllis got off the phone, she was not thrilled at the thought of the lesson the new man was about to learn. He was rather a good looking man for his age. He had hair and no huge belly. And he seemed to be single. No wife would have let him run out and yell at helpless women who were only walking their dogs.

She thought she might allow a week for him to learn about the lawns and get over his indignation, and then go by again and try to get into a conversation. She was awfully tired of having no man around.

"I think Phyllis is interested in someone," Bridget said one cocktail hour when she was visiting Jessie and John Roger.

"Really?" Jessie was barely interested in news about Phyllis. "Who?"

Only Bridget, because she saw Phyllis all the time, could appreciate what a change it was in the recent widow (well, two and a half years) to show interest in a man.

"I can't tell but she's looking in the mirror again and she's thrown away some of those awful sweatsuits she usually wears."

"Well, I suppose that's good." Still Jessie looked baffled as to why she should be interested in a woman with wild hair, who wore no makeup, and baggy sweatpants to the market. If you didn't make an effort, you obviously had decided you weren't worth it and who should be in a better position to know.

A couple of weeks later, Phyllis casually let Bridget know she had been talking to the new man occasionally.

What new man?

"Well, the one who lives at the corner of Shady and Alms."

"That's the one who didn't want dogs on *his* lawn."

"Yes, that's the one. He's alright now. The Office settled him down, and I pointed out to him that I always pick up the turds."

"What's he like?"

"He's a very interesting man. He's thinking of becoming a volunteer fireman for the town. Isn't that good of him?"

"I don't think they take anyone old enough to live here. Maybe he should just volunteer for the hospital or deliver Meals on Wheels."

"That's a good idea. I'll suggest that. Not the Meals on Wheels. I tried that and it's all too depressing. But the hospital part."

"What's he like?"

Phyllis was on guard. "Understand, I'm not a Jessie, doing anything to get a man interested in me."

"No, of course not."

"We have just been talking a little. And we're going out dancing Friday night."

Bridget almost gasped. Here a man had come on the scene and was being snatched up already and she had never even heard of him. You had to be quick in this over-fifty five life, everything went much faster.

"But what's he like?"

"Like?" Phyllis tried to think. "He used to work for the phone company. He just got divorced two years ago and his wife moved back to the Midwest but his son lives in the city."

Bridget could see she was not going to get the kind of information she was interested in – did he like going to the theatre, did he like fishing, could he play bridge?

Chapter Ten

Jessie and John Roger had a fight. At first it didn't seem so momentous, at least not to Jessie. It started over the way he dressed.

She had put on a new dress for him, hoping he would notice it, though John Roger was not much of one to comment on what she wore. It was a dark rayon print with puffy sleeves and a low neck. She had almost passed it over in the dress shop. On the hanger it had looked like nothing in particular but she liked the print and there was nothing else interesting on the rack so she had taken it to the dressing room. But once it was on, she could see the way she had looked thirty five years ago.

Pleased and excited, she had bought it and, at home, had dug out an elaborate silver necklace from Nepal, something she hadn't worn in years. She twirled around to make the skirt swirl out, and was suddenly impatient for JR to arrive, for them to start the evening, a totally new evening, the kind of evening in which anything might happen.

When he showed up, slightly late, in blue jeans and a much-faded work shirt, his expression was grumpy.

Jessie was poised to kiss him. Instead she backed away and said with dismay, "We're going out to dinner!"

"I know we're going out to dinner."

"Then why are you wearing that?" She was now close enough to see that he hadn't shaved today.

"Because I'm tired and I didn't have time to go home and change."

"It's all right. We can go an hour later. I'll call and change the reservations. That will give you time."

"Goddamnit, you're not telling me what to wear! I've had a hard day," he yelled suddenly. He stomped across the dining room away from her and turned near his favorite chair, ready to plop into it. But he stopped to glare at her first.

Jessie was furious. "I *am* telling you what to wear. I'm not going to the Red Chimneys with you in that outfit." She didn't mention the part about shaving. If she won on the clothes, surely the shaving should follow.

"Lady, this is California. You go in any restaurant and you're going to see men dressed like this."

"Not the places I go to!" If she had been, at that moment, devoted to telling the truth, she would have had to say that some men in town did go to all the restaurants and everywhere else, just like that. Especially those who had made a lot of money; particularly in ranching or contracting but also in high tech. They seemed to enjoy immensely the freedom of dressing the way they wanted. Most women put up with it. Jessie hated it. What was all this dressing down in aid of? Why did they all want to look like stevedores or bums? She remembered when men wore hats most of the time. If she had her way, they would have all worn suits and white shirts during the day, and black tie in the evenings.

She remembered Edgar, always so carefully dressed, and had a moment of dislike for this cowboy. Short too! She passed him and sat down on her couch with her arms firmly folded, at war but possibly willing to discuss it. She had pointedly not offered him a glass of wine though she had one in front of her, which she had poured before putting on her make-up.

"Then I'm not going," she declared.

"All right, don't go!"

He glared fiercely at her. When she did not seem to be relenting, he turned around. "Well, I'm not going to skip dinner because of you."

"You're going to leave....just like that?"

"I told you, you can't tell me what to wear. Damn bossy women. They never let a man alone!" And he was out the door, which he slammed loudly behind him.

Jessie took a sip of wine, thinking this was the kind of time when one regretted giving up smoking. She sat and waited for him to return. This was new. He hadn't ever slammed out before, though of course this sort of thing happened once in a while in every relationship. Maybe he had had a bad day.

How could he get so upset when he was so clearly in the wrong?

She had forgotten that men were often like this. When you least expected it, they burst out in some form of "leave me the way I am" in totally unreasonable bad temper. Didn't men have their way most of the time as it was?

After some minutes, she heard his car start up and drive away down the street. She flushed in confusion and stood up to go to the window. He must have been sitting out there in the car, waiting for her to come out and smooth things over. Maybe she should have. Not apologize but just go out and try to rescue the evening. Not likely that she'd apologize when she was in the right! When she got to the window it was too late. His car had already turned onto the highway and was out of sight.

Belvy raised her head and whined. The clock ticked. Jessie waited forty-five minutes and then got up and was about to take the dress and the necklace off. But why waste the effort she had put into dressing up?

Instead she went to the phone and called Bridget. "John Roger got stuck over on the other side of the county. I'm all dressed. Do you want to go out to dinner?"

Bridget, of course, said yes.

Later that night, when Jessie got in bed and turned on the television and was watching a rehash of the day's news plus the most gruesome of the local traffic accidents, she began wondering about the quarrel, even berating herself. It had been nothing at all. A disagreement over how to dress for dinner. But what did it all mean? Was he tired of her? Was he worried about something else? He was having a spec house built. That was usually his excuse for arriving dirty. He had been over to look at the house. Though usually he didn't have to do anything there, just see how it was coming and talk to the contractor. Something had gone wrong and caused him to be out of sorts. She probably should have asked.

Both dogs sat up and gave the smallest of whines. She had forgotten to take them out for their evening walk when she got back from dinner. She had intended to do it with John Roger just before they left for the restaurant. She got up again and let them into the garden. Tomorrow she would have to hose down the corner where they would pee, to get the smell out.

She stopped to admire the almost-full moon. Her confusion and regret abated. Wasn't it quiet and peaceful when there was no man around? She listened for the small sounds of her neighbors and heard a car on the next street. When it had passed, the silence was thicker than ever, a pleasant weight on the night world. It was novel to stand in her garden in the moonlight with the dogs nosing around the bushes, snuffling, their chain collars clinking slightly.

She should enjoy this. John Roger had been with her nearly every evening for the past several months. It was a little tiring. She needed some space now and then. He would come around tomorrow or the next day and they would sort this out and she would hear just what it all had meant.

The next morning she lingered over her toast and coffee, waiting for a call from him but none came. Probably he had gotten up early and was out doing something. It was a day she was not going in to work so she washed her hair and put on shorts and went out to the garden to cut off dead blooms. She puttered all day, sewing a button on a blouse, paying a few bills, filing the various papers which couldn't be thrown out. There was a peculiar ache inside her.

Still no word from him.

It was Bridget who was alarmed. She arrived at the usual "wine time", bringing some camellias from her garden. Jessie had forgotten she was coming. Of course, last night at dinner she hadn't said anything about a difference of opinion.

"But where is he?"

"I have no idea."

"Did you quarrel?"

Jessie hesitated and then decided it was simpler to say yes.

"Oh, that's terrible. Oh, you're going to make it up, aren't you?"

"I don't know."

Bridget was near to squeaking in her distress. "Oh, you have to. You two are so good together."

This was not something Jessie wanted to hear. "Come walk with me while I take the dogs out!"

Tibby and Belvy erupted when they saw Jessie take out the leashes. They cavorted, dancing around her, barking loudly.

"QUIET!" she yelled. "SIT!"

They tried to sit but were too excited and kept jerking away to rush to the door and back. Bridget tried to help but mostly got on the way.

"I don't know how you can do this," she said.

Jessie whacked Belvy over the head with the end of the leash and got her to sit long enough to fasten the leash on the collar. Seeing it accomplished, Tibby bowed his head and waited more patiently.

"Key!" Jessie reminded herself, reaching for it.

The four of them finally got out. After some emphatic SITS and STAYs, the dogs finally calmed down enough to walk sedately along the street in front of the women as they headed toward the playing fields. Jessie considered whether she would let them loose when they got to the fields. She wasn't in the mood for all the games they could play when they weren't ready to quit their run. Maybe it would be better just to walk them.

They walked for half an hour, faster than the women would have chosen if they weren't being dragged. Bridget was beginning to breathe hard. But the exercise relaxed both women, and even the dogs seemed willing to turn around toward home.

"They really are handsome dogs," Bridget said at one point, and Jessie who was used to most people disapproving of the pair, was grateful.

At the end of the evening, after they had had a glass of wine and a slice of peach pie, Jessie confided: "I guess he's mad at me. But I didn't really say anything except 'change your clothes.'"

"He'll be back," Bridget told her confidently.

"I suppose so." Jessie thought almost fondly of Edgar. Anytime they quarreled, he was always explicit about how he felt about everything, why he thought he was in the right.

Five days after the quarrel, when John Roger had still not appeared, Jessie was limp with regret. She stumbled through her work days, forgetting half of what she needed to know. All the years before she knew him had evaporated from her memory and she could only remember his potent presence in her house. Was she ruining her life by letting a man become too important to her? She thought back over her long, unhappy marriage, accepting that John Roger would have seemed unobtainable happiness then. And now she had thrown it away.

As a defense, she began to count up his bad points so that she would have them to remind herself not all had been perfect and, perhaps, she could find someone more suited to her. He was not a good lover. A major disappointment. Number two. She knew she would never be able to persuade him to go into San Francisco for the opening of the opera or for the Black and White Ball, two events that glimmered in her head now and then. He was older than he said he was; she knew that for certain without knowing exactly how old. His table manners were not all that she would have liked.

Probably she was better off without him. This thought brought on a pain at the back of her head and she went to take two aspirin and lie down. She had been seriously caught in the old familiar trap of caring too much about a man.

She sat an extra open house for her friend Sandra, storing up the favor, and read all the new directives from the office.

In the second week, she tried out some small consolations. She bought a new asparagus fern and hung it on the patio. Probably it would die in a couple of months. They never lasted long for her. But for now, it hung its long delicate tendrils down beside the teak bench in a way that pleased her. That was good for about ten minutes of pleasure. She rented a couple of movies but couldn't sit all the way through either one. They were comedies, not suited to her present frame of mind. Movies had gotten better, yes, but she had gotten worse, less interested, more impatient. She dug out a big brass and copper pot an aunt had bought in Turkey long ago and put it on the mantel, taking off the pewter mugs she was tired of seeing. Distractions didn't distract the way they had when she was younger. Vases and pictures and all those things she had yearned for when she was young had lost their power over her.

Maybe she would never get over him, would die still feeling like this. She was plunged in gloom.

She was trying to admire the brass pot when she heard a car in the driveway. Not just a car, an SUV. It had been twelve days since she had heard it.

Now there was an abrupt knock at the kitchen door.

She felt her hair to see if it needed combing. Too bad she had put on these old white pants this morning. She wasn't going to change now. She went to the kitchen door and opened it. John Roger was there. With a frown on his face.

"Well, hello," she said neutrally.

"Can I come in?"

"Of course."

Inside, he stood uncertainly in the dining room.

"Sit down."

He walked towaard the living room but didn't sit. "Okay. How are you?"

"I'm well."

"Well, I'm not. I don't want to quarrel. Okay?"

"That's all you're going to say?"

"I don't believe in quarreling. Okay?"

"You're not going to say you're sorry for stomping out like that?"

"All that stuff! I'm not good at that. Let's just patch it up"

"You hurt my feelings. I didn't do anything wrong."

He waited.

Mournfully, Jessie decided she didn't have much choice. She was afraid he might walk out again. Finally, she said, "Okay."

He nodded, satisfied. "I have to go over to the ocean to pick up some building materials. Would you like to go?"

"I have to change my clothes," she said rapidly. "How long will we be gone? Should I run the dogs first? Are we going to eat over there?"

"I don't know," he said. "Let's take the dogs and run them on the beach."

He hardly ever offered that. That was a major concession. "Oh, they'd love that. Just give me a minute to change."

"Just beach clothes," he called after her as she hurried down the hall. "And a windbreaker. We'll buy sandwiches at the store."

Her heart glad, Jessie hurried into her white denims. She forgot about his table manners and the Black and White Ball. He was here and life was full of movement and anticipation again.

Chapter Eleven

Phyllis waited patiently for two weeks before trying to strike up a friendship with Don Dorfman. This was after she mentioned his name to Alice Egan, the half-time secretary in the Association office, and found out that Dorfman had indeed gone in and complained bitterly about the dogs on his lawn.

Alice had been alone in the office when Don had slammed in.

"I knew just what it was going to be about. I've had this job four years now. It's always the men." She used her pen to push her glasses up, leaving a small blue dot at the top of her nose.

"Right away he started yelling: 'Shitting all over my lawn. It's got to stop'... and more of the same, all very loud as if I had done it myself."

Phyllis nodded in sympathy.

"And then I told him, gently of course, that it wasn't his lawn." The lawn belonged to the Association, and the dog owners were perfectly entitled to do just what they had been doing. As long as they picked up the turds.

Don's face had become red and his eyeballs bigger. He had never heard of anything like this. Of course it was his lawn, he had it right in front of him, he had to walk across it to get to his mailbox on the street. Didn't he set his lawn chair out on it? Et cetera, et cetera.

"Do you know how many times I've been through this?" Alice asked Phyllis. "I just switched my computer over to Solitaire and played a few games while he walked up and down and yelled at me. They should give hazard pay for this job."

He was going to take it up with his attorney.

"Look in your CC&Rs," Alice finally told him.

"What's that?"

"The Association regulations. You got a copy when you signed for your house."

"I did not."

She got up and dug through a file drawer, finally locating the particular file she wanted. "Your signature, right here, shows that you received it."

From the stricken look on his face, she saw he knew he had been bested. After a minute to recover, he lowered his voice and tried to start over again.

"And what about all the pee?"

"Sometimes this job really isn't worth it," Alice said to Phyllis. "I even lost three games of Solitaire in a row by making mistakes. I hardly ever do that."

Finally he ran down a bit but kept glaring, demanding an answer, so she said: "The sprinklers wash it away."

"I've never seen any sprinklers sprinkling."

"Is the lawn green?"

"Yes."

"Well, then they're sprinkling at night."

Don finally gave up. He slammed out of the office and got in his car.

"I thought he would have an accident and that would serve him right," Alice finished.

"It is terrible what you have to put up with," Phyllis said gently, and then she left.

*   *   *

After his unsatisfactory visit to the office, Don drove into town for a six pack of beer. Normally he didn't drink any alcohol before five o'clock but today was definitely different. How was he going to stand this place? He hated all those neurotic little dogs and their asinine old lady owners. He couldn't watch them go by day after day, pausing just long enough to dirty his lawn. Back at his dining room table with the beer in a glass, he brooded.

If he sold the house, he would lose all the money spent on closing costs and have to pay a realtor's fee besides, reducing what he could put as a down payment on the next house. Then he'd have to find that house. He didn't like dealing with real estate agents. He always thought they were trying to put something over on him and, face it, this had really been the best house available for the money.

After three beers, he developed a headache and, waiting for inspiration, lay down for a mid-day nap.

He spent the next few days in a foul temper, brooding over his lawn while he put down shelf paper and unpacked all the dishes. He growled silently at anyone who walked a dog past his house. Then, a friend, Alec, called and invited him to go fishing at Clear Lake and he accepted.

Alec thought Don should throw a fright into those women so they were afraid to come back to his lawn but Don was already less pugnacious than he had been. He could see all sorts of trouble from trying to frighten those old ladies. Plus, they didn't look very frightenable.

When he got back from the three-day fishing trip, he was somewhat resigned to dogs on the lawn. He got to talking to a man who lived several doors down and found out there were regular bridge games. Don hadn't played bridge since the Navy but maybe now he would take it up again. He called in and signed up as a substitute.

*   *   *

Phyllis walked past the corner of Shady and Alms three weeks after the first time. She carefully kept Pudgie to the street side, away from Don's lawn. There was no sign of Don but she thought the aura of the house looked more peaceful. The brass mailbox slot had been polished and this morning's free newspaper had been picked up. Encouraged, she came back the next morning. She had decided to leave Pudgie at home. This time she was rewarded with the sight of Don walking across the lawn to pick up a stray newspaper.

"Good morning," she said.

He merely nodded at her.

"I really like the color you painted your house."

He growled. "That's more than the Association did. They say I have to paint it again…one of the prescribed colors. You know what that's gonna cost? Who ever heard of prescribing colors?"

"I know. They can be difficult, can't they? It's because it's a development, all designed at one time, supposed to all look alike. Though what good that does, I don't know."

He was happy for the opportunity to let out some of his stored-up resentment. "And they don't want the bushes to grow up and cover the windows. What if you like your windows covered by bushes?"

Phyllis tsked-tsked, and nodded sympathetically.

"Is it worth it, just to live here?"

"It really is very nice here. And there are lots of women. You might like that."

"Why would I like that? All of them with dogs!" He had secured the newspaper. He crossed the lawn in front of her and went into his house, giving the door a small slam for emphasis.

Phyllis went on home well enough pleased. He had talked to her, she had shown she was on his side. Next time should be better.

She waited another few days before passing his house again. She had left Pudgie at home again, though he barked his disapproval. Don was outside, painting the house a recommended "warm beige." It was the color of at least a quarter of the houses in Shady Acres.

"Oh, that looks very nice," she said. "Although not as nice as the color you had it before."

He turned around growling. "That was a perfectly good color but it doesn't suit the office."

"Oh, I know. They're terribly fussy, aren't they?"

He seemed to recognize her. He nodded, although not with much warmth. "I'm glad some people around here agree with me."

"Oh, absolutely! You know what you could do? The Association has a Board and they are elected every year. You should get to know a lot of people here and run for the Board and then you could change things."

"Is that right?" He had stopped painting long enough to consider this point. The paint began running from the brush down his arm. He shook the arm in irritation. "Well, I'll keep that in mind."

"My name is Phyllis."

Now he needed a rag to wipe his arm. He said gruffly: "All right, you can tell me about it some other time. I have to paint now."

"Oh, absolutely." Phyllis was of the mind that when a man wanted to do something, a woman should not make judgments about it but also help him do it. That had been her mother's opinion.

She waited another two days for the painting to get done. Then she donned her new aqua sweatsuit. She looked at Pudgie unhappily. If she took him, it might cause problems. If she didn't take him, Pudgie was likely to react by peeing on something in the house. She compromised by locking him in the garage.

It was four blocks to Don's house, not far for a frequent walker like Phyllis, but it seemed longer this time. She noticed everything as if she hadn't seen it for years. The Shasta daisies had bloomed, brightening several yards. That Miller woman who was always traveling must be home because her garage door was open and there was a strange car in her driveway. On the other hand, that could be a burglary in progress.

Should she investigate? Absolutely not. She might be hit on the head and left for dead.

In the next house, the pinkish tan one, there was a new widow. Not anyone Phyllis knew but she had read it in the Association newsletter. Already her bushes were looking shaggy. In Shady Acres, the greatest number of residents were single women. Next in number there were married couples, and lastly, just a few single men. All her life, Phyllis had preferred the company of women. But that was when she had had a man at home. Without that, you could get too much of a good thing.

At Don Dorfman's house, he was not in sight. The painting was done, though not the clean-up. There were still sheets over the bushes and blue tape around the windows. She walked past slowly and on up to the next block, and then walked slowly back. He could just have gone inside for something. Unfortunately, he did not appear when she walked past again. She went home disappointed but she would see him another day. He was painting the house over again to make the Association happy. He wasn't going to move away.

After she got home and let Pudgie out of the garage, she fell into a brown study. What she needed was an excuse to knock on his door.

She consulted Bridget, although without revealing her purpose, when Bridget dropped by. "Are you collecting for the Heart Association now?"

"No, no, that's not until April."

"For the hospital?"

"No, I've quit doing it for them. They're too hard to please."

"What about voter registration?"

"What's this for?" Bridget eyed the bear claw on Phyllis's plate. She had finished her own and Phyllis had hardly started.

"I just think I should be doing something."

"Well, there's always Meals on Wheels."

"Everybody getting meals is so sick and downtrodden, I get depressed."

"They need help in the hospital gift store."

"I don't think so." He wasn't likely to come into the hospital. The smell of rubber came back to Phyllis and she remembered her long tedious hours in the auto parts store. And that had been when she was several years younger.

"They're starting a Neighborhood Watch. You could go out campaigning for that."

"Perfect."

Two days later, armed with pamphlets, Phyllis knocked on Don's door. She had also secured his full name, his phone number and his former address. Don was home and tractable enough.

"Neighborhood Watch? I heard they had one of those in San Leandro but nobody paid it much attention."

"Oh, we take this one very seriously." She liked his eyebrows, full and bushy. He had a nice mouth too, straight and firm. She didn't much like the sleeveless undershirt but he had been in his own house, not walking around outside.

"What would I have to do?"

"I see that you've just painted your living room. What a nice color!"

"I picked that out and they can't tell me to change it."

"Of course not. Your home is your castle. It's lovely."

"I did the dining room in bright green."

"Wonderful!"

"Actually my son did the painting and I did the clean-up. Would you like to see it?"

"I'd love to." She was in the house. She turned on him with a wide smile.

"This is beautiful."

Don spent several minutes looking her over. Phyllis had no idea what judgments he was making but held her breath and smiled brightly. She flashed her bright blue eyes at him. Outside a single car passed on the street leaving silence behind it. Don continued to look at her a few seconds longer while some thought of his, some intention, got completed. "I just made some coffee. Would you like some?"

"What a nice idea!"

An hour later, Phyllis walked home in a delighted daze. The man was lonely. That was all that was wrong with him. When you got past that, he was very decent, polite, anxious to know things about his new neighborhood. He had signed the Neighborhood Watch application and maybe later would even be amenable to running for the Association Board.

He hadn't asked her any questions about herself but Phyllis didn't think men often did. He mostly talked about himself, about his divorce and his retirement and about how he had picked out Shady Acres. Obviously he hadn't had anyone to talk to for months. Any woman that is. Men never told things like this to other men.

Yes, yes, she knew the world was changing. Her daughter told her that numerous times. Women were getting more like men so they could compete for jobs. They had to. Men had stopped supporting them. So the world was changing, but did that mean men would no longer look to women for tender sympathy? How would she be able to make friends in that new world? She didn't know and didn't much care, she would be happy with her few more years in this one where she knew what was what.

She was going to go downtown to McCulloughs and look for a new outfit, something other than a sweatsuit.

Chapter Twelve

Jessie was on the phone. "What are you doing today?"

Bridget came alert. "Nothing much."

"I want you to come over this afternoon. Around five. John Roger will be here. He wanted me to call you."

"You're back together? That's wonderful."

Jessie's voice was like birdsong, notes melting into each other, up and down. "He got over his mad, I guess."

Before going to see them, Bridget drove into town and purchased an especially good cabernet in celebration. What an improvement this was from yesterday! She had had another session with Marion. How had she gotten into being the only prop of a woman who sounded as if she would shortly take a dive from the Golden Gate Bridge?

Not that Marion talked suicide. Probably she wouldn't think of it till just before she did it. But then she would actually do it. She wasn't one of these women who would threaten suicide to make people feel sorry for her. Bridget thought that Marion was like many she had met who had grown up on the Great Plains - to them words meant exactly what they said, never more or less, never something else.

"You have no idea how glad I was to hear from you," Bridget burst out as soon as she was inside Jessie's house.

"Why is that?"

"You remember Marion Frewalter?"

"Yes, how's she doing?"

But from the tone of her voice, Bridget guessed Jessie wasn't much interested, and so let the story go. If people didn't show a certain amount of sophistication, Jessie wasn't interested in them. Marion had not made the cut.

Jessie was happy because she had sold another house. Or at least put it into escrow. Things could still go wrong but it looked good. This meant money for extras for the next several months. This success had imparted a certain glow to her skin and her smile.

"You look wonderful," Bridget said. "And you look as if you've lost weight. Lucky you." It was the thing to say, but now that she looked at her, she thought Jessie too thin.

"I've decided to eat nothing but fruit for breakfast. A friend told me that was much healthier than cereal."

"Mmm." Bridget had a policy never to comment on other people diets, or talk about her own. "What brought John Roger back?"

Jessie hesitated. She didn't usually talk about matters so personal. "Who knows! Isn't that like a man? Gone one day, then here the next without a word of explanation."

"Exactly."

They went into the living room, which was spotless as always; Jessie seemed never to leave things lying around. It looked wonderful to Bridget who had been missing the times spent in it. "I love this room."

"Thank you. If the sale goes through, I'm going to have the couch recovered. The dogs have gotten it very dirty and even torn it a little."

"Maybe you can just get it mended."

"Probably, but it's nine years old. Time for a change."

At this point, a car could be heard in the driveway, and in a moment JR appeared in the kitchen doorway, and walked in without knocking.

"Hello there, Red. How've you been?"

"She brought us some good wine. Come and open it."

"Always glad to do that. How are you, love?"

Jessie went into the kitchen to receive a kiss while Bridget got up to go and look at a wooden Japanese box she hadn't seen before. Bridget's living room was full of all sorts of objects, everything she could possibly find room for, while Jessie would only put out one or two things at a time, and then changed them every month or so.

"Well," John Roger said, as soon as they were all seated. "Guess what we're up to? We're going to go to Europe. I haven't been there in twenty five years. Everything will be different, that's for sure."

"JR, wait…"

"Where in Europe?"

"I've got a travel agent looking for a tour. I like those two days in each of ten cities kind of things. You see a lot. Mostly churches, but that's what they've got so no complaining."

"It sounds wonderful."

"It's not all decided yet," Jessie said stiffly.

Afraid of a disagreement, Bridget started telling about a school she had gone to in Southern France when she was a teenager. With the second glass of wine, they all relaxed and John Roger began telling a long story about trying to sell the spec house he had been building. The people who came by wanting to buy it were all odd types. He was beginning to think there was going to be another hippie revolution.

*   *   *

After Bridget was gone, Jessie said, "You shouldn't have talked about Europe yet. It's not decided."

"Don't you want to go?"

"Not unless this escrow closes. I need the money from that."

"Hon, I will pay for the trip. Forget about the money."

Jessie frowned. "I don't really like anyone else paying for me. I like to take care of myself."

"Well, that's a good way to feel, but we can maybe do twice as many things if sometimes I pay for you. That's worth it, isn't it?"

There was a note in his voice which was saying he hated having the same arguments over and over. She knew it was true, he would rather pay for her than wait around till she could pay for it. But it was just that impatience she disliked. It said her desire to pay for herself was not very meaningful. Which translated into – the money she made was negligible. Her ability to support herself was not at all important. She was just a woman who could be annexed by superior wealth. A headache was developing at the back of her head.

"All right, let's say we're going to go on a trip but not necessarily Europe."

He looked confused. "I thought that's what you wanted. Sure. Where else would you like to go?"

"Santa Fe!"

He looked doubtful. "It's all art galleries. I don't give a damn for art galleries. It's all right but… How about Honolulu?"

Jessie shook her head. "It's just like L.A. Cuernavaca?"

"I've always heard about it and never been there." He was intrigued. "All right, get me some brochures. What is there to do there?"

"All the things you like…swim, play bridge, ride horses. And loads of jewelry stores for me."

He gave her a rare slow smile, acknowledging that she knew him and what he liked.

Jessie's mind was not on Cuernavaca but on John Roger. It was amazing how little difference his absence had made once they were back together. Jessie had trouble remembering what she had done during those empty days. How had she been able to stand it, not knowing if he would return, thinking it might all be over? She would never have told anyone but she thought of him first thing in the morning when she woke up. Not important thoughts, stray thoughts – what is he doing now, is he up yet, does he still have that cough, are all the clothes he was wearing yesterday scattered on the floor? Who changes the sheets? What is he eating for breakfast? Every night, when she lay down to go to sleep, her mind drifted to the last things he had said to her. Whether in person or over the phone, the sound of his words was like a talisman that let her sleep.

It was very likely that he hardly thought of her when she was out of his sight. Or if he did, it would be purely practical thoughts about when they were next to meet or whether he would be able to fix her oven that had been broken forever and ever, or the tomato plants they were supposed to plant in barrels in her patio. He had brought them explaining that he grew tomatoes every year, always had, and this year it looked as if he wouldn't see them unless they were in her yard. He had said that before they quarreled, and then he had gone away and she hadn't seen him. Now that he was back, he had promised to put the tomato plants in tomorrow, saying it was very late for them to get started, but it didn't really matter. What was important was that he planted them every year.

*   *   *

Three days later, the trio of Jessie, John Roger and Bridget were back drinking a new bottle of wine, this time on Jessie's patio, and discussing Cuernavaca. Jessie had gotten some brochures from the travel agent and they had all spent an hour looking them over. The sun was lowering, casting shadows through the magnolia, but the birds still gossiped as chirpily as if it were morning. There were no sounds from the other houses or the street but Jessie had left a jazz CD on the record player inside. Maybe that was why the birds were having so much fun.

"All right, that sounds like the best hotel," Jessie said with finality.

"That's not bad." He gestured with his wine glass toward the music.

"It's not just not bad, it's very good," Jessie corrected. "It's Miles Davis."

Bridget, a classical music fan, shook her head to get the trumpet out of her ears. "I haven't been to Cuernavaca but I have been in Mexico City and Taxco. Twenty years ago. I have no idea what it's like now. It sounds wonderful."

"Do you want to deal with your travel agent, Jessie?"

"My travel agent is out of business. Now that the airlines won't pay them, the whole industry has dried up."

"How did you get the brochures?"

"From Triple A. I'll go back there. They'll book the trip for a fee."

"Maybe I'll go to Mexico this fall also," Bridget said, excitedly. "Don't we have to wait till the hurricane season is over?"

"That's just on the West coast, September, October, November."

"Oh, yes. Right. I haven't been for a while."

The other two passed over the suggestion that she might tag along.

"Jessie, do we fly or bus from Mexico City?" John Roger asked.

"I don't know. I haven't gotten that far. I'll have to ask."

"I've never been to Cuernavaca."

Jessie said, "Bridget, maybe you could get someone to go with you. Maybe this Marion."

Marion, right, who had barely enough money to buy food. Bridget sighed. Jessie was telling her clearly that she couldn't tag along on their trip.

"Well, that's an idea," Bridget said with as much enthusiasm as she could muster. "I'll ask around."

After some silence all around, Bridget said, "I have to tell you about the white elephant sale at the Methodist Church."

Bridget, still in search of an occupation, had volunteered to help out. People had jumped at the chance to empty their closets, donating the weirdest stuff....Bridget couldn't think who would buy it. But here they came, tons of people, purses open, buying up nearly everything. Some of the poorer families she could see they would really need extra mismatched glasses and plates and old irons, but the clothes? The clothes weren't worn out but Bridget thought most of them so odd they had likely been bought at sales, where the reduced prices had overcome objections to bad style and awkward fit. And yet they were snatched up eagerly because of the opportunity to get something cheap.

"Are we eating out or in?" John Roger asked. "I've had enough wine. I need food."

"Out to dinner. I didn't have time to get to the store this afternoon."

"All this talk about Mexico, I'm ready for some tamales."

"Tamales, ugh," Jessie said. "But I could eat some Shrimp Diavolo." She stood up and shook out her skirt.

"Bridget, do you want to go with us?" JR asked.

Bridget shook her head, but not too emphatically. She wouldn't go unless Jessie asked her. It was up to Jessie if she wanted to share JR for the rest of the evening. "I need to eat very lightly tonight. I went out for lunch."

John Roger's attention had turned wholly toward Jessie. His head was cocked to one side, watching his mistress for any sign of what she might be thinking, waiting for the smallest indication that they were about to commence a new activity. Bridget could feel the strong flow of energy between them.

On Jessie's part, her head was bent slightly and she was looking up at him through her lashes, her expression deliberately enigmatic, a suggestion of teasing.

They wouldn't want her tonight.

"I guess I should go and leave you two."

"Another time then," Jessie said, "You must come when I cook my famous Tamale Pie."

Bridget almost laughed. Jessie's oven had been broken for months, and in spite of JR's best intentions, wasn't getting fixed anytime soon. It might be a long time before there was a Tamale Pie. But the invitation was kindly meant. "That sounds wonderful."

She got up, and picked up her purse, and blew a goodby kiss to Jessie.

Okay, she was a third wheel. She knew she was a third wheel. It was a certain something special in their relationship which allowed her to enjoy it. Watching the two of them together, seeing their delight in each other, was warmth enough.

When she got back to her house, the curb next door was filled with cars, and an ambulance was in the driveway.

The ambulance driver was leaning against the van with no sense of emergency. From this she guessed that Sweetie Switzer had finally passed. Bridget pulled into her garage with a sudden sense of panic. Everything went so fast. One moment you were a freshman in college and the next you were about to die and you couldn't remember what all had happened in between.

Chapter Thirteen

Once Jessie and John Roger had left for Cuernavaca, Bridget fell into a slump. She was very happy for them, really she was, but there would be no wine get-togethers until they got back. She still hadn't found another volunteer job to get excited about. What would she have to look forward to?

She decided to share with Phyllis the fact that Jessie and John Roger were back together, and already off to Mexico. Their exciting hopes to build a house at the shore. All that. Would Jessie object if she knew that Bridget was spilling her life out to Phyllis? Well, maybe she would only hint at some of the details, skip over spots that Jessie might consider too private. Like… She couldn't think of any of those right now.

No need to call Phyllis. If Bridget arrived between 9:00 and noon, Phyllis was sure to be home. Phyllis walked Pudgie at 8:00 and then went back to the house to – do what? For Phyllis never read the newspaper or a magazine as far as Bridget knew, and never watched television, and talked to very few of her neighbors. In the middle of the afternoon, she drove into town to run a few errands, drycleaning or groceries or such, and at six o'clock she cooked her dinner. Was her life as boring as it looked?

Was Bridget's much better?

Bridget went back upstairs and changed her clothes. She had put on new camel's hair slacks but she didn't like wearing anything new to

Phyllis's house because Phyllis never had anything new. After changing into old plaid pants and a white shirt, she would run to the bakery and buy cinnamon rolls. Not croissants. She had had trouble buttoning waist bands several times lately. All that butter taking its revenge on her.

Phyllis had a buzzer on the outside of her patio gate. Not until someone rang the buzzer, did the mistress of the house come out and unlock the double locks on the gate. Bridget always wondered – who was she expecting? But when Phyllis came out this time, her wide smile made up for the uncomfortable feeling of standing outside the castle. Bridget's irritation vanished.

Phyllis seemed equally pleased. "Well, this is a surprise! The coffee is still hot."

Warmed by the welcome, Bridget followed her happily across the flagstone patio to the house. This was what she wanted…some cheerful companionship. No comments on the futility of everything, please.

Once inside and sitting at the round table, Bridget looked her hostess over and thought Phyllis was looking world's better than usual. Not her skin of course, but her movements were perky, and she had washed and set her pretty pale hair which was fading from blonde to gray. Her sweatsuit was not new but also not so old and limp as many of them were, showing wrinkles because they had been left in the washer too long before being transferred to the dryer. With it, Phyllis was wearing a bright cotton scarf which Bridget had never seen before.

"Everything looks so nice," she said, looking around, wondering.

The kitchen seemed cleaner than usual, and there was a bowl of cut geraniums on the dining table. The table itself gleamed from a recent waxing.

Phyllis had poured the coffee and accepted the rolls with interest. She put them out on two plates and hesitated with two butter knives in hand.

"Shall we have butter with them?"

The two women looked at each other. It was a hard decision.

"It's only margarine anyway, and whipped at that."

"Oh well, in that case, I guess it's all right. What's been happening to you? Something good, I can tell."

Phyllis wasn't going to give up her news so easily. She stirred her coffee and reflected.

"You'll never believe this. I just took a jacket back to Macy's. It's been hanging in my closet for a month, and I looked at it and thought I don't like it. So I took it back and they gave me back my money. Isn't that amazing, after all this time?"

Phyllis had bought a jacket at Macy's instead of the Goodwill – that was amazing in itself. It must have been a super sale. "Had you worn it?"

"No, I hadn't worn it. I wouldn't do that. But they were very nice. After they looked it over and saw it wasn't dirty or damaged. I had saved the tags and put them back on. You wouldn't take something back if you had worn it, would you?"

Bridget had. On more than one occasion. But she wasn't going to admit it. "What else has been happening? Just returning a jacket wouldn't pep you up like this."

Phyllis sipped her coffee. "Let's see. Oh, I did go dancing with that man. Maybe it's that."

Bridget gasped. With her worry over whether Jessie and John Roger would make up their quarrel, she had forgotten all about Phyllis' single mention of a new man in the neighborhood. How long ago had that been?

"When was this?"

"Saturday was the second time, no third time. He's really very nice. He had a terrible wife, just ruined his life for years."

Third time! "Or he ruined hers. Whichever. Now tell me again who this is."

Phyllis had a small smile that she couldn't quite hide. "Don's his name. He has one of the small houses at Shady and Alms. He's really good looking. Well, not good looking as we would have called it years ago, but nice looking for his age."

"Which is what?"

"I don't know exactly. Maybe late fifties. He took early retirement, he said. He's quite healthy and not fat."

Bridget acknowledged silently that these were the two things mostly wrong with the men in Shady Acres. Those two and bald, though she didn't find bald entirely unappealing. Norm, her second husband, who had split a considerable fortune with her in order to marry his young and beautiful Hawaiian stewardess, had been quite bald early on. Now they were all shaving their heads. "Retired from what?"

"Something in the telephone company. Something technical."

Then he could probably make my DVD player work was Bridget's thought but instead she said: "And dancing with him was fun?"

"Oh, yes. He's very good."

Bridget wondered if she could get over her shock and be gracious about this. After all, Phyllis deserved some good fortune. Finally she cleared her throat and with effort managed a happy tone. "Well, I think that's wonderful. Congratulations. And you're going to see him again?"

"He's taking me out to dinner on Friday."

It was not too long after this news that Bridget decided to end the visit. She never got a chance to talk about Jessie and the house at the shore. Instead she heard quite a bit about Don and his virtues and his problems with the Homeowners Association. Phyllis was taking his part in this and had written an indignant letter for him.

Bridget waited a decent length of time, until the cinnamon rolls were half eaten, then she announced that she had a doctor's appointment. She really didn't want to hear any more about the wonderful Don who had promised to put new batteries in Phyllis' remote.

"Have a great time on Friday." She had already heard that they planned to eat at the Irish restaurant, which was known for nothing but cheap prices while the food was poor.

"Why don't you come back tomorrow," Phyllis said energetically. "There are a lot of things we haven't talked about yet."

Bridget went back to her house and put on the new camel's hair slacks to comfort herself. Someone recently retiring from a technical job at the telephone company was not someone she would be interested in. Just the same…

That afternoon, she went to see Marion, reluctantly, but with a sense of duty and the sobering thought that she still hadn't accomplished anything there.

Marion greeted her with a look of resentment. Not a happy beginning. It was clear she had come to think of Bridget as the author rather than the messenger of her ill-fortune.

"Well, what is it we have to do today? I haven't got a lot of time."

"It's up to you, Marion. You decide."

"What can I decide? Either I pay the electric bill or I buy groceries for the week. There doesn't seem to be much choice there, does there?"

Bridget sat down on the couch. "Well, you said you had enough food for a week or two. I think you should pay the electric bill. You can't live here with candles."

"And then what do I do?"

"You need to sell the SUV. Did you get an estimate on it?"

"That was Jeb's car. How can I sell it? What would he think?"

"Marion, if he knows, and we don't know that he does, he wouldn't want you to go without food or electricity, either one." Then she thought over for a moment whether he might know how things were going here at 750 Spice Drive. That would be definitely odd, wouldn't it? And very upsetting to the recently deceased to know what was going on but be unable to do anything about it. Especially to a man like Jeb who had always liked being in charge.

"I don't even know how to sell it."

Bridget took the phone and called her bank and got a Blue Book figure on the value of the SUV.

She turned away from the phone with delight. "Marion, you can get fifteen thousand dollars for it. That will give you spending money for all year. Better, we'll put it in a money market account and make a little interest."

Marion was somewhat mollified at that.

"And as soon as it's sold, your insurance payments will be cut in half."

"In half?" Marion looked at Bridget as if she made a habit of making up figures to confuse her friends.

"Well, I don't really know but from two cars and two drivers to one car and one driver seems like it should be half, doesn't it?"

"I guess." So Marion, seeing a faint light at the end of the tunnel, made coffee for them.

"Where am I going to sell it?" she asked when the coffee was served.

"Well, you can either put an ad in the newspaper or you can park it at that vacant lot down by the library with a sign on it. It's a nice looking car; I think you should park it downtown first and let lots of people see it. That won't cost any money. If that doesn't work, we can think of something else."

"Is that legal?"

"I don't know if it's legal but everybody else is doing it. There are always cars for sale there."

Marion stirred her coffee. Bridget had had all the coffee she could take in one day and asked for water. She looked around while Marion chewed over and digested the idea of selling Jeb's SUV. The house had changed since Jeb had died. Bridget couldn't decide how exactly. None of the furniture had been moved. Maybe a house just changed when there was no longer a man living there.

"I can't sleep at night," Marion said. "I keep thinking someone is breaking in."

"Marion, I don't think they've had a break-in at Shady Acres in all the years since it was built."

"But it can always happen."

"I doubt it. What happened with your daughter? She was about to come out for a visit."

"Oh, she's busy with her life. I told her not to bother."

Bridget thought this was a bad idea. If you couldn't make demands on your children, who could you get help from? Not that she had ever asked her own for help; she thought they needed a little maturing before they were up to that.

"But you were looking forward to having her here for a week."

Marion tightened her mouth in disapproval. "She comes and tells me all these things about her life I'd rather not know. The young people just don't have any morals any more, even when they make a lot of money."

Bridget had never met Marion's daughter so she thought the best thing was not to comment on this statement. She rather liked her own daughter although she admitted that standards of behavior for young women had changed radically and she didn't think she wanted to know all the things her daughter did.

What she really wanted was to see something accomplished here today. "There's the Association Newsletter," she said. "These ads are free, you know."

Then without waiting for Marion's agreement, she called that office. Nodding at Marion that she could object any time she wanted to, Bridget listed Jeb's car. Marion frowned at some of the details but she didn't object.

"Now get me a number for your insurance company."

Frowning again, Marion got up and went to the overstuffed desk in the living room and came back with a folder.

Bridget called the insurance company, read off the policy number and informed them of Jeb's death. How much would Marion's payments go down when his car was sold?

"More than a hundred dollars a month, Marion. There's your money for food," she crowed happily. If they could just stick it out in this direction, get the SUV sold and the insurance company informed, Marion would be all right.

Marion's face, usually rather blank, developed a distinctly upside down U at the mouth. "You wonder, don't you, about insurance companies! I've been paying car insurance for forty years and never collected a dime."

Bridget decided it was time to leave. "When you get calls and are making appointments, call me and I'll come over when the buyers do. That way, one of us can stay here and one of us can ride with the buyer. We don't want anybody driving the car on a test without one of us along."

"Can't they just buy it? Do they have to drive it?"

Bridget rubbed her temples. "If you can sell it to someone who doesn't insist on driving it first, more power to you."

Shortly after that, she went home with a headache. She had received not a word of thanks. And now, no evening of wine and conversation at Jessie's. She would have to entertain herself.

As she poured her single glass of wine, she thought over the fact that working with Marion depressed her. So why did she do it? Probably, she was still working for those A's, accomplishments, as she had in school. And in this case, the difficulty of staying with the project would make the success even better.

*   *   *

The next day, Marion changed her mind twice but finally agreed to parking the car down by the library. After they reached this agreement, Bridget went to the hardware store and bought a For Sale sign. Then she followed Marion while she drove the SUV downtown to park it with the sign on it in the vacant lot which had become an unauthorized used car showroom.

Marion had shown uneasiness about driving the SUV, possibly just because it had been Jeb's. Maybe he had forbidden her to drive it? Bridget hadn't known him well but remembered him as rather absolute in his decrees.

When Marion climbed out of the SUV in the weedy and gravelly lot, her expression was a mixture of guilt and resentment. "You sure they're not going to break in and steal it?"

"Not on a main street in the center of town."

"Seems like a lot of trouble."

"Not too much to make fifteen thousand dollars!" Bridget was beginning to think if she could just get the SUV sold and the insurance reduced, she would cut back her visits with Marion to maybe one a month. Or less.

They left the SUV at the end of the row of vehicles with For Sale signs on them, waiting patiently like a row of single women at a dance.

"Do you want to stop at the video store on the way home? That new Jane Austen from *Masterpiece Theatre* is out."

Marion had a weakness for Jane Austen. "I suppose we could. But it's awfully hard to get them back on time."

"I'll bring it back tomorrow. I have to come in for a dentist appointment."

"Oh, I can't promise to see it tonight. I might have to do something else."

Bridget drove past the video store without slowing down. "Well, the only time you can get two days is their end of the month special."

Marion was wearing one of her oldest dresses. It had faded across the shoulders and was ripped slightly at the buttonholes. She had tied back her now-bushy half-colored hair with a piece of yarn. Here she was only in her early sixties, outstandingly healthy, the owner of a

$400,000 house, the mother of several breadwinners, and she looked the next thing to a street person.

Bridget's patience was wearing thin. "Marion, why don't you put on a decent outfit? You have plenty of nice clothes. Why do you go out looking like that?"

Marion gave a little intake of breath and then a sob. "How mean of you! Bridget, you know I'm doing the best I can."

"Well, if you are, it doesn't show much." The car slowed and kept veering to the center of the road; Bridget's driving was suffering from emotion. "I'm sorry. I shouldn't have said that. I just think you would feel better if you made an effort to look better."

"I can't stand this any more." Marion's voice was sliding toward screechy. "I'm so tired of having you tell me what to do. You have no sympathy. You don't know what I'm going through. I'm just a chance for you to boss someone around."

Bridget was fighting back tears. "Marion, I have spent hours trying to help you. How can you say I have no sympathy? I think I have too much!"

"Just let me off. That's all. Just let me off in front of my house. And then don't come back. Please. I've had enough of all this. I have a family. That's all I need. My sister can do anything you can do."

Probably she can, Bridget thought, but will she?

"Happily."

She pulled up in front of Marion's house in silence and Marion got out without saying anything more. She was obviously crying. Bridget wanted to ask if she had her key because Marion hadn't brought a purse; it would have to be in her pocket. But she wasn't going to ask. If Marion didn't have it, she could go to a neighbor and have someone help her break in. Bridget was not going to do anything more for her today.

She watched Marion walk up the sidewalk with a great sense of sorrow. The majestic California oak in her yard was rustling overhead in the slight breeze. There was a twittering of house finches and the daylilies were nodding at the wind. With a day like this, who needed a Marion lousing it up?

Maybe you couldn't do anything for anyone else, after all. That was all she had wanted. To make Marion feel better. Marion turned around and looked back, and Bridget, afraid the quarrel was about to continue, pulled away from the curb.

When she got home, she took two aspirin and crawled into bed with the day's newspaper. How would Marion pick up the car? Would she remember about the ad? It was difficult to let go of the projects she had started in her friend's life.

Former friend!

Chapter Fourteen

Phyllis's bell rang one morning at 10:00 while she was in the bathroom brushing her teeth. She really hadn't expected to see Bridget again so soon. She had looked forward to confiding more about Don, but then she had thought, what if it all came unraveled and Bridget asked what had happened to the new romance she had boasted about? What would she say then? She had better keep quiet about him till it seemed more certain. She ran a brush quickly through her hair.

Not anything she could do about it – her hair which needed cutting or Bridget coming to visit and making inquiries. It was flattering that Bridget, with all her money, took the time to come see Phyllis. She was not going to pretend no one was home.

But when she looked out the window beside the door, it wasn't Bridget. It was Don, standing on the other side of the locked gate to her garden. She was alarmed. She looked down to see what she was wearing. At least the sweatsuit was clean if a little worn.

What was he doing here so early?

She opened the door a crack and called out: "Just a minute. Give me a minute to put something on."

"Sure. No problem."

She hurried back to the bathroom to look at her hair, her lipstick, her nails. Peeled off the old grey sweatsuit and pulled on some flannel trousers and a cotton shirt. Ran the brush through her hair again; applied lipstick; decided there was nothing that could be done about the nails in a short enough time.   Racing back through the living room and dining area, she grabbed up yesterday's newspapers to put in recycling, and dumped her knitting into a drawer. It would have to do. Because she was having trouble with the lock on the back gate, she opened the garage door and led him in that way. Luckily Pudgie was asleep in the other patio.

"That lock is getting worse and worse," she apologized.

This route brought him past her dirty laundry which was half sorted on the floor. Phyllis could feel her face flush as he looked over her garage. She had seen Don's house where everything was always put away.

"Maybe it just needs some WD40."

Phyllis filed that away. She hated asking him to do more repairs for her.

In the dining room, he looked around again with curiosity. Phyllis flinched, wondering how it looked to him. On all their previous dates, she had met him at the living room door. He hadn't been this deep into her house. Well, everybody looked around the first time they were in someone's house. Or at least women did.

"Please excuse the mess," she said, although there really wasn't much mess remaining. Just some magazines, and a stack of bills on the sideboard.

"No problem. You must sleep late."

"Here. Sit down here. Shall I make some coffee?"

"Okay."

She got the coffee from the freezer and rinsed out the pot. What if he didn't like decaf? It was all she had. She decided not to mention it, just wait and see how he reacted.

"You must get up early," she said while she worked over the coffee.

He nodded. "Six o'clock. Can't seem to break the habit even though I'm not working any longer." He looked over at the coffee maker which was now burping dutifully. "I've had three cups already. I hope that's decaf."

"Yes, it is." Phyllis came toward him where he sat in the dining area and set down a tray loaded with the sugar, creamer, paper napkins, cups, and saucers.

"Oh, you don't have to go to all that trouble."

"It's not trouble. Have you bought any more plants for your front yard?"

When the coffee was ready, she poured it and he watched with interest. She had brought out the fat, olive-colored Heathware cups and saucers, seconds which Phyllis had collected in the sixties whenever there was a sale, and then saved rather than use. A fellow householder, alert for new ways of doing things.

"You keep a nice house. How long has your husband been dead?"

"Over two years. Almost three." She sat down across from him and noticed his ears, which were large but lay flat against his head. Up close, his complexion was more pink than tan.

Don added plentiful amounts of cream and sugar to his coffee. "Too bad he checked out on you. Early was it?"

Phyllis thought this over. "Early? You mean was he young. No, he wasn't particularly young. But he had survived his first wife's illness and death and there we were, looking forward to a new life. I guess it's always early if you're in love."

Don digested this. He examined her. Phyllis held her breath. She hadn't expected, when she got up this morning, to be judged so thoroughly so early in the day. The sun was shining into the pale blue diningroom and on the mahogany table which had come from Sam's first wife's mother.

"Trouble is…:" Don's eyes wandered away from her face, the cup, the table, and focused on the trumpetvine growing just outside the window. "A fellow gets used to getting up in the morning and going to work. I haven't gotten a handle yet on this retirement business. What is one supposed to do all day?"

Emboldened, Phyllis reached over and touched his arm. "Well, come to see me and have coffee, of course."

He laughed at that so Phyllis joined in.

"No. I haven't bought any more plants but I want to get some. Someone told me there's a nursery out on Route 10 that's better than the others. Is that true?"

She nodded encouragingly. She liked encouraging a man. "Well, there's one there but if it's better, I don't know. I haven't bought anything there."

He sipped his coffee. "I see you have trumpetvines. You know, the rats hide under them. Love eating the flowers. You'd better be careful."

"Oh, I don't think they'd have any rats here. I would have heard about it. Not much happens in Shady Acres that I don't hear about."

"I'd better stay in touch with you then so I know what's going on."

"All right." Phyllis smiled. "I'll be your informant."

He started on a long story. He was still ruffled over having had to re-paint his house. They had come out and approved the new color. The man who came out had tried being comforting, even though he was the same man who had come out soon after Don moved in. He made an effort to soothe Don's feelings, but Don was still resentful.

"If I hadn't done it myself, it might have cost me fifteen hundred dollars just to put another coat on."

Phyllis nodded. "That's what I was quoted last year. But then I never got it done. Couldn't afford it."

"What if I'd held out and made them take me to court? What would have happened then?"

"They just keep piling up fines against the property and then they file a lien. At least that's what someone told me. I don't really know. Would you like another cup?"

"I'd better not. That's four this morning. I'll get an upset stomach." He stood up abruptly.

"Oh, you're not going to go, are you?"

"Better get back. I've got things to do." He turned toward the door.

"Don't go out that way. Go out the front." She hurried ahead of him, bumping against him as she rushed to open the front door. "So sorry you're leaving so soon."

"Well, let's go out Friday evening, what do you say? Dancing."

"Dancing? That sounds wonderful." She could feel herself blushing.

Only a week later, when Phyllis got up in the morning and walked into her kitchen, her first thought was whether it was neat enough for Don because he would be here shortly. His own house, she had found, rarely had anything out of place. Would he object to the fact that yesterday's free newspaper was still on the counter as well as her coffee cup from last night, a ball of twine, a stack of mail that came to Resident, and twenty cans of catfood? Not that he ever said anything, he just looked uncomfortable and she could tell he was itching to put them away himself but didn't want to presume when he was in her house.

She put them away before she made her oatmeal.

Then while she ate, she began to wonder what they would talk about today. She lapsed into a happy daydream until she happened to look at the time. Then she hastily put her bowl and cup in the sink and rushed to take her shower.

It was astonishing, wasn't it? How many widows were there in this half mile? Plenty. But somehow Don had selected her. God must have arranged this because she had had such bad luck before.

Not that there weren't problems. Don always ate breakfast at 7:00. He then did his dishes, swept the breakfast area with a broom, looked at his newspaper, the front page and the sports section only, and then he was ready for his day. That was so early that there was not much he could do in town.

Where once it had been Bridget coming over every other morning for coffee, now it was Don and he came earlier than Bridget ever had. He apologized once when Phyllis was still in her bathrobe, and the next day did not appear until 9:00 but in two more days, he was back to 8:30 or even 8:15. That was as late as he could find things to do in his own house, he confessed.

Phyllis tried to think of something he could do during that half hour. She might have suggested dogwalking except Don didn't much like dogs. Finally, she just set her alarm earlier and made sure she was up, dressed and ready before 8:30.

Don didn't much like Pudgie and Pudgie was developing a real hatred for Don. When Don walked into the house, Pudgie, who had always had an uncertain temperament, would start growling.

"Better train him to stop that," Don said stiffly. "Start out that way and you'll have a mean dog on your hands."

Phyllis would obediently scold Pudgie, who would retreat resentfully under the couch. Phyllis suffered from conflicting feelings; sorry for

Pudgie, afraid Don would get angry. She couldn't think how to sort this out.

From his post under the couch, Pudgie could still see Don when he was seated at the dining room table, and the two at the table could still hear the dog growling intermittently till he fell asleep. After he fell asleep, they could hear his snoring over their conversation. When this quieted down, Phyllis would try to convince herself the problem was solved, until the next morning when the conflict was repeated all over again.

By this time, she was allowing herself to be kissed each time Don left. Other, more interesting, thoughts began to occupy her head, especially in the last few minutes before she went to sleep at night. With all this going on, she didn't really think much about Pudgie.

Everything was proceeding comfortably until Don arrived one afternoon when Pudgie was napping in the sun from the dining room window.

He had come in the afternoon because he had been to the hardware store and found the plug he wanted to put on Phyllis's washing machine. "This will work much better," he promised.

"Would you like coffee?"

"No, I've had plenty."

Just then Pudgie woke up from a sound sleep and dreams of conquest, and heard a man's voice in his own house. Alarmed, indignant, he jumped to his feet and began barking.

"Pudgie, stop that!"

Pudgie's eyesight was not good and there was a table in the way but he located the invader across the room and made a frontal assault on the stranger, teeth bared. Without hesitation he clamped those teeth on the part of the enemy available at his height of sixteen inches. This was Don's left shin.

"What the hell…" Don stepped back with the dog firmly attached to his leg. "Ouch. Get him off me!"

"PUDGIE, STOP THAT!"

Pudgie was much too full of triumph to pay attention to commands. He had the enemy in his grip and he meant to make it count. He growled deep in his throat. Phyllis was frantic. She picked up the closest thing which was that day's newspaper and began hitting Pudgie with it.

"Stop that! Do you hear me?"

"Hey there, let go!" By this time, Don was holding onto a door handle and stomping his foot up and down trying to shake Pudgie loose. The teeth were clamped around his shin bone. It seemed possible that if it weren't for the bone, the dog might tear out a section of flesh.

Pudgie was not happy with his position either. His elderly teeth were getting ratcheted back and forth in his mouth by the stomping up and down. At the same time, there was this irritating newspaper attacking his head. But a dog worthy of his name didn't give up the fight so easily.

"STOP! STOP!" Phyllis shouted and this time connected with her hand in a hard slap on Pudgie's haunch.

An assault in the rear stung him, and injured his certainty of victory. Letting go, he howled in indignation. Then he retreated to the other side of the room to regroup and consider his next sortie.

"My God. He drew blood!" Don exclaimed. He rolled up his pant leg and showed Phyllis the teeth marks in his shin with blood dripping from several of them.

Phyllis took command. She made him sit down and prop his leg on another chair. Then she hurried off and returned with a wet paper towel and some Neosporin. Don soon lost his indignation in all the pleasant ministrations. Phyllis even bandaged the worst two punctures with gauze squares and strips of adhesive tape.

"Have you had a tetanus shot?"

"Yeah, yeah, this year! That part's okay, but, Lady, you're going to have to do something about that dog."

Phyllis merely nodded comfortingly. She knew something would have to be done, but right now she was sitting close to Don and they were breathing in and out together, sharing their relief at the crisis being over and comfort being given and received. Their eyes met. Things could be worse.

Later that afternoon Phyllis looked at Pudgie sadly. He had been the best friend he could, given his limited understanding and his difficult past life. Still, it wasn't going to work. Surely they would find another home for him. One tear slid down Phyllis' cheek.

The dog knew it was serious. Something critical in his life had gone wrong and he didn't know what it was. He began to bark his protest. That was a mistake.

"Stop that!" Phyllis stood up and wiped off the tear.

In only a short time, Pudgie found himself in the car on a leash, along with some cans of food and his bed. He turned a mournful look at Phyllis, trying to convey his conviction that there were always some flaws in life. Phyllis sighed regretfully, but she was not going to change her mind.

In short order, he was unloaded at the Friends of Animals.

"He bit a guest," Phyllis explained and they nodded. They would try and see if he could be trained out of it. They didn't like to give up on a dog. However, if not, then…

Phyllis relented to some extent. "He was good for months and months. He doesn't like men."

Having done the best she could for him, Phyllis went home to wait for Don to come again.

*   *   *

Don was in his own living room, entertaining a tall young man who kept walking back and forth to the kitchen to peer in the refrigerator.

"No more beer?" the young man asked.

"It was all right there in front. If you can't see it, you've drunk it all. So what are you planning to do now?"

The young man, who looked a great deal like Don except he was skinnier and his hair was dark brown, threw himself back in a chair. "Don't know. Have to think things over. I thought I had that job for years to come."

"Can't you tell when they aren't happy with you?"

"Unh-uh. It must have been this other guy – Samuel – who didn't like me."

"Well, what about your own work. It must not have been good enough."

"I was plenty good when they gave me a chance."

"You have to do better than that. You have to be better than most of the other people. I've told you that before. You can't always expect the union to haul you out."

"Hah, the union! They didn't do a thing. Anyway, I can't pay my share of the rent this month. I was hoping I could stay here for a while till I get straightened out."

Don sighed. He had been expecting this for the last half hour. And he couldn't refuse. Couldn't let his only son sleep in the street. "I don't know... You young people never save anything."

"Pop, how could I save anything? You know what my car payments are, plus the union dues, and my rent and food, those did in almost my whole pay right there. I hardly ever got any entertainment out of it."

"Okay, for a month. There's the second bedroom but there's no bed in there. You'll have to bring one. And you'll have to buy your own food."

"It's okay. I have one more paycheck coming. I'll save half of it toward a new place, maybe try to get one of my own. And my car, shit, the value has dropped on it already..."

"You young people all think you have to have brand new cars. I don't see that. When I was your age, all I cared about was it got me there."

The younger man looked stubborn. "Damn it, can't you ever do anything nice without chewing me out about something else."

Don stood up. "If you're not happy with the arrangement, you can go to Kansas and stay with your mother."

Chapter Fifteen

Bridget had promised to pick up Jessie and John Roger at the airport on their return from Mexico. Turning into the Arrivals lane, she wondered why she had ever promised such a chore. They had been revamping this airport for years now and had managed to obliterate everything she remembered about it.

At least she should be able to find Continental. It might be in the International Terminal but maybe not. Cars sailed by while taxis pulled in and out with abandon. She was forced to constantly switch her attention from the signs on the front of the terminals to the cars in front of her.

She drove anxiously, irregularly, through the whole stretch of four terminals, forced to keep the pace of the traffic, without seeing the sign she wanted. Now she would have to cross the flow of exit traffic and go around again. Probably by now they would be standing outside waiting, tired and impatient.

On the second pass through, she slowed way down and let the other cars honk madly or go around her, and finally saw the right sign. Fighting several taxis that were trying to pull out, she took aim at the curb lane and at last achieved it. She peered through the crowd on the sidewalk for some glimpse of Jessie.

No sooner had she done that than she heard an angry police whistle. Was it for her? No fair, no fair at all - you were supposed to be able to pull in long enough to load passengers. She could feel her dress going damp under her arms. She could see the cop stalking toward her along the line of cars. Why her? There were cars everywhere. She looked up at the nearest sign and saw she had pulled into the area for taxis only. Full of guilt, she put the car in reverse and hit the gas. It responded by stalling. Sweat broke out on her forehead.

The cop definitely meant her because he had now arrived and was leaning in her window.

"What's the matter, lady?" He was young, bulky. His manner was forceful but, thankfully, not hostile.

"It just stalled. It never stalls. I'm sorry. I'm trying to pick up my friends." She began to think about tow trucks, about tickets and missing John Roger and Jessie.

"As are all these other people. But you're in a taxi area. You'll have to move. Just turn it off, wait a minute and try it again." He took a look at the car, a Volvo station wagon, almost new. "You're going to be all right."

She was relieved to have her car approved of. "It's really a good car," she said, half so the car would hear and behave.

A car pulled in behind her, beeping loudly. The cop stepped away from Bridget and straightened up so that the driver could see him, and blew his piercing whistle only a foot away from Bridget's ear. She had to shake her head hard to get the shriek out of her head.

When the offending car pulled hastily out, the cop came back to Bridget. "All right. Try it again."

Bridget turned the starter and the car responded.

"See that white van up there. Pull in right behind that and you've got five minutes to wait for your friends. No more or you'll have to go around again." He straightened up and walked back to deal with a taxi driver who was beeping angrily behind her.

"Thank you," Bridget said to his back.

She pulled the car in behind the white van, avoiding several taxis which were coming in one after another like planes to a carrier after a raid on enemy ships. She was past the Continental sign but it didn't matter because, as she could see through the glass doors, all of this was baggage claim area.

She was never going to drive to this airport again, no matter how much someone needed her. She would drive to a nearby hotel and whoever was coming in could take a van to it.

"Oh, thank goodness, you're here." Jessie was opening the car door before Bridget had caught her breath.

"I don't think I could walk another five steps. I'm absolutely done in."

Jessie was wearing a Mexican dress, an elaborately embroidered thing of peacocks and roses in red, green and white that made her look gaunt. Her hair was tied up under a hat that showed her face as thin and red. Maybe all that time in Mexican sun wasn't the best thing for her.

Bridget leaned toward Jessie to give her a kiss but Jessie's shoulder bag had caught on the car door. Untangling it, she fell into the car, bumping Bridget's outstretched face away.

"Sorry."

"Where's John Roger?"

"Right there!"

Now Bridget could see John Roger at the back of the car motioning to her. She pushed the button that popped open the trunk, and it opened fast, nearly catching him under the chin.

"I'm sorry," she yelled.

John Roger had the bags in and the lid snapped down in a matter of seconds. He gave a shove to the airport cart, pushing it toward the building, but someone else grabbed it, saving himself a fee. The back door opened, and JR was in the back seat. Bridget turned around happily to greet him. "You're here!"

How old he looked, wrinkled like an old apple! The door slammed. The cop was waving her out. She had had her allotted minutes.

"Bridget, you're a life saver."

All her anxiety now seemed worth it. "Did you have a wonderful time?"

Jessie turned in her seat to look at John Roger. "Yes, yes we did but JR is not doing well."

"What's the matter?"

They had an hour and a half trip ahead of them. Bridget fought several lines of traffic to get away from the terminal, past the next one, and onto the lane toward the freeway.

John Roger grunted. "Nothing much. Just an upset stomach. Which everyone gets in Mexico. We should have gone to Italy instead."

Jessie ignored this. "You spent a day and a half in bed. That's more than an upset tummy. I've got to get my messages. Bridget, do you have your cell phone with you?"

"Yes, it's right there in my purse. I'm so glad to see you both again. Dinner at my house tonight?"

"As long as there's no beans, no rice, no tacos and no avocados!"

"That's easy," Bridget said. "I'll order Chinese."

Jessie grinned and all their pleasure in each other reappeared. "Perfect. Bridget, you're a dear. JR, your car is at my house. You can take a nap before dinner."

His growl was gentler. "I'll have to go home right after dinner. The mail will be burying my garage."

Jessie had Bridget's phone out and was taking out her own address book, already preparing to return calls. "I had the Post Office hold my mail. Why didn't you do that?"

"Not as smart as you, obviously."

"That's right!" Jessie said, dialing her number.

Bridget smiled happily at them, so grateful to have them back.

*   *   *

It was a few days before they could get to the kind of convivial evening they all liked. Jessie put in long hours at the office to make up for clients she might have missed and one of JR's tenants was giving him trouble. But Bridget waited patiently and plans were finally made for an evening at Jessie's. Bridget brought some shrimp coated in cocoanut to celebrate.

Jessie peered at these. She picked one up tentatively. "How sweet of you. I'm sure they're wonderful."

"They're not really that many calories," Bridget begged.

"What is in the coating besides cocoanut?"

"I don't know. Probably just regular breading."

"You didn't make them then."

"No. I get them from the Hungry Cat deli. Vincent makes them up especially for me."

"How lovely."

Jessie took a tiny bit of the one she had picked up.

"Jessie, for God's sake, will you just eat the thing and stop fussing. Here, I'll have one. They look delicious."

The wine was poured and Bridget ate her second shrimp and then her third.

"I know you don't usually eat things deep-fried but I love these."

"It's absolutely wonderful, Bridget." Jessie smiled warmly. "Now, let's talk about something fun. We've been to see an architect about the house at the beach we're going to build."

"Are you really going to do it?"

"Looks like it," John Roger said. "Put it on land I already own. I'm taking the architect a plot plan tomorrow."

He sat back smiling. "Said I'd never build another house and here I am dying to get started."

"It's going to be double the size of mine, built around a big room."

Jessie's words were almost drowned out by a knocking at the door. "Nobody ever comes at this hour."

When Jessie opened the door, a youngish woman in a light blue running suit stepped in, her expression angry.

"Dorothy?" John Roger squeaked. The expression on his face turned indignant. "What are you doing here?"

Dorothy pushed past Jessie and entered the room. Her eyes swept over all of them.

"Dad. I thought I'd find you here. I need to talk to you. I've left you several messages and you don't call me back."

"Baby, this is not the time or the place. I've been away. I told you I'd be in Mexico a while. Why don't you come over to my house after dinner tomorrow night and we can talk?"

Dorothy stared at Jessie. "Is this her?"

Jessie began to draw herself up, looking daggers back at the younger woman but her voice was soft. "Yes, I'm Jessie. I've been so wanting to meet you. I've heard so much about you. "

"I brought you some silver earrings from Taxco," John Roger said.

"Well, I don't want to meet you. I want you to let my father alone."

John Roger recovered some composure. He stood up and advanced on his daughter. Dorothy was forced to step backwards toward the door.

"Dad!"

"Pumpkin, this is not the time or the place. We'll discuss this tomorrow night."

Dorothy had released her space reluctantly. Now she was being forced out of the house. She tried to push back with her anger. "That's my land at the shore. I take the dogs out there and run them. Bobby said you were going to put a house on it, but you can't do that. It's mine. It was my mother's. It's not your money anymore."

"See you tomorrow about eight," he said, still advancing on her so that Dorothy was forced out the screen door.

When Dorothy was out the screen, he closed the door. He looked at the two women but they were silent. Jessie went back to her chair and took a sip of her wine.

Bridget spoke, mostly in order to break the silence. "How many children do you have?"

"Just two and the boy is no trouble at all."

Bridget and John Roger looked cautiously at each other, trying to restore normality, but Jessie was close to shaking.

"What did she mean it's not your money anymore?"

"She doesn't understand. Everything is in a trust. She's an officer of the trust but that's no nevermind, just allows things to go smoothly when I die."

"And this property was her mother's?"

"Well, that's not really true either. I bought it long ago. Then when I was having some problems with a couple of partners, I put it in my wife's name for a while. But when she died, it came back to me, so it doesn't matter."

Bridget stood up. "You people want to discuss some private matters so why don't I go and let you do that. How about coming over for dinner on Thursday?"

Chapter Sixteen

Bridget sat at her desk, facing her computer, a flat screen Mac with all possible add-ons. It was lavender which was what had attracted her in the first place. She was delighted with it though embarrassed because she used it so little. Sitting in the midst of this, she could feel in control of at least some aspects of her life. Her only excuse for this expenditure, aside from paying her bills, had been to keep track of her investments. She did have a file of all the annual reports, and occasionally, when she was bored, she might track a stock on the computer. However, the investments were mostly monitored in the office of David Soto downtown.

This morning she had a real need for the computer. She had to write a letter to Elaine, the advice columnist in the local newspaper. Ask Elaine, it was called. Bridget was in the grip of such a strong emotion that her hands shook a little on the keyboard, making opening a blank page difficult. Nevertheless, she was not going to give up.

She had wakened in the night, suddenly in a panic, her chest heaving. She had gotten up and got a glass of water and an aspirin and tried not to think. It was not her fault, not something she had willed, but had just happened.

Last evening she had gone to the Red Chimneys with Jessie and John Roger. Jessie had been distracted, not talking much, acting as if she wanted to be let alone, and Bridget had felt the conflict between the two. Apparently, the problem of the land at the shore was at the center of it. Looking equally unhappy, John Roger had turned his attention to Bridget. He ignored Jessie and talked to Bridget at length, teasing her about how often she changed her hair style and about being May Queen all those years ago. Then he had gotten pretend-serious, wondering out loud why she didn't have a man in her life and offering to find one for her.

"Stop that," Jessie said abruptly. "That's Bridget's business. When she wants one, there will be one there."

Their dinners were just then placed before them. They might have turned their attention to the plates but they were stirred up. John Roger was uneasy, embarrassed.

Bridget dropped her eyes to her dinner, two small lamb chops perched on a bed of something, and then turned back to John Roger ready to apologize. And there she had surprised a look of warmth and sympathy that brought a flush to her cheeks, her neck, her breasts.

"Dear Elaine," she typed slowly. "I've fallen in love with my best friend's lover. It's terrible. I can't go on seeing them together. It would make me miserable. But I can't not see him. That would make me more miserable. What should I do?"

It was only because she had felt safe enough with the two of them that she had let her slowly-growing regard for John Roger blossom and probably begin to show. All the defenses she had built against the possibility of attraction to him had come down without warning. Had she, without meaning to, let him know that she thought about him a hundred times a day?

Of course it would never work out. There was no way that he would leave slender, stylish Jessie for overweight Bridget. And even supposing that he did! Jessie would not give him up without a fight – look at how she sold houses in bad times as well as good! No. Jessie would banish Bridget and probably use a few thousand words beforehand to indicate what she thought of someone who posed as a friend and acted as a thief. And Jessie might even use that capable tongue on John Roger.

Tears began to drip on the keyboard, turning the black metal darker. Bridget hadn't expected to cry, she didn't often. She had come into the study without a tissue. Now she had to go out to the bathroom and pull a handful from the box.

She could sell this house and move back to San Rafael. It would give her an excuse to stop seeing them. She sniffled and blew and wiped. Would she be able to do that? Give them both up. Jessie had become her best friend, even without John Roger. There wasn't anyone else in Shady Acres as interesting to talk to.

She went back to the computer. The sun was sneaking around the drapes and there were sounds outside - a power mower had started work somewhere in the block, and then a car had fired up and backed out of a garage across the street. The day was starting.

What would Elaine say in answer to this? She was a good read, sometimes caustic, but usually sympathetic, and always had an answer. Or maybe she only had answers for the letters she published. Maybe there were many others that she threw out because she couldn't think of something to say.

"I'm willing to move if you think that is a good idea. But how far away do I have to go?"

Maybe it was a good time to go to Key West for a month. But that would only put off the problem. And Lisa, her sort-of-friend there, was always something of a trial.

"What do I want? I want to go back to being a friend to both of them, to spending evenings as a threesome. To drinking wine and laughing about our neighbors and arguing about what should happen in the elections. Is that too much to ask?"

It was, wasn't it?

She read over that paragraph and then highlighted it and punched Delete. No point in pretending that things could be put back as they were before.

Thoughts of John Roger unfolded. She remembered his droll look when he thought one of them had said something ridiculous but he didn't want to point it out, just wait for them to admit it and then he could tease them. His excitement when he talked about a fuel cell that was in the works that would power a whole house without PG&E. His stories about being a reluctant rancher.

She couldn't think of anything to add to the letter so finally she typed Sad in Sonoma and punched the Save button.

It was after she had printed the letter that she began to get nervous. What if someone guessed who had written it? Recognized the stationery? But they couldn't. She didn't know anyone at the newspaper.

Bridget washed her face and found something to wear, anything would do. What if she ran into John Roger? Of course she didn't plan to. She planned to go out the other entrance to Shady Acres.

It was only after she was in her car, backing out of the garage, ready to start her day that she began to cry again.

The town was bustling, cars hurrying in all directions, people greeting and conversing, like a cheerful nest of ants, without any need for a Bridget. Just after she parked in the newspaper parking lot she happened to look in her purse and see that her cell phone was blinking. That was interesting. She almost never got phone calls. She must have given the number out to someone she never saw.

Unable to restrain her curiosity, she took it out and opened it up. It said 'new message' and when she punched it, she could not recognize the number. It seemed suddenly safer and more interesting to look at the message than to go into the newspaper office and turn in her letter to Elaine. In fact, now that she thought about it, the letter to Elaine had a lot of problems. What if it was accepted for publication and Jessie read it? Would she recognize who it was from? Bridget's whole pose of enjoying her single status would crumple. And what name had she given John Roger? Surely she hadn't used his name, had she? Or Jessie's?

Maybe she had better take the letter home and re-read it. She pressed the button for messages.

"Say, Birdie," came a rasping voice that was oddly familiar. "I'm in your town. Why don't I take you to dinner?"

She knew the voice as well as her childrens' but it couldn't be, could it? Impossible, wasn't it? All right, probably it was Norm. Her second ex-husband who had made tons of money and then turned her in on a new model! Surprise raised her eyebrows while she looked at the grape stake fence that covered the back end of the parking lot. What on earth was he doing around here? And what was the current wife up to that she let him visit former wives? Norm. He of the balding head and the fierce competitiveness that had built up a fortune before the two of them reached forty. When he had decided to marry a twenty-year-old

Hawaiian stewardess, Bridget had not been ready to give him up and the two of them had had a long series of violent arguments both in and out of court.

It was some time later that she realized she was still in the parking lot, had not returned the phone call or taken in the letter to Elaine, while the day had advanced enough to increase the sunshine coming through the driver's window. She started the car and drove out to the street.

Norm. Why on earth would he want to take her out to dinner? They had no children; they had no property in common; they hadn't seen each other for – what? - five years at least. Curiosity overcame her and she parked by the road and called him back. All right, she would go out to dinner with him.

"Okay, about dinner. But what are you doing in this part of the state?"

"Just traveling through."

That alone was suspicious.

Norm arrived at 5:30 that evening, earlier than Bridget had wanted. She heard the car in her driveway when she was still upstairs, just out of the shower, powdering herself and trying to decide what to wear. Then the doorbell. She was not going to go down and greet him without her hair curled, her makeup and clothes on.

She leaned out the upstairs hall window. "Norm!"

He finally came out from under the porch and found her up above. "How are you, Birdie?"

He looked the same. Short, wiry, nearly bald. There was an exotic yellow sports car behind him in the driveway.

"I'm not dressed. Go around the house to the back patio. That door is open. I'll be down in fifteen minutes."

She banged the window shut, angry that he had come early. She would not have time to use the curling iron.

"Okay," came floating up.

Now that he was here, she hesitated over her selection of clothes. She had put out some "slimming" black pants, a ruffled white blouse and a red sash, sort of a matador costume. That made her laugh. Did she think they were going to have a fight? Or that he would need fighting off? She always had strange reactions to Norm, not at all like her reactions to Edgar. Or to her third husband who was after all the father of her children, but of little interest otherwise. She backcombed her hair to make it fluffier and stood over the clothes while she considered them.

The matador costume would not disguise her extra weight. Nothing would. The new bright blue outfit should do.

Dressed and made up, she stood in front of the mirror, examining herself relentlessly. Just a little discipline, that's all it would take to lose the pounds. And what would happen if she did it? Would she be engulfed in a new, unhappy affair?

It was something of a relief to get down to the living room and see Norm thoughtfully examining the South Seas sculptures.

"Are you looking to take some of them back?"

"No, no," he protested. "Say, Birdie, you look good."

"Thank you. I've gained weight."

"I wish I could. The doctor keeps telling me I need a little extra, but I can't seem to get it on."

They were still standing in the middle of the room, sizing each other up. Bridget thought he looked much older than he should. He was her age, sixty two. But then he had relentlessly pursued a high-stress life. He had always reminded her of a greyhound, quivering with energy.

"Would you like some coffee or a drink? It's early for dinner."

"Tea. Maybe herbal tea. Do you have any?"

"Yes. Peppermint, I think. That's a new trend for you. Is that from your latest wife?"

He shook his head. "Not married at the moment."

Things were definitely different. "Sit down."

Instead of sitting, he followed her out to the kitchen and wandered around, looking out at the yard, at her collection of cookbooks, which never got used, at the watercolor from Martha's Vineyard.

"Everything looks good, Birdie. Nice looking house, you were always good at decorating. What have you been doing? Have you been traveling? Did you go to China yet? Now that is a kick."

They talked about China, which Bridget had hated and Norm found fascinating, mostly because he thought there was money to be made there.

"Do you still have an importing business?"

He accepted the cup of tea and shook his head. "No. The opportunity came to sell it at way over its value so I did. Good thing. Then came the dot-com bust and it took all the values down."

"I can't believe you're doing nothing."

"Not really nothing. I've got another start-up, still in the garage stage. And I've been building this house at Palm Dessert. And I spent six months in the Stans, advising businesses."

"The Stans?"

"Krygistan, et cetera." He began to talk about his adventures there.

Bridget was enjoying herself, in spite of her misgivings. It had always been true of Norm, that with his lively mind and his brimming energy, he could keep her interested like no one else. She wished she could meet some women with lively minds. Or was it really only men who would excite her?

Back then, just when she had gathered enough confidence to stretch a little to meet his mental pace, he had fallen for the Hawaiian stew.

"How many times have you been married?" she asked.

"It's not that bad. Four. Just four. This last one, we never actually got around to getting married, waiting for her divorces to come through, and then she wasn't happy with that property settlement. Nothing would ever make her happy with a property settlement. I got really bored and left. How about you?"

"Well, you met David. That was number three. Since then I've given up on marriage."

"Well, we live and learn, don't we? How are all those kids?"

"The question is, do we learn. The kids are fine, mostly pursuing artistic careers that pay hardly anything but are in glamorous places. They have fun and they let me alone most of the time."

He laughed. "You know, you're almost the only woman I can have a conversation with."

She took him to the old hotel for dinner. That was a good choice for out of town guests whom she hadn't seen recently. The hotel had a wide menu, accommodating all kinds of tastes and dieting regimens.

Norm brought out glasses to read the menu and Bridget thought again how old he looked for his age. The glasses were small squares, unframed, and gave him a medieval look. Maybe greyhounds didn't live a long life.

"The little T-bone is quite good," she said.

"Do you think they would fix me scrambled eggs? I've been having a little stomach trouble." He said this with a diffident air, but Bridget thought this was not like Norm at all. He must have some trouble he wasn't letting on about.

The restaurant did scramble eggs for him, and serve it on a handsome plate with potatoes, sliced tomatoes, and a green salad. Norm ate only the eggs and not much of those.

Bridget ate pot roast with gusto. When they were finished, Norm had more herbal tea and Bridget had coffee and brandy.

"What's the matter, Norm?"

He looked away and then back at her, embarrassed to have such minor concerns and yet worried too. "Well, yes, I've got a little problem I can't seem to get rid of. Disgusting, isn't it? I never used to think about my body at all."

"Like all of us. What kind of problem?"

"It's nothing. It's not cancer. But the climate in Palm Dessert is beginning to bother me. I'm thinking of moving back to the Bay Area."

"It is a lot milder, but why not Southern California. That's even milder."

"Do you mind if I spend the night?"

Bridget hid her surprise. "No, that would be all right. I have two guest rooms. You can have your choice."

But when the time came to show him a room, rather than give him a choice she took him to the downstairs guest room, which had its own bathroom and was abloom with giant orchids on drapes, bedspread and chairs. Norm had grown quieter since dinner. He was obviously tired and barely seemed to listen to her instructions about towels and extra blankets.

"This is very handsome, Birdie, and good of you. Thank you. I'll be more talkative in the morning."

"Well, you earned the money," she said as she left.

She thought about that as she went to bed. Norm had earned the money, lots of it, and he had not been happy about giving her half, but he and his attorney had not tried any tricks. Though there were no children of the marriage, they had been married ten years. It was odd and upsetting to see him less than he had been. Something was obviously wrong. Maybe it really was cancer. Or maybe it was only an ulcer. Anyway, something bad enough to keep him from finding another stewardess to look after him. Men, especially men with money, could always do that. On the other hand, women kept their health longer so maybe it was even in the end. She lay in the dark, thinking for the first time in a long time, that she was almost content with her life.

In the morning, she waited for Norm to wake up and then fixed him a good breakfast and served it on the patio. He looked better this morning and greeted her with some of the old affection. Bridget felt only pity.

Norm nodded his head over the pretty blue tablecloth from Mexico, the bacon and eggs, the steam coming from the silver-plated coffeepot, and the bright red bougainvillea which climbed the wall of the house.

"It's very nice here. A man could get used to this." He looked up at her appealingly. Just a man who needed to be comforted, taken care of for a while.

"No, Norm," Bridget said sternly. She remembered those looks. They didn't last long. Her life was too good to bring in a wild card like Norm. "There is no here for you here. We've been over a long time."

"I suppose so," he said diffidently. He really did seem different but Bridget didn't trust that at all.

*   *   *

There was a phone message from Bridget when Jessie got home from work. "I'm sorry. I can't come tonight. I just don't feel well enough."

Jessie was concerned. When was Bridget ever not feeling well? She was the picture of health.

John Roger was already there, having arrived a few minutes before Jessie, and let himself into the patio where the French doors were open into the house. This was safe enough because Belvy and Tibby would attack any strangers that tried to get in that way but of course he was no stranger. He had been wrestling with the cork, and had the three wine glasses already out.while Jessie picked up her messages. Before she could relay Bridget's message, he had the glasses filled and on the coffee table, one each in front of all their usual chairs.

"You must have said something that upset her," Jessie said to him. "She's not coming."

"Me? I didn't say anything!"

"Think about it. You must have said something."

"Why should it have to be me? It's either you or her. Women are always upset about something and none of it matters. My day's been bad enough without that. I couldn't get the goddamned tire off the truck."

Jessie frowned at him. "It's no use asking you to think about people's feelings."

He frowned back at her, hard. He sat, took a couple of long swallows, looked at Jessie admiringly, if resentfully. "We could go over there. She always likes that. Take the wine and everything."

Jessie mulled that over. "I don't know. She might feel...I don't know."

"We could take dinner to her. Everybody likes that."

"Unless they're on a diet. Okay. I'll tell you what. I've got some mushroom thingys in the freezer. I'll pop those in the oven. We'll have to buy another bottle of wine. This one's half gone."

John Roger liked sitting and talking in Jessie's handsome livingroom but he also liked rushing around on some grand plan, getting things done, and then sitting again. He stood up, anticipating that pleasure.

"All right. Let's do it. What are thingys?"

Jessie was not as quick to jump up. She had put in a hard day, and was already husbanding her energy to last through the evening, but she was concerned about Bridget. Surely she wasn't out of sorts; that wouldn't be like her. It was hard to remember that only a few months ago she had seen Bridget as a nosy parker. Now she was nearly Jessie's only friend besides John Roger, and who wanted a man for a best friend?

Finally she stood up, brushing down her skirt, hoping that the mushroom "thingys" could be cooked in the microwave.

The mushrooms wrapped in filo dough required fifteen minutes in a hot oven. This was all right because it was just about the time it would take for John Roger to get into town and buy another bottle of wine. It also gave Jessie a chance to change her clothes and take two aspirin for the headache that had been coming on since she left work. Some days she thought she wouldn't have enough energy to make it all the way till bedtime. Maybe she should see JR only every other night and on the alternate one go to bed right after dinner. But this plan required advance planning; what usually happened instead was than when she got home, JR was already there and Bridget already invited. They would all have a glass of wine which would mask her tiredness and she would be launched into the social part of her day.

She was putting the still-warm hors d'oeuvres in a tin just as he pulled into the driveway. He came through the door with a blast of energy, his nose pink, his eyes bright. "Ready?"

"You love rushing around, don't you?"

"I do."

She kissed him for that, and thought how sad it would be not to see him every night.

When they arrived on Bridget's doorstep it was late enough that they were already in shadows from the trees and the tall stand of bamboo by her front door. No lights shone from the house.

"Maybe she went to bed. She wouldn't go to the hospital without telling us, would she?"

"No."

They rang the bell.

It was several seconds, and another ring before the light went on in the window overhead, making bamboo stripes across the yard behind them. "Who is it?"

"Bridget, it's us. We wanted to see if you were all right."

A few minutes later, the door opened and Bridget stood there in a dark pink bathrobe, her face shiny with cream. "You came to see me? I look frightful, I'm sorry. Come in."

"Are you all right?" Jessie asked as they went into the house.

"This is so sweet," Bridget said, her eyes filling with tears. "I've had a hard day."

Indeed she did look undone, her usual bravado gone. Her hair mussed into odd shapes.

"Now, come on. None of this silly crying! Just go get your corkscrew because I bought a really good bottle of viognier and you damned well better drink it!"

Bridget giggled a little as she led them into the living room. "I'll get out my Irish crystal wine glasses."

"Plus a corkscrew."

"And a plate for something hot I just made."

Bridget turned on lights as she led them through the shadowy house with the two trailing behind her. When they reached the living room at the back of the house, they surrendered the cheering food and drink to their hostess.

Jessie and John Roger sat side by side on the maroon velvet couch while Jessie looked around her, trying to decide what had been added since she was here before or had she only missed things because there was so much to look at. What were these fancy little shoes, only about six inches long and elaborate with silk bows and tiny rhinestones? If that was a new collectible she had somehow missed it.

"She buys so much. She told me she goes down to the auctions in the city at least once a month."

"Hmph!" John Roger said to show he heard her but had no opinion on the subject. He hated gewgaws.

Then Bridget was back with a tray holding the requested corkscrew, goblets and a plate holding the mushroom thingys, even little napkins. Her hair looking combed and she had wiped the cream from her face.

"Are you sick?"

"No, not really."

While JR fought the cork with a few sharp words to it, Bridget fussed around, plumping a pillow, turning on another lamp. "Just getting a cold and feeling depressed. I had a strange visit from the past."

"Never be depressed," John Roger said. "Just think you could be dead instead."

Jessie rapped him on the knee. "Stop that. That's supposed to be cheering?"

He finally got the recalcitrant cork out and poured the wine.

"This wine really is good," Jessie said. "I always thought it was just a con game, asking for thirty dollars for a bottle for wine."

"All pretty much tastes alike to me," John Roger said. "But if you like it, I'll buy a case."

"I can taste the difference," Bridget said. She had seated herself in a dark orange chair, leaning back almost at ease, forgetting to worry about how she looked with her make up off and her hair mashed down. "Thank you so much for coming."

"So it was a bad day? Do you want to talk about it?"

"I guess not. That might make it worse. Let's just forget it."

The guests nodded and settled back to enjoying the wine.

"We should spend more time here," Jessie said. "I never get to look at all your interesting things."

"Is all this stuff insured, Red?"

"No, and not all of it itemized, though I try to. I just insured a couple of the paintings. They told me to photograph and make a list of the other stuff and keep the list, and take out household goods insurance that was pretty high, so that's what I did."

Jessie got up and wandered around, picking up a glass paperweight with thistles inside and examining it. "I never have anything worth insuring. It's all fake, just for looks."

"I don't know that it makes that much difference," Bridget said. "I mean I like to look things over once in a while and then I think about where it was made and who likely made it. But only about once a year. Most of the time, all of it just sits there and gathers dust."

John Roger also got up and tested several chairs, finally finding a deep one he liked even though it made his feet come off the floor when he sat back.

"Probably it's like the wine. Only matters to some people."

Jessie said, "We all want beauty in our lives. Look as the people who spend their whole lives on that! Different people have different ideas of beauty is all"

After a while, Bridget added, "It's fun to learn about things. My father used to collect first editions but if you didn't know it was a first edition, it just looked like another old book. I prefer paintings but everything authentic has gotten so expensive. I keep meaning to take a course on American art."

"Well if you want the best in beauty," John Roger said. "There's a sailboat or there's a horse. After that, there's a big drop-off."

Jessie laughed. "You also care about beautiful houses, I know you do. How can I build a house with you if you don't care? You're just trying to start an argument."

Bridget's expression was solemn. The wine was getting to her. "It all depends on where and how you decide to spend your life. And mostly you decide that before you know all the choices. I have a cousin who has spent his whole life working with the American Friends Service Committee in all the most Godforsaken places in the world. If I see there's a disaster somewhere in the world, I know he'll be there soon. He doesn't have time to collect anything."

"How did he happen to do that? Was the family religious?"

"Not particularly but Matt was always worried about people, concerned with who would help people who needed it. I guess he was born for that. But doing what he does would make me feel worse, seeing so much ugliness and only being able to cure a little of it. I guess I'm better off with my head in the sand."

John Roger. "I think you have to do your share. I used to do that… if I saw something that needed doing and I could do it, I would."

The women smiled at that. "Does anything stay done?"

"Mostly I only give money," Jessie sighed. "I never feel as if I have much to contribute except that, and not much of that."

This was a new JR showing himself. "I give money too but every once in a while I feel as if I have to do something more. The Congregational Church back home was good for that. If you just went down there, they had all sorts of opportunities for doing good…right away and short term."

"What was it you used to do, John Roger?"

"Oh, go out and help repair the private roads, help round up someone's herd that had gotten away. Organize a group to help a widow with house repairs. There's usually lots of that kind of thing around in ranch country. Or used to be. Maybe not any more. I've been gone for a while."

"I wish I could find something like that now." Bridget said.

Jessie nodded. "When you find something, let me know. I'd like to get a feeling I was useful." Jessie looked around the bright red livingroom which seemed to enclose them so comfortably that they could reveal themselves.

143

"You know we're drunk, don't you?"

"That's for after you quit work," John Roger said, ignoring her last comment.

He re-filled their glasses. "Hey, for thingys, these are pretty good. Did I ever tell you how I got into ranching? My father decided I was going to flunk out of college so he put a down payment on a ranch nearby. Then I got married and my wife wanted a more educated man. She talked me into going back to school and the first thing you know, I'm a teacher as well as a rancher, two things that are about as hard work as a man can do until you combine them and then they're five times as hard. There I was getting up at five a.m. to go and feed the stock, and then grading papers till midnight. It's no surprise that I moved out here and went to speculating in land once she died."

"What did she do?" Jessie asked. "I hope she contributed."

"She paid all the bills, got the loans when we needed them, and kept a nice neat house, with plenty of good food on the table."

He nodded, remembering. "There were times when it didn't seem enough to match how hard I was working. The kids saw that, they wanted nothing to do with ranching; the boy went off to the big city as soon as he got out of high school. I had hoped he might join me. After that, it was nothing but chores. So I left after she died."

The two women looked at him, seeing more than they had seen before.

"I guess the critical thing," Bridget said, "is where you grow up. That usually gives you only so many choices. Then you make one before you know what all the other possibilities are. I think I would really have loved living in Paris or New York and working some small job in the fashion industry. But when I grew up, I didn't even know those jobs existed."

Jessie said, "That's true. I made a choice before I knew what other possibilities were around. I went to work right after high school, and then got married, just cuckoo for this man. And it took him a long time to get settled into a job he liked, and I had a baby and mostly worked part time at dumb jobs. We were always struggling and miserable."

John Roger looked her up and down. "I can't believe that. I bet you were a beautiful young mother with a beautiful baby and in love with her husband. I wish I'd seen that."

Jessie shook her head in disbelief. "Men are so sentimental, aren't they? And the whole time, I didn't know why I was so unhappy, didn't have any idea that what I would really like was having a good job and supporting myself."

Bridget also doubted her. "That past doesn't sound like you. I always see you as so sure of what you are doing."

"It took me years to get there."

"But you did," John Roger said. "I guess that's why you won't give it up, even though you should."

"Why should she?"

"Because she's getting too tired, and too thin. Can't you tell she's lost weight since we came back from Mexico."

"Yes, I do see it. Can't you work just a little less, Jessie?"

"My office doesn't really give me that choice. Either I work a full schedule or I quit, which I'm not ready to do yet. JR, it's about time for us to go home and give this subject a rest."

"All right. See that, Red? As soon as I get to say something, it's time to leave."

Bridget smiled at him, a warm smile but one with the tiniest bit of 'women know best.' "Well you got it said anyway. Jessie will come around to quitting when she's ready. I trust her to take care of herself."

"Thank you, Bridget, whether that's true or not. Now, let's go, JR!"

"All right. All right." He got up, stretching a little, looking Jessie over.

When they were gone, some of Bridget's melancholy returned. She picked up the wine glasses and the plate which had held the mushrooms and carried them into the kitchen. Her house seemed cavernous and as quiet as a tomb. If Jessie didn't know what she wanted, then who did? If Bridget didn't want Norm, with all his charm and intelligence, then probably she didn't want any man. What did she want?

Chapter Seventeen

Once his son Nick had moved in with Don, Phyllis's neighbors saw more and more of his white pickup in front of her house.

Being unemployed, Nick stayed in the house a great deal of the time. He got up around eight o'clock, wanting coffee. After that and some breakfast – he preferred scrambled eggs fixed by Don - and out to the back patio for a cigarette, he wanted to talk. If Don wouldn't talk, Nick talked on the phone to various friends or watched sports on television. He preferred baseball, and after that football, but he would even watch tennis if he couldn't get anything else. He drew the line at golf though. He was really glad Don had gotten cable so you could pretty much get sports any time of the day.

Don had just gotten used to living alone. Nick had left home right after high school, almost ten years ago. Don hardly remembered what his son had been like then except endless arguments over using Don's car and chores Nick was supposed to do for his mother but seldom did. Now, Don, who had developed fond feelings for Nick while he was elsewhere, found his constant presence an irritation.

If Nick was taking a shower, Don worried over his water bill; if Nick wanted breakfast cooked, Don resented the number of dishes and pans it took. The slamming of a door would set Don's teeth on edge. Nick was not really destructive but Don found himself examining doors and tables and dishes to see if there was any sign of damage.

If he wanted a little peace and quiet, he had to retreat to Phyllis's house. He had found it necessary to apologize for this by explaining Nick's presence.

"Well, isn't that nice of you to take him in! Of course you're welcome here. Why don't we have him over to dinner here one night?"

"No thanks," Don said. "It's bad enough seeing him at home; I don't need to see him everywhere."

Some days Don arrived at 8:30 for coffee and stayed for an hour or two, and then came back at 3:00 or 3:30 and stayed through dinner. Phyllis scarcely had time to get to the store and get the house vacuumed and her laundry washed and put away. Also her food bill had doubled.

They were having their before-dinner glass of wine. Phyllis had heard that the thing to drink before dinner was sherry but Don didn't like it. He had suggested beer and Phyllis thought beer was low-class so they had agreed on a glass or two of locally-produced, moderately priced red wine. They were sitting outdoors under the awning at the glass patio table, a more expensive piece than Phyllis would have bought if she had ever felt rich enough to acquire one. This one had come from Sam, her unfortunate second husband, and she liked to stroke it now and then and remember him.

"Are you a Republican or a Democrat?" she asked almost as soon as they were seated there early one evening.

Don pondered and examined the question for hidden meanings. They had never discussed politics.

"I'm registered as a Democrat but I often vote Republican. Why?"

Personally she thought that the better class of people were Republicans but you couldn't get around the fact that the Democrats were usually right about things. She nodded acceptance of this.

"Are your parents still alive?"

"No. No. They both died about ten years ago. They lived a good long life though."

"How old were they when they died?"

"Just shy of eighty. At least my mom was. My Dad was a couple of years younger."

She nodded. "Do you have other children besides Nick?"

"No."

She wondered what it was she wasn't asking. "Does he usually hang around? I mean, has he in the past?"

"Not really. This is the first time he has moved back in. But his job went away – what could he do? Hey, nice roses there. Your bush looks very healthy."

Phyllis nodded and thought again. There really wasn't anything to say about the roses. "When you were married, did you do all the repairs around the house?"

"Well, sure. Usually. No point in paying someone if you can do it yourself. And I don't spend a lot of time in front of the television."

"That's good," she said.

Don was pleased at having pleased her. "Don't know why they write most of that stuff. It's so dumb. The only thing I can watch now and then are game shows or college basketball, but I don't watch all of a game, maybe just the final minutes."

She frowned, basketball was so noisy and the players were always bumping into each other. "Have you had a checkup this year?"

"Sure. My doctor in Oakland won't let me out of that. Get one every year, the full works. How about you?"

"Oh yes. I'm in excellent health."

"That's good. That's good. You look healthy."

"So, how are you? Are you healthy?"

"Fit as a fiddle."

"Have you ever smoked?"

"Just a couple of years when I was twenty. Then I was laid up with bronchitis and couldn't smoke. I began to think the smoking was making me sick. When that was over, I never went back."

Phyllis gave him an approving look and they sipped their wine some more. "That was when they knew how bad it was and they weren't telling us!" she said, nodding.

The smell of roasting meat was coming through the screen door. Pot roast.

There was a longish pause then Don spoke. "What else do you need to know?"

She took her courage in hand. "Would you consider buying some of the food? It doesn't even have to be half, just some."

"Of course. I've been thinking about that. Didn't want to insult you. Would you like for me to give you money or would you prefer I go to the store when you do."

"Go to the store with me. Then we'll get what you like and we can split the bill right there."

She paused and turned red. She had just thought about running into one of her neighbors in Safeway. And what would the clerks at checkout think?

"You okay?"

Phyllis reconsidered and remembered that old Mrs. Simpson next door didn't do her own marketing but had it done for her, and the woman across the street got Meals on Wheels every day. That left only snoopy Gladys. Well, it was none of their business, any of them.

She refilled their glasses and they sat in a comfortable silence for a while. Then…

"Do you pay your wife alimony?"

"Nope. But she gets part of my pension. They send her that. I don't have to. It was only fair. We were married all that time, back to when I joined the company. But it's not very much."

"As long as it's fair…"

"That's what I say. It has to be fair. She didn't work for years and years so when she went back to work, she didn't make much. I was ready for the divorce quite a while before we got around to it, but no denying she put in her time. Only fair."

"That's a very nice attitude."

He beamed. "I'm glad you approve of me."

"Can you cook?"

"Nope. I leave that to the ladies. I don't try to muscle in on their territory."

Well, you couldn't have everything.

*   *   *

Their first shopping expedition went well. Phyllis found out that Don much preferred beef and pork to chicken and fish, and that he was wild about stuffed bell peppers. He confessed to the bell peppers right in front of the meat case, with the cold air blasting out at them, so she looked over the varieties of hamburger. She had never made stuffed bell peppers; Sam hadn't liked peppers in any form and neither had her first husband. It couldn't be too difficult, there were recipes for them in every cookbook, and cheap besides. She turned to him about to say something like, would you want them tonight?

However, his eyes were fastened on her brightly. "I like the way you've been curling your hair lately."

She flushed and lowered her eyes. Oh my!

Things must have been going too well for Fate to be contented. Only a day or two later, Don appeared, just as she was about to serve up dinner, with a gloomy face.

"What's wrong?"

"My wife!"

"My ex-wife," he said when he saw the effect of these two words on Phyllis, the sudden flash of her bright blue eyes. "She's very worried about Nick because he's been laid off. She's coming out to see him and she wants to stay with me."

"How can she do that? You're divorced." The smell of burning potatoes rose from the pot on the stove and assaulted her nose but she refused to be deflected.

"I can't refuse her. She doesn't have much money. She can't afford to go to a hotel."

Phyllis took hold of his large pink hand, with the nails always cut down to the quick, and felt the distress racing with his blood. "Sounds like she's asking for a free vacation, staying with you. Sit down and let's eat."

When she took the lid off, the potatoes sizzled and she could see the burned bottom of the pan. Now they would be stuck for good. She took a fork and pricked out a piece from one on top the pile, and put it in her mouth. Sure enough, they tasted bad all the way through.

That was a man for you, getting his news out just at the right time to burn the dinner. She set the pot in the sink and ran some cold water in it to loosen the burned part.

Don had taken his place at the table but he protested her interpretation. "She's not looking on it as a vacation. She's worried. She thinks Nick is in bad shape. He's not even hunting much for another job. You've heard me say that!"

Phyllis sighed as she took some cottage cheese out of the refrigerator to substitute for the potatoes. "If she's going to wait around until he gets another job, she may be here a while. Where's she going to sleep?"

Don was embarrassed. Color rose in his fair face. "There's only the two rooms and Nick is in one of them. I guess I can sleep on the couch."

She carried their plates to the table while her mind raced. In her experience, ex-wives were often up to no good. "When is she coming?"

"She didn't say. I don't know what to do. You're not mad, are you?" He looked at his plate as if not seeing any of the food she had put on it.

Phyllis's spirits lifted. At least part of his distress was on her part. It was amazing how easy that made things. A bus went by outside, its high whine making the stillness of the evening more pronounced. "You can stay here. There's the second bedroom which I just use for ironing. That way she can have your bed."

The red and the stiffness began to leave his face. "Can I? That would be wonderful. Thank you."

They began to eat. He looked at her inquiringly – did she really mean it? Would everything between them be all right? And did this have some other meaning?

Phyllis answered with a comforting bland expression. An awkwardness that had come over their relationship as it waited for the next step, was now gone. She knew exactly how she was going to proceed. She would make up the bed in the guest room for him, but she wouldn't close her own door. She had been through this process with Sam.

"I don't know how to thank you, Phyllis. You are so great. It sure is lucky you walked in front of my house when you did, otherwise I might not have found you."

Phyllis smiled comfortingly. Didn't men understand that those things were never accidental?

Chapter Eighteen

It was only a few weeks after the return from Mexico, that Jessie called Bridget late one evening.

"I hope you're not in bed yet."

"Well..." Bridget had put on her nightie and her face cream and was sitting on the edge of the bed. It was nearly midnight and normally she would have been asleep by now but it had been such a beautiful night with moonlight so bright she could see every flower in her yard, and she had sat on the back deck a long time, moonstruck. She had begun, for no real reason, to remember her first year of marriage to Edgar, the quality of it, the music which was different from any other time in her life. How she had struggled over cooking for him, even breakfast, and how, when it was warmly received, how exciting that had made her day. She could remember a moment when she had set a small green vase of geraniums on the table with the conviction no group of flowers had ever been so beautifully arranged, and right then she had trembled with the thought that from here on she was always going to live in this magical happiness.

Well, that was a joke, wasn't it? Was this memory why she was still tempted to look for a man; was she trying to recapture something that had once been perfect but never was again?

"What's the matter?"

"JR's on the floor and can't get up. I'm not sure what to do." Jessie's voice was very low and slow as if she was trying to avoid any semblance of panic.

There was some noise in the background.

"What was that?"

"He says he's all right, he'll get up in a minute, but really, Bridget, he can't!"

Bridget could feel a little muscle in her face twitch. She had known something was going to happen. She had thought ever since they came back that his color was bad, that he looked pinched and ancient. Hadn't she watched her mother and seen her go from a vague stomach ache to angina? "Did you call the ambulance?"

Jessie sounded confused. "I didn't think about an ambulance. I left a call for my doctor with his service but I haven't heard from him yet."

More sounds in the background. Of course, JR was protesting.

"How's his color?"

"I can't really tell. He's not in the light."

How could she sit there and do nothing? "Do it right now anyway. I'll be there in a minute."

"Does it matter which ambulance?"

"Not an ambulance! Call 911 and get the medics there."

"All right," Jessie sounded less vague now that action had been initiated.

Bridget threw on a muumuu over her nightie and rushed to the car. Then she went back in and wiped the cream off her face and put on some lipstick. If she was a couple of minutes late it wouldn't matter. It was the paramedics that mattered.

Surely Jessie would know a heart attack if she saw one. But then she spent her days in a real estate office, not in Shady Acres where heart attacks took such a prominent place. How old was John Roger anyway? That was the trouble with men, they went on as if nothing had changed with age until something was big enough to knock them to the ground.

She could see the flashing lights sending arcs through the darkness even before she turned the corner. The Fire Department medical van was in Jessie's driveway, its bright red lights on, its turn signal still blinking. The kitchen door was wide open. Bridget walked through it to see two tall, healthy, young men in dark blue uniforms, standing over a figure on the floor. When she looked down, she saw John Roger, small and awkward, crumpled in the space between the dining room table and the kitchen counter, a scowl on his face, his head propped on a dog cushion.

One of the men flipped on the dining room switch and the scowl was illuminated, his color was tinged with purple.

Near his head were Jessie's bare feet with her bright red toenails. "Bridgie," Jessie wailed, surrendering to her fear now that others were here to make decisions.

"Just let me take your blood pressure," one of the young men said.

"My blood pressure is fine!"

"JR, stop that!" Jessie said. "Something is wrong. If it's not, then stand up! I dare you."

"All this fussing around..." He raised his head for a minute, then let it drop back to the floor. At that, he eased a hand up and surrendered to the blood pressure wrap.

"What are you doing here, Red?"

"I go wherever there's some excitement!" Bridget sat down heavily in the nearest dining room chair.

"Be quiet, JR." Jessie twisted her head toward Bridget. "He was just working himself up about something, the Nature Conservancy or something like that..."

The young man with blond curly hair who was operating the blood pressure unit, brimming with so much earnest energy he might have been a star athlete, had wrapped JR's arm with effortless competence and was muttering over the numbers.

"There it is. Pretty low. Grandpa, we're going to transport you to Emergency. Call them, Kevin."

The other young man, dark and thoughtful, nodded and went out the door to their truck.

Jessie began to shake with fear. "I want to ride in the ambulance with him. Bridgie, will you come along behind us?"

"Yes, of course. But let me carry your purse. I forgot mine and I don't have my driver's license."

Jessie looked at her in confusion – the subject of a driver's license had thrown her off balance. .

"Get a dress on!" Bridget commanded because Jessie was in a lacy robe.

Jessie paused a moment to look down at herself, and then went back to the bedroom hastily enough. When she reappeared a minute later, the robe had been replaced with a dress and her hair brushed down a little.

The young men had rolled in their high-tech stretcher and lowered it on its scissor legs. After they had gently picked up John Roger and brought him into better light, Bridget decided that his color was worse than she had thought. Also his face looked to have fallen in.

"Why don't you ride with your friend!" the young man said to Jessie.

"Will he be all right?"

"We'll take good care of him."

Bridget took a jacket and purse out of the closet and handed them to Jessie. When their hands touched, Bridget felt the tremble in the pale bony hands. The paramedic put away his equipment and shook out a blanket to put around the patient.

From the patio came a low whine.

Jessie reacted angrily. "SHUSH. Be quiet. It's not walk time."

The moon had gone behind a cloud and the night was very dark. The red van sounded its siren only briefly, at the intersection with the highway. There was little need. The only car in sight passed in front of them silently and was gone. Bridget clung close behind the van; she knew she had done this at some time in the past but she couldn't remember when or where, or who it was had been in the van that time. Not anyone who filled her with this dread. She knew that.

When they got to the hospital, she dropped Jessie off at the Emergency entrance and went to find a parking space. By the time she got into the Emergency room, a bland place filled with chairs and devoid of nurses, Jessie and John Roger were out of sight.

Bridget tried the wide door to the inside but found it locked. Resigned, she selected a seat facing the desk so she would know the minute someone appeared and would be able to get her questions answered quickly. To keep her hands quiet, she picked up a tattered magazine.

It was *Rod and Gun.* She put it down again. A young man in surgical green came through the door. When he positioned himself at the desk, she got up and went over.

"My friends…"

"They're right inside waiting for a doctor. I'll tell them you're here."

"How is he? Is he in danger?"

The young man humphed. "I'm not a doctor You'll have to wait and ask them."

She would never have thought he was a doctor. He didn't look intelligent enough. An aide at the most. Bridget went back to her seat, angry, wanting to insist on seeing Jessie. If she made a fuss, she might get thrown out before she had any answers. What if she just walked through? Had the door locked automatically behind him? She was very conscious of her muu-muu, its red and orange Hawaiian flowers and flaring sleeves, no aid to dignity there.

The trouble was she didn't have any rights. She was only a friend of a friend. She needed to be quiet and patient. She gritted her teeth and tried to think about other things.

The chairs were not bad, blond wood, with well-padded seats in blue tweed, almost soft enough to spend hours and hours on as must sometimes happen. Refusing *Rod and Gun,* she took her checkbook and calculator out of her purse and began to subtract the expenditures from her account that she had been making all week. Then someone else came in, an older man in dirty jeans, who was holding a blood-soaked washcloth to the side of his face. Small drops of blood marked his progress from the door to the clerk's window.

The sight of blood raised her anxiety. She put away her checkbook and calculator. She got up and walked across the room to see if there were any magazines on the other table. Here she found *Parents* and *Child's Play.*

She went back to her seat and settled for reflection. The clerk had told the bloody man to take a seat and had phoned someone, presumably a doctor on call. Shortly afterwards, a nurse came to the door and gestured the man in.

Bridget jumped up but the door closed again before she got there.

She watched the clock, wondering how John Roger was doing and whether Jessie was holding up. Had JR ever been a smoker? Had he worn his heart out in other ways? Or maybe it ran in his family, the sudden fatal heart attack in the middle of a seemingly healthy old age?

It was amazing how the hands on the clock did not move for long minutes and then took a little hiccuping step to catch up.

Two long hours later, Jessie came through the door. She looked fractured, limp, as if she had been battered by waves and left on the beach to dry. Bridget rushed to her.

"They told me to go home!"

"Why? What's happening?"

"They say he's stable for the night." Jessie was so clearly near to collapse that Bridget hadn't the heart to question her further. She put an arm around her.

"Let's get in the car."

"Yes, yes. I'm just going to take a pill and crawl into bed."

When she fell into her own bed half an hour later, Bridget merely peeled off the muumuu. She pulled up the covers and turned off the light and stretched out, too exhausted to do anything but close her eyes. Still, JR's pinched face stayed with her into sleep.

*   *   *

The next day it rained. This was odd because it was too early for rain. There were calls all over town as various plans were cancelled. Canvas lawn chairs got soaked. Bridget tried to call Jessie in the morning but there was no answer. Probably she was at the hospital. Bridget decided to spend the day making soup and bread. It wasn't something she did very often but it seemed appropriate to the day and could be done while waiting on news. Jessie finally called her at eight in the evening to say that JR did seem better but was discouraged and mostly slept.

The next morning...

"Bridget, can you take me over to the hospital? I can't find my contact lenses anywhere."

"What time is it?" Bridget was refusing to open her eyes, sensing that it was light in her room, more light than she wanted to look at.

"It's seven thirty. I need to talk to the doctor and I have to catch him on rounds. They won't give me any information because I'm not a relative. All the nurses will say is that he did have a stroke but he's doing okay. They also said he wanted them to call his daughter and did I have her number."

"What did you tell them?"

Jessie made an unhappy sound that crackled with anxiety. "I found the number for them. I don't want her there but I suppose she would have a fit if she wasn't told. I didn't want her getting angry at him."

Bridget opened one eye. Sure enough her bedroom was bright with sunshine. "You have to give me time to shower."

"Fifteen minutes? Is that enough?"

Bridget groaned silently. Her normal morning routine required forty-five minutes but she thought she could rush it. "I'll be there as soon as I can."

Jessie came out of her door the moment Bridget's car turned into her driveway. Anyone looking at her would question whether she had slept at all in the last two days. Her eyes were red and swollen, her hair pulled back in a ponytail. Not the usual Jessie.

"Thank goodness you're here." She was in the car already. "I can't find out anything over there. Except JR did tell them he had a stroke several years ago. That's bad, isn't it? A second stroke."

"I don't know. Can I see him too?"

"Probably. But I don't want Dorothy alone with him."

"What would be wrong with that?"

"You saw how she is. She will do anything to get her way. She might start a fight over that property right there even though he's so weak."

"They wouldn't let her do that, would they? Isn't he in Intensive Care?"

"They were moving him out this morning. I don't trust Dorothy."

Bridget thought that he had asked for Dorothy, therefore there must be a reason. Did she control his money?

As they passed Emergency to go to the main entrance to the hospital, they saw a private ambulance there with the doors open. Bridget slowed the car and as they turned to look, John Roger was brought out on a stretcher. Bridget couldn't see his face but knew it was him because walking beside him was Dorothy, looking pudgy and sleep-deprived, in rumpled jeans and a man's workshirt.

"Stop!" Jessie yelled.

Bridget slowed the car, not sure what to do.

"Let me out," Jessie said quickly.

The brakes squealed as Bridget obeyed. Jessie was already half out her door, and in a minute Bridget joined her, banging shut her own door and rushing in the wake of her friend, leaving the car across a driveway with the passenger door still open. Two bad nights wasn't keeping Jessie from running like the wind across the flower beds and back to the ambulance.

Dorothy had hurried forward, blocking Jessie's rush toward John Roger.

Jessie screeched: "What are you doing? Can't you see he's sick?"

"Just stay out of the way. He's my father. I'm taking him to a hospital in Marin."

Jessie stepped around her, reaching a hand toward John Roger who was still feet away. "NO, YOU CAN'T DO THAT."

The two men from the ambulance looked at each other, took their hands off the stretcher and moved in to block the women from each other. "This is not a good thing to do," one of them said, trying to sound calm and reasonable.

Dorothy was crying and started beating on the chest of the medic who had stepped in front of her, his arms out to stop her progress toward Jessie.

Jessie's face was red and one of her shoes had come off. She tried to move around the man who blocked her progress toward Dorothy. "Let him alone. I love him."

By now Dorothy had been backed six feet away from Jessie but toward the ambulance and the stretcher. "Get out of here. He's my father and I will take care of him."

The man who was trying to push Jessie away in a different direction was having his hands full. He was shorter than she was and she had managed to get close enough to John Roger to take his hand and would not let go. "No, no."

"Hey, this is not good for him? He needs to keep quiet. You're distressing him. Let us get him in the ambulance and you two go over there in the parking lot and talk this out," Jessie's medic was saying.

"All she wants is his money," Dorothy said.

"She's the one who is after money," Jessie cried, her face now red and covered with tears.

The two young men looked at each other and some signal between them energized them.

Dorothy had been backed against the side of the ambulance. Overpowered, she stood still so the man who had pulled her away now returned to getting the stretcher into the ambulance. At this, the young man who was still blocking Jessie firmly pulled John Roger's hand away from her and she relinquished it, tears streaming down her face.

"JR, I love you," she cried.

Now working together hastily, the men got the stretcher inside the ambulance. If JR responded to Jessie, the sound was lost in the interior. Bridget came up behind Jessie and put her arms around her. The back doors of the ambulance banged shut on John Roger and one man while the other went around to the driver's seat.

Jessie was sobbing. Seeing the job accomplished, Dorothy had run across the parking lot and was getting into her own car. The ambulance backed out faster than seemed normal, as if the men were afraid of being pursued.

"It's all right," Bridget kept saying. "We'll find out where he is and go see him. She can't keep you from seeing him if he wants to see you. And he does."

Jessie made no answer but sobbed all the way back to her house, tears streaming down her cheeks unchecked.

"I'll never see him again."

"That's not true. It's going to be all right."

Chapter Nineteen

When Jessie and Bridget came back from the hospital, it was not yet 10 a.m. but might have been midnight for the way they felt. Bridget turned into Jessie's driveway, then afraid to leave Jessie alone, turned off the key and got out too.

"Thank you," Jessie said, without looking back.

Holding the door open for Bridget, she said, "Do you want a glass of wine?"

The thought of wine before breakfast made Bridget nauseous. "No, I don't think so."

"Well, I'm going to have one, or maybe three." Jessie dropped her purse on the kitchen counter. But instead of reaching for the cabernet that was still sitting out, she opened a cupboard and pulled out a bottle of brandy. She got a glass from the dishwasher and poured it half full of brandy, looked at it briefly, and at the last minute added a little water from the tap.

Bridget thought it was the first time she had ever seen Jessie admit to needing a drink. Did that really ever do anything for you? All it did for Bridget was to upset her stomach.

Jessie leaned crookedly against the counter, her hip wedged against a drawer pull, and had several sips of the brandy. She interpreted Bridget's thought. "Would you like some coffee?"

"Nothing, thanks. I'll go in a minute and let you alone." Bridget wandered through the dining area and into the living room. Should she leave her alone or not? She crumpled into the closest chair and stretched her legs out on the ottoman, trying to remember what it was she had to do today. Nothing occurred to her. She had stepped out of her life. The doors to the patio were open framing the sunshine on the garden, too familiar to be of interest. The only thing in her head was the image of John Roger's pale face and the harsh sound of Dorothy's voice. She had a sudden urge to call all her children and make sure they were all right.

Jessie was making coffee. The smell wafted into the living room with the first perk. "How about some fruit salad?"

Bridget went back to the kitchen propelled by the thought of food. "Well maybe just a little. If there's nothing sour in it."

Some time later – Bridget had no idea how long it had been – two empty bowls which had contained the fruit salad plus two nearly empty brandy glasses sat on the coffee table. The sun had moved so the room was darker than it had been. Jessie was curled up on the couch opposite Bridget who was back in the chair with the ottoman, contemplating her ankles which seemed to have doubled in size since she last looked at them. Tibby and Belvy were snoozing on the carpet, only occasionally opening an eye to see if there was any sign of a move toward the out-of-doors. The whole charm of the room, the view of the garden, the smell from the lavender planted near the doors, none of this beauty seemed meaningful.

"Has Dorothy ever been married?" Bridget asked.

"I have no idea."

"That's what she needs. A husband to worry about. And why doesn't she have any children? She looks to be thirty at least."

There was no response to this.

"I'd better go soon."

Jessie's voice was calm, but her face was haggard. "I'll never see him again."

"You can't say that. You don't know. They're doing wonderful things for stroke now." I'm drunk, Bridget thought in amazement. I haven't been drunk for several years, maybe more.

"Yes but now Dorothy has him and she'll never let him go. You saw how she treated me, as if I was a Jezebel leading her father astray. As if what he wanted was nothing. She'll pop him somewhere unlisted and have him hidden away."

The sudden vision of John Roger peering up from under a blanket rose in front of Bridget's eyes. She closed them to get rid of it. "How can she do that?"

Without warning, Jessie began to cry, soundlessly. "How can she be that cruel? I should never have given the hospital her number."

"He won't allow that. He will call you. I know he will. He's in love with you."

She should go back to her own house, even to her bed but what would Jessie do if she was left alone? Then there was the whole question of whether or not she herself could even stand up.

"But look how weak he was....putty in her hands. And he asked for her. He wanted to contact her. That's the worst part. He had me, but he wanted Dorothy there."

"Why did he do that?"

"I don't know."

"How old is he? Do you know?"

"He told me he was seventy but I know he lied."

The whole ugly scene rose up before Bridget again. The ambulance, the two young men – maybe they were medics, maybe not - the huge Bird of Paradise plants lining the sidewallk, all this framing the conflict – Jessie looking distraught, John Roger's helplessness, Dorothy's violent anger. Had they passed out of adulthood and into some dependent state, helpless in the hands of their children? Dorothy's young strength had left Bridget feeling old and here she was in perfect health and only sixty-two.

"Give him a few days. He'll call you."

"I suppose he could be eighty." Jessie's voice was trying to show she was the soul of reasonableness but, belying this, there was a bleakness around her eyes and the residue of pain on her cheeks.

Bridget stood up with some effort and went across the room to plant a kiss on her friend's forehead. "Maybe you need to go to bed for a couple of hours. You've had a rough few days."

"Maybe later."

Bridget went back to her chair, not willing to leave Jessie yet, although she felt she was the one who needed a couple of hours of sleep.

Suddenly Jessie was angry. "Why go through all we've had together, all that hopefulness, if it's going to end like this?"

"But look at the wonderful months you've had together." Bridget wanted to add – I haven't had that, but didn't.

"It's not enough."

"Jessie! What else is there? Just enjoy every moment as it happens, marveling at them. Nothing lasts." Do I do that, Bridget wondered, and knew she didn't. Don't I spend my life afraid to try things for fear they will turn out badly.

"That's not enough."

Bridget was almost angry. "How can you say it's not enough. You and me, we're among the fortunate people on this planet. What would be enough?"

Jessie lowered her tone. But she wasn't going to back down. "Maybe another five years. Maybe."

"I think you'd only say the same thing at the end of another five years."

"Probably. But don't I deserve it? Haven't I gone off to work day after day, week after week for all these years. Isn't that worth something? Why shouldn't I be happy?"

With that, Bridget gave up. Who did this remind her of? "We all deserve it, I guess. Let's talk tonight. Call me if you hear from him."

She staggered to her feet again and went home to her own bed. Which she didn't enjoy very long because she had forgotten the men were coming to clean her carpets and she had to get up and put away all the small things so that they could move furniture and do their work. In the process, she broke a wine glass and knocked over a plant which spilled dirt all over the newly-cleaned carpet, and generally had a day out of hell.

However, that evening she called all three of her children just to hear their voices.

Chapter Twenty

"You can put your keys down there," Jessie told Jack, and he obediently laid them on the end of the kitchen counter where John Roger had always set his keys. She had shooed the dogs into the garden and was considering denying them dinner because they had misbehaved. Also because she wanted to concentrate on Jack. Why had she said she would fix dinner for him? It was going to take forty-five minutes at least and she was not at all hungry.

"And come in here and let me get a look at you." Then because that sounded funny, she amended it. "Let me see if you got any leaves in your hair from those bushes."

For they had walked the dogs because, Jessie had said, this was a chance to get to know each other, and would give them a good appetite for dinner. Then those adolescent Afghans had showed their usual naughtiness. Belvy had run off after a rabbit and Jack had obediently gone after her, finally running her to earth in a thicket where he had torn his shirt. Belvy had then laid down, acting as if she had done nothing wrong, wagging her tail and pretending to welcome the leash which Jessie snapped it on her choke chain with an angry pull When they got back to where Tibby was waiting with seeming patience, he was eating something so probably nasty that Jessie refused to look at it.

Jack's hand lingered over the keys as if he thought he had made a mistake. He was a tall, thin good-looking man with a head of thick grey hair and a strong nose. When he had found her name and photo at Togetherness, they had talked on the phone several times but this was their first time meeting in person. As he turned toward her, Jessie couldn't be blamed for thinking that she had struck gold this time. Jack might be in his early seventies (he claimed to be sixty-nine), but he walked with the vigor of a much younger man. He was wearing a blue checked shirt and a red necktie, and Jessie was warmed by the formality of the tie. She had had to fight with John Roger nearly every day about the wrinkled and disreputable clothes he wore.

"Thank you for going to all that trouble with the dogs. They are terrible children, aren't they?"

"No problem." He looked around. "I like your house. Did you have a decorator?"

Jessie shook her head though of course she had consulted several times with her friend Mimi who belonged to the A.S.I.D. and was therefore a cardcarrying decorator. "All by myself."

"You're very talented!"

"There is a leaf in your hair. Bend down."

He obeyed and she brushed it out, enjoying the feel of his springy hair. As he straightened up again, he sent her a flash of interest from wary brown eyes. What was going on?

Much might have happened then but Jessie woke up. Woke up with the knowledge that there was no Jack. All of that, even the leaf in his hair and the misbehavior of the dogs had gone on in her sleeping mind.

There was no John Roger either. Not here in her bed, not at the end of a phone line where she could reach him. She had heard nothing from him but an aborted phone call, since he had been loaded into the ambulance. After all their months together, their love affair had been turned into a dream while the only reality that remained was the scene in the hospital parking lot.

Her heart beginning to race, she sat up in bed in a violent rush, springing to readiness to protect herself. The white cloth blinds glowed with morning sunshine. But, sure enough, there it was…a pain in her chest. She fell back to the bed and punched at the pain to see how deep it was. Was she going to die right here without ever knowing where John Roger was?

She began to cry because now she had hurt herself with her fist. The first pain seemed to have left so maybe it wasn't a heart attack after all. She had better get up and start her day and not lie here grieving. No, and not fancifully making up stories about a new man to comfort herself.

She cried for a while in the shower but the business of getting clean and getting dressed comforted her some, the sameness of it, the need to pay attention to details of her body, though through it all her chest still hurt. She had hit it too hard. When she was in her underwear and a robe and her hair wrapped up, she went out to the kitchen for breakfast.

The house was full of sunshine, lying about the true nature of the day, pretending that it wouldn't be like yesterday, hours of nothing but heartache. She wanted to call Bridget, get some comfort just from conversation, though she feared she might have been leaning on Bridget too much. Anyway, first she had to call the office because she had promised that she would be in today, and now she wanted to put it off another week. If she stayed home today, perhaps JR would call.

Jessie did this, talked to the receptionist who was the first person in, shielding herself from the curious inquiries. That over, she chopped oranges and bananas together and sprinkled some muesli over them and added some plain yogurt. More breakfast than she usually ate because she sensed she hadn't been eating enough. This, with a cup of green tea, she carried out to the table on the patio to eat while she looked at her garden.

The garden was not a lot of comfort. It showed signs of neglect. There were leaves all over the patio and the walkway, and the dead roses needed cutting off. There were plenty of weeds among the geraniums. Perhaps she would do that today since she was staying home.

Oh, JR, why did you want Dorothy there when you had me?

The morning seemed endless while she worked away at all the boring jobs that collected after weeks of neglect. While her hands were busy, she dreamed up dramatic things she might do – bold strokes which would prove she was in charge of her life, and it was satisfying and much to be envied.

She would sell her house and use some of the money to decorate a new one. She would hunt out a travel agent who would do a trade with her for some decorating and then she could take a trip while her newly-decorated house was rented out to a vacationing family for some fabulous amount of money.

She made the bed and did a load of whites in the washer. She swept the front sidewalk and put away the clean dishes from the dishwasher, and loaded it again. She picked up the scattering of newspapers and mail, and ran a quick dustcloth in the living room and dining room. She felt the memory of John Roger's departure in the ambulance as a huge weight pushing her toward the ground, stifling her ability to breathe. He had tried to hold onto her hand but had been too weak. He might even die and Dorothy would never tell her. She would go on expecting to hear from him for years and never know that he was gone.

With this thought, she lost all energy. She couldn't start any new enterprise because she was not up to even the smallest steps in her current life. The dogs followed her from room to room, making sad faces and tiny whimpers trying to coax her into a walk, while she started small tasks and then abandoned them. The weight of her thoughts was too much to bear alone. Finally, she called Bridget but she was not at home.

She was tired out before noon and lay down on her bed and pulled up a cover. Her back ached. The blinds were open and the light was too bright in the bedroom so she pulled the cover over her head, wondered if she could fall asleep. The dogs lay down on the floor by the bed in positions where they could see her if she did anything more interesting. Seeking escape, she fell into a deep sleep.

When she woke, the sunshine had changed position and no longer made the white bedroom too bright. She looked at the dogs for comfort and they stared back fondly. It was her own fault she had so few friends. She always grew impatient with the worries and foibles of other women. Bridget was the only one who had pushed herself forward and insisted on friendship but Jessie did not want to wear out that friendship.

The fact that Bridget had been married to Edgar long ago had made her more interesting. Edgar. She began to remember bits of phrases, things he had said that she had appreciated. True, he had lots of unfortunate habits but he was intelligent. She could stand to see Edgar right now.

She needed to see someone. That afternoon she called Edgar and made pleasant noises. The next day, Edgar himself sat in her striped satin chair and looked around him, perhaps to see what differences had appeared in the months since he had been there.

"You got a new painting."

Jessie nodded peaceably and handed him his martini. "Someone in my office was selling off her things, moving to San Miguel Allende. I liked it. I don't know anything about the painter though."

"You should never buy a painting without knowing its provenance. At least not an oil."

"I guess the provenance is that it belonged to Gail Eisenstein who bought it in a shop in Paris."

"Probably a copy. It looks familiar to me. I'll look it up."

"That's nice of you. What have you been doing, Edgar? Are you still a mentor?"

He frowned. "Had to give that up. I've gotten too old for teenagers. The things they say make my teeth ache."

"I was always too old for teenagers. Even when Naomi was that age."

"Where is Naomi now?"

Jessie shook her head wonderingly. "She's in West Africa giving hygiene lessons for the Peace Corps. I try not to think about all the diseases she could catch."

"You should never have let her go."

"Let her? You seem to have forgotten about young people. She didn't consult me, didn't even tell me till the week before she was leaving. I could stand to see her right now."

"Jessie, you were always too permissive. Are you still working?"

Edgar was beginning to seem more and more familiar. She could almost predict the words before they came from his mouth. She sipped her martini and looked at him. At his cropped hair and tight mouth. There were new wrinkles around his eyes but his stomach was as flat as ever. He would become more and more like a straight steel beam till he died, probably from chagrin.

"I *am* still working." She glared at him so strongly he blinked and set down his glass.

There was silence in the room for long minutes. Finally, Edgar stood up.

"Have to be getting back. Meeting someone for dinner. Nice to see you, Jessie. Thanks for the drink."

"Nice to see you, Edgar. Have a good evening."

She didn't mean a word of it. Seeing Edgar proved to her how right she had been when she had stopped seeing him. And how much better a man John Roger was.

After she washed out their glasses, she lay across her bed and cried for a while.

Chapter Twenty-One

A man named Martin Morton bought Jeb's Navigator. Marion had thought she didn't know anything about selling a car - she might have to call Bridget after all – but when Martin Morton arrived, he seemed quite capable of managing the process without her help. He told her immediately that he had looked the car over when it was parked in town, had decided that was the one he wanted, and written down her number.

"But to make sure," he wiggled a finger at her, "I have to drive it. If it seems to be all right, I have cash with me."

The mention of cash brought Marion alert. Not that she had been uninterested but several men had come by to look the Navigator over and then explain at length why it wasn't the car they wanted after all. Money from the planned trip to Alaska had not been returned to her yet. She was down to $4.44 in her checking account plus Jeb's poker winnings which she hadn't yet touched.

Morton was a short, chunky man with such a decided air, Marion began to worry what she would say if he announced he wanted to pay less than the fifteen thousand. She knew she wouldn't be able to argue with him. But if he planned to offer less, wouldn't he have said that over the phone?

Following Bridget's advice, Marion announced she would ride along while he took his practice drive. He nodded pacifically and after she got her sweater and climbed into the passenger seat, he carefully went through all the buttons on the dashboard. Marion clutched her seat belt when he started up to keep it from cutting into her neck, and began to wonder if maybe she was being kidnapped. There was no money in the pocket of her sweater. He couldn't go off with the Navigator without her signature, could he? But there was her house; he could demand of Alice or Bro and Letitia that they turn over the house if they ever wanted to see Marion again. On reflection, that seemed a little far-fetched so she dropped the thought and watched her neighborhood go by.

Morton was a good driver if a bit faster than Jeb had always driven, and his braking was abrupt. He hummed to himself and frowned occasionally. Marion kept quiet and focused her mind on the money; she didn't want to say anything that might give him an excuse to disagree with her. He was exceedingly thorough, trying various speeds and various turns, and she was just beginning to wonder again about kidnapping when he turned back toward her house. She breathed out a little of the breath she had been holding. He must have decided everything was all right.

When they parked in front of her house, she slid carefully out of the high seat, hating it as she always had, wondering how she would get through this awkwardness about the money. Maybe it would be all right if she took less. He would hand her a stack of bills and she could pretend that was what she had wanted all along. Wasn't it Bridget who had set the price? Probably too high.

Morton got out and raised the hood and was brandishing the dip stick in preparation for checking the oil.

She had never checked oil; didn't know how the stick was supposed to look. She waited quietly by the curb for him to finish. He looked at the end of the stick and nodded so apparently it was satisfactory.

"Okay, I'll take it. Shall we go inside?"

Indoors, he took out a thick envelope and began to count out 100 and 50 dollar bills. Marion sank into a chair at the table and watched.

"How about fourteen thousand, five hundred?" he asked when he handed the wad of cash to her.

There it was and she was too intimidated to protest. Wasn't this just like the rest of her life? She always had to take what anyone offered because she had been taught when very young not to argue with grownups. Now everyone was grownup but she had somehow remained a child.

Morton looked at her rather fiercely. What would Jeb have done? He hadn't really liked fighting about anything either. She thought of what a difference five hundred would make in her budget, and opened her mouth for some kind of mild protest.

"My husband…" she said timidly.

"Oh, all right. I plan to drive it the rest of my life so I guess it won't matter if I've overpaid."

He reached in his pocket. "But you'll have to take five hundred in a check."

Marion nodded humbly. He wrote out the check leaning over her dining table. When he handed it to her she looked at it carefully to make sure he had signed the check and the name was the same he had given before. It looked all right.

"Thank you." She added the check to the wad of cash. She thought she should really count it all again herself. That would look more professional. She picked up the wad and began taking each bill and laying it back down on the table, turning them all the same way like they did in the bank, though she knew she was not remembering her count.

"It's all there." Morton stood in front of her, seething with impatience. He reminded her very much of Jeb at that moment. There was never enough time to let a woman make up her mind.

She continued picking up the bills and putting them down one by one but she had lost her count completely. It would take too long if she went back to the beginning so she gave it up and nodded her agreement.

She had put the pink slip in the cut glass fruit bowl on the sideboard so it wouldn't get lost. She handed it to him.

"You have to sign it," he said.

He showed her where to sign that the car was now sold. Luckily the Navigator was in her name as well as Jeb's. While she was doing that, he produced a piece of paper, already made out, saying she had gotten the fourteen thousand, five hundred in cash. Marion signed her name again.

"Is there anything in the car you want to get out?"

Marion tried to think if there could be anything; Jeb had been fairly neat about leaving things in the vehicle. She shook hands with Morton. The stack of money on the table glowered demandingly. When had she ever seen that much money in cash? What was she going to do with it? For just a moment, she wished that Bridget was there.

Then suddenly, after he was out of the house and near to climbing into the Navigator, she remembered and ran out calling…'wait, wait.' Her grocery bags! She usually took old grocery bags back to the market in order to get a nickel off her new groceries. Morton was just at the curb, hadn't gotten in the car yet. He nodded and opened the back for her, and Marion took out the stack of wrinkled bags.

"Thank you. Thank you. I hope you like the car."

He merely nodded, now impatient to get away. Marion stood by the curb, clutching her stack of bags, and watched him drive away, taking a piece of her life with Jeb.

She dropped the bags on the kitchen counter and went to look at the pile of money on the dining table. What on earth was she going to do with it? It was six o'clock – the banks were closed. She would have to hide it someplace.

It took her half an hour to settle on a hiding place but she was rather proud that she had thought of it. She took the table cloth off the dining table and spread the cash neatly and evenly over the pad that went underneath the cloth. She then carefully laid the table cloth over the money. It was hard to get the table cloth on without disturbing the bills, and it looked a little bumpy but what intruder would bother to look. A woman might but most burglars were men, weren't they? They always looked in drawers and under the mattress and now, she heard, they looked in ice cube trays for jewelry.

She took a cup of tea and went up to her bed in exhaustion.

*   *   *

Marion slept nearly twelve hours and woke up at six the next morning. Immediately she knew that something was different and she tried to think what it was. There was sun coming through the drapes in the usual way. And there was her cat sitting on a chair opposite the bed neatly washing her grey and white face. From outside she could hear some blue jays arguing. Marion got up and took a shower, and decided that the difference was good if a little strange. She felt lighter, less encumbered.

While she was eating her oatmeal, she wondered vaguely about the day ahead, what absolutely had to be done – take the money in to the bank – and what she might want to do – spend a little of it. That began to seem interesting.

She changed her clothes twice, putting on a newer blouse and slacks, and when she brushed her hair, twisted it up in a knot, which looked not bad. Riley's was having a sale on knit pants and tops. But did she really want another one of those? Maybe she should get a nice pair of grey pants and a good looking white blouse so she would have something new to wear to the movies - if she should happen to go - nothing fancy, just looking a little better than her last year's clothes.

When she was ready to go, she rolled back the tablecloth and this time she did count the money out carefully. She got confused halfway through and had to start over again when she got to the twenties. Had he cheated her after all? The second time, she wrote down the totals of each stack and it all came out right. He could have cheated her and she wouldn't have known till today but he had given her exactly the amount he claimed. She sighed in relief.

She put rubber bands around the three stacks of hundred, fifties and twenties, knowing the bank teller would count it all again, and then she put all this in an old soft purse and the purse in a shopping bag. Bridget had talked about putting it all in a Certificate of Deposit. While she was in the bank, she would ask about that, what they were paying and how long she would have to leave it. The tellers had always been very nice and probably would have good suggestions.

She picked up the check and looked it over. If it really was all right, maybe she would take it and deposit it in her checking account for emergencies, after she had spent just a little bit.

Marion came home from town excited about the grey slacks and white blouse which, although they were slightly more expensive than her usual purchases, had really been a very good price for the quality, and had both been on sale. Her transactions at the bank had been fairly mundane, the teller not being excited at the sight of fourteen thousand, five hundred dollars in cash. Marion had agreed to put it all in a six month CD, and then had deposited the check into her nearly empty checking account, taking back, at the last moment, sixty dollars for immediate needs.

She laid the blouse and slacks out on the dining room table where the tablecloth was still folded back, and admired them. She also had a smaller paper bag. She had gone into the dime store for some more knee-high stockings and seen a pile of notebooks with spotty black and white covers just like the ones they used to hand out long ago at the secretarial school for exams. The memory had pleased her, and so she had bought one of the notebooks on impulse. She really didn't remember why, only it had beckoned to her from across the aisle and it had reminded her of those long-gone days when she was single and hadn't yet met Jeb or owned a house or produced a child.

She made herself an egg salad sandwich and sat down at the kitchen counter with the notebook. She opened it to a blank page and stared at it while she ate. When she had finished eating, she made herself a cup of tea and then sat down again in front of the notebook, this time with a pen in hand. The blank page teased at her mind for a while till she took the pen and wrote down: *Thursday, September 8.*

What was it she wanted to remember about this day? Finally, she wrote down what she had paid for the slacks and blouse and where she had bought them. While she was at it she might as well write down the weather report, which was '*fog in the morning, clearing by mid-day, high winds and cloud cover in the evening.*' Then she paused. Should she go to the grocery now or wait till tomorrow? She had enough for dinner, only was low on catfood and dishwasher soap. After reflecting for some time, she wrote '*feeling allright, not too bad.*' Then '*Tony Bennett will be on tonight. May call Letitia.*' That seemed to be all she wanted to say but she felt some satisfaction. She closed the book.

And right then she knew what was different about today. Today there was a different voice in her head. There had always been this secret conversation going on. For years and years, one side had been Jeb's voice and one side had been her own secret responses. Now Jeb's was not there anymore. Instead there was a strange voice commenting on everything. It wasn't Bridget either.

The thought of the notebook stayed with her through her chores. She washed the pots and pans and unloaded and reloaded the dishwasher.

She ran the vacuum cleaner around the living room and watered the indoor pots of African violets.

It took her till after dinner to decide the strange voice was her own, her grownup voice had replaced her childish voice. That thought pleased her so much, she went outside to look at what needed doing in the garden, and later she looked in the refrigerator and decided that tomorrow she would clean out the refrigerator and throw out all food that had been there since the funeral.

All those years of her marriage, she had had employment. Taking care of Jeb. Now she had none. What was she going to do with her life? What little of it was left!

That evening her daughter Stephanie called, wanting to know how Marion was and whether she could borrow the Navigator for a couple of days.

"I'm sorry. I've sold it."

"MOTHER! What did you do that for?" Adolescence seemed about to return.

"For money, of course."

Marion thought she would put that in her notebook so that when she looked back she could remember exactly how this moment felt, hurt and love and irritation all mixed up together.

She closed the window to keep the night air out, and pulled the drapes closed. Her bedroom looked peaceful but empty. Lamplight fell across the flowered chair and the velvety beige carpet. And right then she was struck with an odd pain somewhere in her middle. All those years and years of her marriage to Jeb, all thirty-one of them, every day of every year, were gone. And what had she done with them – she had no idea. If only she had written them down in a notebook, she could have them back again, now and then…for a little while.

Chapter Twenty-Two

One day, when the most exciting thing she could think to do was to run down to the department store and buy some stockings, Bridget knew the time had come when she had to look for another volunteer job. This time she wouldn't join a fundraising committee putting on some event. (What she remembered was the gasp and she hated that gasp.) Though they might do a little bit of work such as dealing with the caterers and addressing envelopes, the real excitement came when each member of the committee announced how much money she was giving to the cause.

There would be the gasp – if the amount was large enough for a gasp – there would be a slight pause and then a clapping of hands. The next person who had to announce her gift after a clapping of hands usually made a point of announcing a larger amount. Competitive giving. Bridget liked to compete, but not in that way.

No, what she wanted this time was to actually do some work. Learn something too.

She threw herself into the process of looking. She made lists of people to ask and began taking them to lunch. Of course, a lot of this was money down the drain, entertaining boring people who had nothing interesting to suggest but wanted to gossip about something. The first week it seemed as if there was nothing new to do in the whole town. The second week was better, a few glimmers, then she spent days trying to contact a woman named Rose Allbright. Bridget had been told that Rose was the Volunteer Chief Extraordinaire with her finger in many pies. If she impressed Rose Allbright, she would be swimming in the right wake and be privy to all kinds of novel activities.

Rose, however, was very busy and seldom had a chance to return phone calls. By the time she finally called Bridget back, Bridget had almost given up hope.

"I'm so terribly, terribly sorry I haven't gotten to you sooner. But I haven't been ignoring you. I've heard such wonderful things about you. I've been looking for something special for you – something you won't get bored with…" and on and on. Her voice had a breathy theatrical quality with exaggerated A's. She had really been looking for something worthy of Bridget, something she would find personally rewarding – that was so important, wasn't it – but it was rather a low season right now. In spite of that, she was right on the brink of finding something perfect for Bridget's unique talents.

Bridget's spirits rose, then fell again as Rose went on.

Unfortunately she was so rushed right this minute, she couldn't talk about anything till later; she had to be somewhere in fifteen minutes. But she was eager to get acquainted; she was sure Bridget would find working with one of her groups very rewarding.

Bridget was to come down Thursday around nine, to the second floor of the building next door to the movie theatre. She was to go up the stairs that were to the right of the theatre and, at the top of the stairs, go through the door even though there was no sign on it. There would be lots of empty desks. If no one was there, Bridget was to help herself to coffee, make a pot if no one else had, and sit at one of the desks, and Rose would be along shortly.

Bridget went to her closet. Should she look like a business woman, or should she wear something fashionable or dress down, looking like someone ready to dive into any kind of work, even cleaning out closets? Volunteer work could be like that. You thought you knew what you were getting into but when you arrived, they needed an entirely different kind of effort. Sometimes they liked you to be humble.

While looking in her closet, she got another call back, this time from the Boys and Girls Club, asking if she would be willing to oversee a study room for two hours twice a week. She had said she would take anything, so now she had to say 'of course'.

The Boys and Girls Club was not really to her taste. She had maybe had enough of children after the three of her own who had all managed to be hellish in their high school years and each had to try out several colleges before finding one that fit. The thought of her children, who were now all handsome and idealistic and employed in artistic pursuits for next to no money, filled her with purpose, and she was reconciled to the study room.

She appeared at the Boys and Girls Club at the time requested and put in the required two hours and found it not too bad. Aside from a tendency to giggle, the children behaved themselves and, though a few spent the time staring out the window, many of the others seemed to be doing their homework. Maybe this would be pleasant enough if what Rose Allbright was working on did not come through right away.

Then the day before she was to climb to the second floor and meet Rose, she got another call. This was to help stuff a fundraising mailing for the hospice. The hospice had just moved and needed money to fix up their new quarters. When she joined the mailing party, it looked attractive enough, consisting of three well-dressed women Bridget's age. Talkative too. While they folded and stuffed and sealed envelopes, they exchanged their experiences of the town – the stores, the restaurants, the traffic tickets, and the very unpleasant man who handled mortgage loans at the local bank.

"I think one of my neighbors is about ready for the hospice," Bridget contributed when there was a pause.

Three pairs of eyes looked indignantly at her. Bridget was grateful this was a one-time only event. How was she to know the real work of the hospice was not an acceptable subject.

Now here she was at nine on Thursday morning, climbing the long straight steps next door to the old movie theatre, hoping she had found the new phase for her life. The staircase had been recently painted a nice combination of beige and pale green. So that, although it was clearly an old building, with embossed tin lining the staircase below the hand rail, and worn depressions in the wooden steps, it seemed that someone was hoping for another fifty years from it. The steps were rather steep and, with no landings, soon had her panting a little. Probably she was too eager.

The door at the top had a frosted glass window and a slot which had once held a nameplate but did so no longer. Tentatively, Bridget turned the handle. It turned easily and let her in. She was here!

Here turned out to be a small waiting room with no pictures on the wall and no chairs. She stepped through the next door into big room full of rows of wooden desks just as Rose had described.

Bridget looked around eagerly but there was no one else in the room. Where was Rose? Where was the group she had been promised?

The desks were outfitted with desk pads, calendars, and rings of white, evidence of past coffee cups or pots of flowers. On the wall was a calendar still turned to January though the current month was not.

"Hello?" Bridget called.

Clear across the room, there was one window open and faint noises of traffic and voices came from the street downstairs. She walked around the desks looking for one that showed signs of recent occupancy, but couldn't determine that any of them did. The desk pads and upright files were rather cheap and somewhat out of date, as if whoever owned the office didn't replace such things very often. Well, of course this was just the kind of office people used for temporary campaigns, mailing parties, planning sessions for fund raisers.

There was an alcove on the back wall, which turned out to contain a sink and some big coffee urns. There was even a three pound can of coffee standing waiting to be used. Bridget took the coffee maker apart and assessed its workings. Then she filled it to ten cups from the tap, put in a reasonable amount of coffee, and plugged it in. Sure enough, in a few minutes, it began to chug.

That was all very well for activity but didn't promise that she was ever going to have anything more interesting to do. While the coffee perked, she walked around the office again and even looked out the window which showed that ordinary life was still going on in the street she had just left.

She tried to ascertain what activity the office had been intended for. There was only one computer, rather an old one. There were a few pencils out on desks. Pencils, not ball point pens. The calendar pads had mostly not been opened, but were still clothed in their cellophane wrappers.

Discouragement settled like a chilly cloak around her shoulders. She had believed Rose but that was the way she was…easily taken in.

When the coffee was ready, she poured herself a cup and selected a typist's chair where she could see out the window. There were people going by on the street down below, hurrying into the bakery, stopping to chat with friends, a small woman pushing a stroller. Bridget felt like opening the window further and yelling out at them – what should I do next?

After a while it occurred to her that it was rather peaceful to sit here and drink coffee. She could reflect on her life and it occurred to her that at one time this would have been heaven – say when she had had three toddlers - a big sunny space, plenty of paper and pens, silence, and nothing in particular she had to do.

Was this whole idea of hers wrong? She had wanted a volunteer job to feel useful, create change in the world, fill up that emptiness she felt sometimes. Maybe the way she was going about it was not the right way. But she was just one woman and not brilliant and how else could she go about it?

She felt tears in her eyes. "I don't have to change the world," she said out loud. Just do something so she felt useful.

She took out a packet of tissues and mopped her eyes. Saw that the mascara was running just a bit. Okay, yes, she had been thinking about her end, her death, and what other people might say about her at her funeral. Maybe all that because Norm had appeared and reminded her of how much of her life was gone. And that had made her wonder, what had she done with her life so far?

She had raised three children and it seemed as if they had become reasonable citizens of the world. In the past that was all most women had ever thought they had to do. But this was the 21st century. A woman who had been to college, who had enough money not to worry about survival, who was healthy and energetic, should be able to do more.

All the causes she gave money to, all the volunteer work she had done in the past, the PTA and the crossing guarding, and the fundraising, had been very petty, only barely of use to the world.

The breeze from the window was chilly. She got up and forced it down. It was an old style window on ropes and went down crookedly, protesting. No one on the street below heard the noise and looked up. She might as well be a ghost, just haunting this office because she had been sent here to get her out of the way.

There should be something more coming to her life, some excitement of some kind. "I count for something!" she said.

"At least I *could* count for something."

Women of her age didn't accomplish much because they started out with low aspirations. It was Norm who had pointed that out. She thought about things she had started to do which were maybe a little out of the ordinary. But she could see now that anytime she tried to do something new, after a while she would be taken over by boredom and petty worries and the excitement of the new enterprise would fade away.

This time that was not going to happen.

She stood up. Her lungs filled, her legs shook a little and she could feel how firmly her feet met the floor. That was the feeling she wanted to have – her feet pressing the floor, ready to take on the world and have a place in it!

A cloud in the sky outside must have lifted because the upstairs room filled with bright blue light and Bridget stepped forward, stabbed with a feeling of happiness. That was worth anything, wasn't it? With this feeling of certainty she could go on and on, looking forever for her place until she found it.

A telephone rang in the room. She laughed out loud. She was being summoned. She found the phone and picked it up.

"Is this the bakery?"

"No." Bridget banged down the receiver. Then she laughed again. She was not going to be snapped out of her sense of joy.

She walked down the aisle of desks, noticing details she hadn't seen before, an old phone book sitting underneath a chair, marks where a computer had sat, an ink stain on a desk mat. All of them spoke of human activity, things had gone on here; whether important or unimportant, people had been working at projects, participating. Her cell phone rang and she dug it out of her purse with renewed hopefulness.

"This is Rose Allbright."

Ahh. Rose was extremely sorry not to have joined Bridget in the upstairs room but she could make lunch if Bridget was still interested. They could discuss what Bridget wanted to do and where she could fit in.

"Yes, yes." They fixed a time and place.

Bridget left the room of desks where no one worked, remembering to first unplug the coffee pot. She walked down the steep stairs, wondering what stray mysterious thought had filled her with happiness. It was good enough for the moment. She would keep searching. And Rose, however erratic she turned out to be, might help her find her way.

Chapter Twenty-Three

Don was carrying a lamp into Phyllis's house; not a bad lamp, he had decided, a straight, tall brass pole with a globe on top and a plain white shade over that. It should look pretty much alright anywhere, shouldn't it? But now he wondered if it was up to the quality of Phyllis's other furnishings. He had laid it down gently in the back of his pickup but, as he pulled it out when he got to her house, the shade caught on a hook on the side of the bed; Don responded with a yank and it came out with a rip in the shade.

"Damn." He let this out as quietly as he could. Now he thought it might be better to just junk the lamp before Phyllis had a chance to see it and disapprove. He was also uncomfortable that Phyllis's nosy neighbors might be looking out and would guess that he was moving in. A lot of whispering would then occur, and maybe Phyllis would be hurt by it.

Not that they were doing anything wrong. They had both gone to the Association office and confessed what they were up to. Don was going to live with Phyllis and his son was going to… It was at that point in their rehearsal that they changed their story. Nick was too young to live in Shady Acres; best not to mention he had taken over Don's house for the time being. Instead they would say Don's former wife was coming to live with Nick.

The beauty of this new arrangement was that it would also solve the problem of Mary Margaret's visit. She could have Don's room in Don's house and visit with Nick (instead of Don) all the hours she wanted, and that would make her happy and Don much happier.

So here was Don, moving the things he needed (if they were not needed by Nick) into Phyllis's house and he was both excited and apprehensive. What if those quarrels, which had been such a major portion of his marriage, suddenly broke out in this new relationship? Thinking of this, he had, over two days, whittled down the number of possessions he was actually moving. Better not to have too much to move out quickly in case there was a sudden disagreement and he had to exit.

It was a grey morning and he looked apprehensively up at the sky which had refused to honor this critical day with sunshine. But when he got through the gate with the lamp and the damaged shade, Phyllis was standing in the doorway, and she was smiling at him. He hastened his steps and tried to think how he would explain the shade.

"That will be useful," she said approvingly, and he was filled with an amazing lightheartedness.

After they had found a spot for the brass lamp next to a rocking chair in the spare bedroom, they went through Phyllis's bedroom, the kitchen, the living room and up and down the hallway all day, moving Phyllis's things out of the way, and then moving Don's things into their place. Was it getting too crowded? They consulted and decided that some things would have to go to the storage shed.

Don had brought his bowling trophies. He didn't bowl much since leaving his job and therefore his team, but he was proud of the trophies, and besides who knew when Nick might accidentally knock one off and break it. Now where to put them? He walked through all five rooms carrying the open cardboard box that held them. Phyllis had a small bookcase in the livingroom under a window but the top was crowded with four pots of African violets. Her sideboard in the dining area proudly held a silver tea service which had belonged to her second husband, Sam, and of which she was very proud.

"I could move the tea service," she offered, but her voice was a tiny bit forced.

"Absolutely not. I'll just park these in the garage."

"No, no. Don't do that." Now she led him to her garage and pointed to a dusty whatnot shelf hanging from a couple of nails. "We could put that in the front hall."

"Perfect." He set down the box of trophies and went home for some cinch anchors.

While he was gone, Phyllis began to worry about lunch. She didn't usually bother with lunch for herself, just whatever leftovers there were in the refrigerator. What was she going to feed him? When he returned with the cinch anchors and a toolbox, she had her apron off and her hands washed; she was going out to buy some cheese for toasted cheese sandwiches. Would that be all right?

"Terrific," he said.

The work went on after lunch but with a quieter rhythm. Once in a while one of them paused because there was something else that needed discussing or required both of them to pick it up. Should Don bring his monster television? Yes, they could put it in the bedroom. And didn't she want his brand new vacuum cleaner? And what about blankets? Did she need more?

Through all this, which could have been upsetting, Phyllis felt as if she was swimming slowly and contentedly in the lake she had lived by as a child. Her arms and legs had that lazy, competent feel they had had then, as if they didn't need to move until the last moment and then only enough to keep afloat. She imagined she could hear the faintest lapping of lake against the piers, feel the layer of lambent water against her skin, and the sunshine on her head. She could have been alarmed that her life was going to change this much but she wasn't at all. Instead it all felt right and pleasantly odd and endearing.

"Would you mind if I moved these magazines?" he asked.

"Throw them out if you want. I've probably read them as much as I'm going to."

"Oh, I wouldn't throw them out. Or I might take them to the hospital." He stopped because they were passing in the hallway, just outside the bathroom. He touched her elbow with one finger.

"Good idea. Let's do it."

"I've got lots of towels. Should I bring them?"

"No, leave them for the boy. I have lots too." She looked down at his finger which was warm on her skin. They stood quietly, contented with only this one point of contact.

Behind them somewhere was the mellifluous liquid sound. "Do you like swimming?" she asked.

"Swimming, sure. In a lake, not a pool. I hate that chlorine smell."

"All right, a lake. Let's go sometime."

"Yes."

Later, she found he had accidentally left the water running in the bathroom sink – that was the source of the liquid sound and her mood - but the knowledge didn't spoil the day.

By seven o'clock, they were tired. Don cooked hamburgers on the outdoor grill while Phyllis made potato salad and sliced tomatoes, and they ate on the patio. It was still light, though the sun was gone, and the jasmine gave off a heady odor. The evening was cool and none of their neighbors were outdoors, which made it quiet. Phyllis brought out a battery operated radio and set it to a music station.

"What's that for?"

"Some neighbors leave their windows open so as to catch all the news," she whispered.

"Wouldn't you know!" He laughed and turned the sound up more. "This should take care of it."

Phyllis's feet hurt from a full day of walking or standing. "I think I'll take a bath and soak for a while."

"Sounds good. There's a Giants game on. Do you mind if I watch."

"Not at all."

She thought they sounded like an old married couple and the thought made her contented. She reached over and patted his hand.

After they had taken the dishes in, Phyllis went to close and lock both doors, closing the two of them in to see what living together was going to be like.

When Phyllis had finished with the bathroom and piled up in her bed with the newspaper, she heard Don come out of his bathroom and, tentatively, quietly, close the door to the spare room. She was contented. She was tired. But tomorrow night, she would leave hers open and see if that was enough or if he needed more coaxing. She bounced her bed a little to test it out. She really needed a new mattress. Maybe she would get a foam one; they were much cheaper and more comfortable also.

All in all, it had been a good day. A very good day. A new start.

Chapter Twenty-Four

"I won't be here the week of the tenth. I'm going away," Bridget said by phone to her housecleaner, Maria Theresa. She was unable to keep the delight out of her voice. She had to tell someone, even if only Maria Theresa.

"Miss Bridget, very nice, where are you going?"

"Honduras."

"Central America? I hear it's very bad there now." Maria Theresa was from Mexico but she thought poorly of anything south of Jalisco.

When Bridget turned away from the phone, she was still full of delight. Wasn't it marvelous what could happen in life all of a sudden?

It wasn't just a vacation trip. No, this was a mission. Something worth spending her time and money on. Rose Allbright had sent her to this group of people who were gathering supplies for a school out in the country in Honduras. This was spearheaded by a woman named Graciela who was originally from there. Cousins of hers there had talked about the poverty of the country schools. The teachers had almost nothing to work with. Maybe Graciela and her American friends could do something to help.

Rose Allbright had supplied the organizational know-how while Graciela, who was married to a prominent attorney, raised money from her friends. Bridget had been sent in by Rose to put it all together, to throw a dinner dance, hire the band and the food, collect the money when it came in, write the thank you notes with receipts for gift taxes, pay the bills, and total up the profits. It was a fundraiser again but for a good cause. With the money in hand, Bridget and Graciela chose supplies from a school catalog, and had them packed for the long trip. The result was several large crates of pencils and pens and paper and paint, of rulers and crayons and three-ring binders, of classroom books in Spanish, of charts on the human body, blank grade cards, solar-operated calculators and various other teacher aids. These crates were sitting in Bridget's front hall.

Graciela had looked forward to delivering these supplies in person and seeing her cousins at the same time. She described with gusto to her friends here the remote river up which she would be poled to the schools her cousins had chosen.

All was set. But then Graciela turned out to be pregnant and her doctor had forbidden her to make the trip. Instead she had a good cry with the group who had worked so hard. They had to look around for someone to go in her place. Bridget had eagerly volunteered.

She had no competition. Bridget offered to pay her own way and no one else wanted to spend all that money in order to take a tippy canoe, actually several canoes, some unknown number of miles up an unknown river, shepherding the crates which were likely to be stolen at any point in the journey. Even Bridget, when she woke up in the morning, too early to get up, and lay in her safe bed listening to the chattering of the birds, had a few stray doubts about the trip.

"You need to take someone with you," Graciela directed. "Actually, a man. It is very difficult to do anything in Honduras as a woman, unless you are a nun, and even then it can be a problem."

Wasn't that the story of her present life? Being directed to appear with a man when there were no men from which to choose.

"You'll have to send me a nun," Bridget said.

Graciela explained that in her present life she knew very few nuns and those she knew were not free to travel. After all their wonderful work to raise money and purchase supplies, was it all going to go for naught?

"Can't we just ship them?"

"No, they'll be stolen immediately and never get to the countryside."

While she was still pondering this, Bridget picked up the phone that afternoon and heard a man's voice. It was Norm.

Bridget sat down by the phone and let her voice become soft. "How nice to hear from you. I have a wonderful idea. Would you like to go to Central America with me?"

"Oh, I don't think so right now. Why don't we just have dinner?"

She should have remembered that he never liked to fall in with other people's plans. What would persuade him?

"I'm not really well," he said when she did not reply immediately.

"What's wrong with you?" Then you'll be better for having something to do, she thought. She began to consider Norm. If he was this lonely for company, it meant that he didn't have a focus right now, something to do and someone to do it for. Why couldn't this focus be temporarily supplied by a trip to Honduras?

"I'm on a cancer watch."

Bridget digested this. She knew she was supposed to be deeply concerned but the boxes in her hallway weighed on her. "It can't be that serious."

"Birdie, its cancer."

"I thought you said when we had dinner that it wasn't."

"Well, I lied. I didn't want people to fuss over me. And it's only maybe."

"Well, there you go…only a maybe. I can't believe you're really sick. When is your next doctor's appointment?"

"Next month. But I'm supposed to lead a very healthy life in the meantime."

"Well, you can do that on the trip. It will only take a week. You'll be back before you know it. I'll watch what you eat and how much you sleep."

"It's not just that…".

"Let's go to dinner and talk about it," she said, striking while his determination faltered.

The next night over dinner at the Red Chimneys, Norm protested before she had a chance to bring up the subject.

"It's really not convenient right now. I'm just about to move. I have to find a place to live."

Bridget frowned a gentle reprimand. They should enjoy the food first, and work out their disagreement later. The frown made him unhappy. "Where is it you want to go?"

"Honduras."

"You won't like it. Heat, poverty , mosquitos."

"But it's for a good cause." And she told him the whole story. "Think about the children!"

Norm looked mulish and applied himself to his meal. Was he really sick? He had always been something of a hypochondriac. His hand was steady and his eyes looked fine. She noticed that he chose the salmon instead of a steak, something he would never have done in his younger days; a doctor must have been lecturing him about the disadvantages of red meat. She sipped her drink and waited.

Only halfway through the main course, he went back to the argument. "I really do have to find a place to live. I'll tell you what! If you'll let me live in your house till the trip and leave my things there till we get back, that would take care of that problem."

"What happened to the house in Palm Desert?"

"It's for sale. Besides, I have a contractor working on it. I can't leave anything there."

Bridget nodded, trying not to let her satisfaction show. He was going to go with her. Of course, being Norm, he would have to win something. "All right, you can stay with me till we go, and then when we come back, I will help you find another place."

Was the problem going to be getting rid of him when they came back?

He nodded his agreement solemnly. His voice was mild and conciliatory; however his eyes were elsewhere. "Birdie, you've become so strong; did you know that? You've thrived on being alone. When we divorced, I worried about you, but of course you married Paul right away."

Maybe she had also been worried then about how she would survive living alone because she had latched onto Paul very quickly, and then, panicked that she was thirty five and her child-bearing years were evaporating, had had three babies right in a row until she longed for a little loneliness.

"That was sweet of you to worry."

"You are going to pay the airfare, aren't you?"

"Okay." She wasn't going to war with him over money though he was much richer than she was. I thrived of necessity, she thought. She noticed he hadn't promised he would move out when he came back. Or for that matter, to pay for the lodging. This was the same Norm who had put a successful company together on his friends' money.

At least the children in Honduras would get their school supplies. It was going to be odd having Norm around, cooking for him. She couldn't remember what he was like to cook for. Was she going to have to resist his advances?

"No sex," she said abruptly.

He looked up from his salmon, startled. "No, no. I'm sick. You don't have to worry."

Had he really changed that much? Somehow she wasn't totally convinced of it.

*   *   *

The very next day, Norm arrived at nine in the morning, a station wagon filled with luggage. The very best leather luggage. Appropriate to a Mercedes.

Bridget was barely dressed. Hadn't finished her make-up, didn't have her jewelry on. She rushed downstairs and out the front door, fussed already though he had just arrived. Wasn't that the way it had always been with Norm? He believed in that old saying about getting the worm; he was always early everywhere, catching everyone off-guard, alarming people (including Bridget) with all the possibilities his busy mind could think up.

"You can have the same room you had last month, but that closet won't hold all this."

He was out of the car, freshly dressed in blue shirt and white trousers, his face still pink from shaving. He had already pulled out two briefcases. "Can we put some of it in the garage?"

"Then everyone will see all this when the garage is open."

"The things you worry about…"

"I have a storage shed out back."

"I hope it isn't damp."

"Norm, this is California. Nothing is damp in the summer."

194

"If you run the sprinklers, it is." He had the rear door on the station wagon up by now.

Bridget picked up a box that didn't look too heavy, and he followed her through the house with another one.

"All right, all right. There's a big closet off the kitchen. You can put some things in there. No dampness."

"Just show me where. Do you have a dolly?"

"No, of course I don't have a dolly. Why would I?"

"Okay, Birdie! Don't get upset. Think about your trip."

But of course the whole day was like that. Moving Norm in was no small task. He needed a desk but there was none in the spare room. There weren't enough plugs for his computer, the charger for his cell phone, his electric razor and toothbrush. There was no plug at all in the guest bathroom. She would have to buy some power strips, or else get an electrician over. It was essential he get on the Internet as soon as possible.

How close was the laundry and dry cleaner?

When she opened the closet off the kitchen, it was full of boxes of discarded clothes she hadn't taken to the Goodwill yet. Luckily, Maria Theresa came through the front door just then.

"Good, we need your help," Bridget said.

The three of them carried all the boxes of discarded clothes out to Maria Theresa's car so she could take them to the Goodwill.

There was a table in an alcove off the living room and Bridget let Norm set up his desk there, and promised to bring him a power strip. She was not used to all this exertion before breakfast. She had to pause and make coffee and put a couple of English muffins in the toaster while Norm and Maria Theresa carried in the rest of his belongings

By the time she had him situated, it was already past noon and Bridget was eager to get out of the house. She hurriedly finished her makeup and gathered up her purse and sun hat.

"I have a lunch date," she lied. "Here's a key to the front door. You will have to leave your car outside; there's no room in the garage."

"I guess I'd better go out for lunch also," he said slowly, waiting for Bridget to invite him. When she didn't, he nodded and went back toward his room.

Bridget went to the salad counter in the market and selected a mound of vegetables and covered them with raspberry vinaigrette. She took this and a bottle of lemonade to the City Park. Sitting on a bench, munching slowly, she calmed down. There was no reason she couldn't make this work with Norm. The arrangement was upsetting because it was all new but it was only for a few weeks. It had been years since she had thought about how one got along with the unique and somewhat difficult person he was.

She tried to remember what their marriage had been like. That was more than thirty years ago now. They had lived in an apartment; that was the first thing that came to mind. That had been unexpected because Bridget had her half of the sale of the house she had shared with Edgar, and Norm had even more cash from an inheritance. They could have bought quite a nice house but he was casting around for a new business to get into and didn't want to spend anything. So Bridget had bowed her head to this and set to work making the apartment really nice. She spent Saturdays looking at furniture and fabrics, painted the walls herself, and took a class in upholstery. She had enjoyed it all too.

She was working then. In Admissions at Stanford. That had been pleasant enough and a short bus ride from the apartment. She had liked the people she worked with, and some girls she had known in college lived in town, so they had had a pleasant social life, going to movies and concerts at the University, taking picnics over the hill to the ocean on the weekends.

She could remember all that but memories of Norm were rather shadowy. She had been freshly divorced when she met him at a Stanford party and was dazzled by his energy and irreverence. She had thought what a joy he was after stern Edgar who concentrated almost exclusively on rules and regulations, "ought-tos" and "shoulds". Norm excited her physically, and she began to think more critically and question more things. He was good for her, even though he could be sharp-tongued. Demanding, sometimes eccentric.

So, as she remembered it now, it had all been fun during the first years. And for a long time afterwards. Then he had suddenly found the business he wanted to go into, high tech of course like most of the people he had been in school with. At that point, he had pressured all their friends into investing in it, and he began spending seven days a week and twelve hours a day working, and their life became less fun. Bridget had comforted herself - she believed him that he would make lots of money and then the good times would return. So, even though she had finished her degree in History, she began taking courses in Art History to fill up her lonely evenings, and applied to have the courses count toward a Masters degree that she never finished. She had also joined various clubs and was relatively contented over the next few years.

What had he been like on a day-to-day basis when he was home? That was the trouble with having been married three times, she couldn't remember the details, or if she did, couldn't remember which husband they were about. Was Norm the one who had taken up wine knowledge and become a bore about it, or was that Edgar? And was he the one who never picked up his clothes till she began sending them all to Goodwill if she found them on the floor? That hadn't been Edgar. She wouldn't have had the nerve to do that when she was first married.

When she had finished the salad, she went to the kitchen store and spent a pleasant hour looking over all the things she might buy if she wanted to become a more serious cook. Eventually she felt serene about returning home.

Norm had moved his car to the curb, so probably he had been out but was now at home. She drove into the garage, and entered the house by the door to the hallway.

"Bridget!"

"Yes, I'm here."

They met in the living room. Her new housemate came in from the back hall with a look of frustration on his face and two light bulbs in his hands.

"What's the matter?" she asked. Then a host of memories returned and she had a flood of amusement and warmth. For all his business savvy and technical degrees, Norm had always been inept at household problems. She had never felt the need of having a child while Norm was around.

"The shower doesn't work and these bulbs seem to be burned out."

"The lights are on a switch at the wall."

"I tried the switches on the lamps."

"I know, but that doesn't work if the switch at the wall is off. Come on. I'll show you."

"And the shower?"

"The water to it is turned off to keep it from dripping."

He was sheepish. "Birdie, how do you know all these things?"

"From having husbands who didn't," she laughed. Actually it was going to be fun to have him around, for a while at least.

Chapter Twenty-Five

Bridget had been careful not to talk to Jessie too much about her new volunteer job. She didn't want to show the excitement she felt about it when Jessie was so low. Also, Bridget rather thought that Jessie had a working person's scorn for volunteer jobs. Therefore when the trip to Honduras became a reality, she only mentioned it as something she had to do as a result of the fundraising, she had to go and deliver the goods. No mention of the fact that she thought her life was finally on the right path.

Then Norm appeared on the scene and she hadn't been able to keep the small happy burble out of her voice. Now it seemed as if she could never reach Jessie. Bridget tried dropping by but each time she stopped, Jessie was not at home. There was no answer to the ring or the knock. The garage was locked up and the shade was down on the kitchen door. The only sign of life was the barking of Tiburon and Belvedere.

Bridget thought she had to see Jessie before she went to Honduras, therefore she drove past her house four or five times a day till she caught her putting out her garbage cans for pick up. Bridget swerved to the side and braked hard with a squealing of tires. She ignored this and jumped out of the car.

"Jess, I've been missing you. How are you."

"Hello," Jessie said limply.

When she got up to her friend, Bridget was so relieved that she hugged her. Then she stepped back to survey her. She thought Jessie looked terrible.

"Have you heard anything from John Roger?"

"No."

"Come on, I'm going to take you out for waffles and strawberries. Because I'm going away."

"Oh, I can't do that now. Going away where?"

"I'll tell you all about it."

At Ron's, they sat on the deck. Sunlight splashed off the blue and white striped awnings and onto the red and white checked tablecloths. It seemed as if all of California sparkled with pleasure. In the distance, the Mayacama Mountains masqueraded as a travel poster, their peaks lavender and grey, boasting that there were no bad mornings in this valley. They lied.

Bridget made the telling brief. She had to make this trip, deliver the school supplies and her ex-husband had agreed to go along as a sort of guard. Jessie accepted this with a look of interest.

"An ex-husband? Is that a good thing?"

"Who can tell?"

The waffles were still warm, piled with strawberries, while the snowy clouds of whipped cream were cold. Bridget tucked into this with real pleasure and even Jessie began to eat steadily.

Better not to talk about John Roger. "Jessie, you never talk about your past. Have you been married?"

"Yes, of course. Hasn't everybody?"

"For a long time?"

"A long, long time. Not happily."

"Tell me about it."

Jessie made a face. "I got married only a year and a half out of high school and things just went on from there. I had a baby...Naomi. We never had enough money. When I saw I had to work some, I got a part time job and my mother baby-sat for me. Joe worked a lot of nights while I worked days. Without knowing it, I began to hate my life, but I didn't know what else to do and Joe was no help. Then one winter after we'd been married seven or eight years, I got a bad case of the flu and had to stay in bed for a week. Naomi was in childcare so I did nothing except watch daytime soaps and look at my life.

"That was plenty depressing. The house was shabby and didn't even belong to us. Naomi cried all the time. My job was at the five and dime - close, convenient but unbearably dull and paid hardly anything. This was not where I had expected I would be at the age of twenty-six.

"When I realized this, I packed up Naomi and went home to my mother to cry."

"The woman who said what you needed was not a man but a job?"

"Right. Of course, she was not very helpful. She was full of old sayings like 'you made your bed', etc."

Jessie had cried even more. On the second day of this sorry scene, her mother said with impatience: "You're a good manager. If he's not what you want, you'll have to make him over."

This totally novel idea – that she could change Joe to fit her objectives stopped Jessie's tears. She packed up poor Naomi again in an hour.

Now Naomi cried because she had just gotten comfortable in her grandmother's house with her cats and orchard and butterscotch cookies. Instead, in short order they were back home again where Joe had plenty of angry things to say about his lonely days of cooking his own meals.

Jessie ignored this and proceeded to work out her plans. It was amazing what having a plan did for her psyche.

"It made me a different person," she told Bridget.

She woke up in the morning eager to get to the day. Little things, Naomi's sulks or Joe's insistence on arranging his evenings without consulting her, didn't bother her. She found that planning for particular results came easily to her. Her first objective was more money in the household; her second was a career for herself. After she had gotten to those, she would look at how she wanted to live.

Over the next years, as slowly but surely as water dripping on stone, Jessie got Joe through a night course and into the position of night dispatcher of the trucking operation, a white collar job where she insisted he wear the white shirts she ironed.

After several false starts, she passed the real estate exam and began to sell houses at a reasonable clip so there was finally money enough to buy a house of their own. Along with this, she pursued a change of friends and activities.

Joe complained fairly often; he didn't like working nights while she worked days. They hardly ever saw each other and he sure as hell wasn't going to do any of the housework she had outlined for him. Jessie made some adjustments to cut down on the complaints – she paid Naomi to do the housework and told her to save the money for college - but mostly she ignored him. Having a house of their own helped. Once they had made this huge step, Jessie set her mind on a handsome wardrobe, as well as new furniture. They took golf lessons together although Jessie was good and Joe wasn't. Naomi got to go to soccer camp and visited colleges.

When Jessie pointed these accomplishments out to Joe, he mostly agreed. He was proud of the house and liked the way Jessie looked and the way she dressed. He liked Naomi a lot better now that she made fewer demands on him, and having reached this plateau mostly because of Jessie's efforts, he quit any further efforts. He wasn't going to try for a better job or change friends, or apply for the country club. This was a better life than he had ever imagined; it was enough. Jessie's reward was that during the days, she sometimes associated with the kind of men she might have married.

When Joe reached 62, Jessie purchased (at a very good price) a rundown house in a charming retirement community. She moved Joe into retirement and got him to working on the house so he wouldn't get bored. For herself, she found a nearby real estate office, and she began to join the kind of clubs she had always wanted to belong to, a bridge club, a dinner group, a theatre-going group, all for herself – not including Joe. She also joined a gym because keeping her weight at 120 was no longer such an easy job.

Through all the crises and agreements and disagreements of their long married life, Jessie had kept firmly in mind that part of her job was to keep Joe healthy, energetic, and in a cooperative mood. A woman needed a man. And if his earning power was no longer a big factor in their life, she still needed him to keep the house and garden in repair and as an escort. Or did she?

Now that they were more or less retired, and Naomi had moved far away, they were spending more time together and Jessie had to admit finally that he bored her completely.

"So what did you do?"

"I left him right there and moved up here."

"So that was just a few years ago?"

"A little more than a few."

"And you got the life you wanted?"

"Yes. And the house I wanted. And even a man I wanted. Until now."

Bridget digested this while she scraped the last dabs of whipped cream from her plate. She had fantasized about this strawberry shortcake for weeks, and now it was gone. Maybe the thing to do was to continue fantasizing instead of eating it.

"Jess, I don't think you should waste this 'Now' mourning over JR. Not that he isn't worth it! But life is too short, look how long it took you to get what you wanted. You mustn't lose it. There are other men."

Jessie's pale face was tight with apprehension. "Very few. And JR was special. After all the time I wasted with Joe and then with Edgar."

"I agree with that. He was special to me too. I don't know when I've had a male friend I enjoyed the way I did JR. Just the same, I think you should look around for someone else. Even if you got by Dorothy somehow, he isn't well."

A few tears seeped from Jessie's eyes but she nodded.

"Don't think about it as replacing him, but about you getting to enjoy your life."

"You're right." Jessie took a tissue from her purse and wiped her eyes. "It will be a little hard at first."

"You can do it."

Jessie nodded. She ordered a second cup of coffee and was silent.

Bridget drank water, recommended for losing weight, and reflected on how nice it was to think about Norm.

"Okay. I'll do it."

"Good."

Chapter Twenty-Six

"Well, I'm finally over him," Jessie said to herself. She was just out of bed, making coffee, looking from her kitchen window at several half wine barrels which had been empty just a few months ago and now formed a thick curtain of staked greenery six feet high.

These were the tomato plants she and JR had planted and which, although it was October, only now had dozens of fat green tomatoes. When they got around to planting the seedlings, they had argued for several days over whether it was already too late. Then it had been a somewhat foggy summer – blame it on that – anyway it was now clear they had acted too late. There wouldn't be enough sunshine before a frost to ripen any of them. It might be better for her to pick them green and make the green tomato relish her mother used to make.

She thought all this calmly while the coffee maker burped, and then it came, the sudden stab of pain in her chest, and she knew she hadn't recovered at all. Maybe she never would. She sat carefully on a chair, wondering as usual if it was a sign of problems with her heart.

There had never been any sign of heart trouble; she always got through her annual physical with flying colors. Maybe this was how she was fated to die. Perfect health all those years of unhappiness and the few short months of happiness with JR, and now with that over, her life would end.

If that was going to be true, there were things she needed to take care of. She stood up determinedly and got a mug from the cupboard.

As she poured the coffee, she reviewed her life. What was she leaving undone that should be done? The thought of her daughter distracted her. Why didn't Naomi come home for at least a short visit?

She had to finish the will she was always making notes on but had never written. Probably she should get an attorney to do that. Or weren't there form wills you could fill out and they would be legal without the expense of an attorney? She would have to ask someone. Who would know things like that?

She took the coffee out to the patio but the day was still too cool to sit there. Besides she needed to get a pad and make some notes. She settled at the dining table with a pad of paper, and sipped her coffee, thinking again that she should take it with milk. Light was reflected from the well-waxed mahogany table. She touched it with pleasure, remembering in what shop she had found it and how much she loved its graceful beauty.

The dogs had slept in. They did that sometimes if they had had a good run the night before. Now Belvy came down the hall from the bedroom yawning, to be followed by Tibby who was peering ahead for breakfast. Belvy wandered into the kitchen for a drink of water while Tibby came and laid his head against her thigh.

She patted his head. If she died, what would become of them? Who would put up with all their foibles? Not anyone she could think of. You were supposed to take care of your pets in your will, but then you had to have someone willing to take them. Eve Sainstbury had left her dog, Muggles, to her friend, Helen. Money too, to take care of it. Not a day went by that Helen didn't curse that dog because he was so difficult.

She had better avoid dying and stick around. That thought was accompanied by a small cramp in her stomach because the coffee was too strong. And probably because she hadn't eaten much yesterday. Light eating during the day had always been made up by having a good dinner. But the last few months, she had found herself unable to eat dinner. Probably it didn't matter. You were supposed to eat less every year as you aged. Didn't the doctors always say thinner was healthier?

She was paying attention to her body. She would know if anything major was going on. This thought was interrupted by the sound of a car stopping outside.

Not the postman; he always parked at the next corner. Not Bridget who was away. Then…She got up and went to the door to look out. There was a taxi, a strange taxi, not a company she recognized.

And getting out very slowly was…someone white-haired… It was JR.

She put a hand up to her heart to still it. It was several moments before she could put her other hand on the door knob. He was walking with a three-footed cane, shuffling along, not the walk she remembered.

He looked up and saw her.

The look in his eyes tore into her heart…as if he wanted to speak but was not sure he could do it. He nodded, 'all right….in a minute,' then looked down again to check his footing on the sidewalk. It was taking all his effort to come toward her and he wanted no mistakes.

He was here. Nothing else mattered. She threw open the door and rushed out. Behind her, the dogs also recognized JR and greeted him with a low whine. She turned abruptly and rushed back.

"Stop that," she said and shooed the dogs into the garden and closed the door on them.

When she got back out to the front, he was still only halfway up the sidewalk.

"You're here." She threw out her arms to grab him in a hug but he waved abruptly that she was to stand away. She might easily topple him over.

To keep from hugging him, she went past him, and slammed shut the door to the cab, which he had left open. Here she was outdoors in her nightie and she didn't give a damn if the whole neighborhood saw her. She came back to walk beside him.

The cabbie turned off his engine.

"He's staying?" she said to JR.

JR did not turn to her but nodded. He was making slow but steady progress toward her open door. When he reached it, he put a hand on the door frame and paused, gathering strength, then slowly lifted one foot and the cane up the one step into the house. After he had managed that, he took a breath, then leaned forward and with even greater effort, shifted his weight to the forward foot and stepped up into the house.

Behind him, Jessie rejoiced at seeing his old khaki work pants and worn white shirt – the clothes she had always hated. Above that was what she loved, his thick white hair that needed trimming. When he was through the door, she stepped in behind him and closed the door while he made his way, painfully, to a chair at the dining table. He sat with a thump, breathing heavily.

"It's so good to see you," she whispered.

"Give me a minute."

She sat down opposite him and waited. Now that she was facing him she could see how he had changed in these few short weeks. His eyes seemed lighter and paler, and blinked frequently, his cheeks had sunk in. The air of command he had always had, even that night when he was lying on her dining room floor, that was lost.

"Well, there we are," he said finally. "I wasn't sure I could do it, but I gave it the old college try."

"I'm so glad to see you."

They looked at each other wordlessly.

"You're not eating, Jess. Shame on you. And your face is flushed. Why is that?"

"I'm all right. How are you?"

"Well, as you can see, not as well as I'd like."

"I don't care. Just to see you is enough. Are you out of the hospital?"

"Not a hospital, I'm now in one of those old folks' homes, assisted living they call it. Which means they charge a lot to come in a couple of times a day and give me some pills and yatter at me about what I'm eating or not eating."

Jessie's mouth set in a stubborn line. "You don't have to be there. You can come here. I can tell you when to take your medicine."

"Now Jessie," he said gently. "You know that's not going to work out."

"Why not? I would do it better. I miss you."

A ghost of a smile appeared and disappeared. "You're not in great shape yourself and you know Dorothy is not going to put up with you being in charge of my health."

"Dorothy," Jess said angrily. "Why do you need her when you could have me?"

He sighed and looked away. It was clear he could have done without this part of their conversation.

"Jess, Jess. Dorothy is my blood and bone. That don't mean I like her particularly, but she gets my money and she has to take care of me. And she will. I trust her to do that. And I'm hoping one of these days she'll get a little wiser. Maybe not before I die but someday."

"But I love you."

He was beginning to look exhausted. "That's why I'm here, woman! We've had a fine love, haven't we?"

"But not for very long."

"Well, we have to take what's given, don't we? When does anyone ever have enough?"

Jessie felt at that moment as if she could do everything. She could convince him and fight with Dorothy and make a home for him here. But she didn't know how to start, and she was afraid of exhausting him. She stared at him wordlessly.

"How are my tomatoes doing?"

"There are loads of them but they are all still green."

"I knew we were putting them in too late. Do you think they'll ripen at all?"

Jessie got up to get a tissue because she was beginning to cry. "I need to find my mother's recipe for Green Tomato Relish."

He laughed. "That would be a good thing to do. Do that if you can. And give some to all your pals. How's my friend Bridget?"

Jessie wiped her eyes. "She's gone to Honduras with one of her ex-husbands."

"Her ex-husbands? Now why did one of those show up?"

Jessie shrugged. "She wasn't giving out any information about that, but she seemed rather excited."

"Someone was bound to come along. She's too much woman to be ignored. Tell her I said hello." He leaned back, pleased about Bridget.

"She will be thrilled. She asks about you all the time."

"And how are those imps of Satan which are whining at the door right now?"

Jessie jumped up. "I'll let them in."

"No, no. I'll enjoy them from a distance. They could knock me over just with a tail."

"I know. But they'd love to see you. They're fine, just more than I can handle a lot of the time. Oh, it's so good to see you. How long can you stay?"

He reached a hand out to her, and Jessie reached across the table and they were holding hands with both arms outstretched. "I have to go in a minute," he said.

"No. Why?"

"Because I'm getting worn out. This is too much for me. I just wanted to see you once more, and know you're okay."

"But you can come again!" Her voice was almost shrill

He shook his head. "I wish we had had more time, but that's all there is."

"You could come once a week, and we could just sit and talk like this…"

He shook his head again. "Now I'd better go before you get me crying. We had good times, Jess."

Jess mopped her eyes and did not respond.

"Come and give me a hand so I can stand up."

She stood up and came around the table and put a hand under his arm and pulled at him. With both of them straining, he got to his feet. This had cost him some effort, and he stood a moment, breathing heavily. Then he turned to the door.

Instead of moving aside, Jessie put her arms around him and her head on his shoulder, and held him tight. He reached up and patted her hair.

"Well now, that was worth all the effort," he said in a low voice.

Jessie released him. "I'm so glad you came." She refused to cry anymore, but threw her head back and followed him to the door.

He negotiated the step down carefully and then turned for one more look at her.

"Call me now and then," she begged in a small voice.

"Bye, Jess," he said and blew her a kiss.

Then he made his way slowly toward the bright green, two-toned taxi from some unknown other town. The driver got out and came around to open the door for him. Across the street, one of Jessie's neighbors stopped to watch.

Jessie stood in her doorway, the sun hot on her face, willing him to say something more, to change his mind and get back out of the taxi and come to her.

When the taxi's motor was turned on, the sound was like a roar in the quiet neighborhood. In the shadow of the taxi interior, she could make out the thick thatch of JR's hair. Then he raised an arm out the window, and waved at her, a defiant closed-fist wave.

The taxi backed out into the empty street and he was gone.

Chapter Twenty-Seven

Her house looked odd. Bridget blinked at it, wondering what was wrong. It looked more brown than gray and more horizontal than vertical, and weren't the windows oddly squared? She squinted, trying to bring it back to normal.

"Doesn't the house look odd?" she asked Norm.

"I don't know. What's odd about it?"

Then there was no time. The taxi pulled into her driveway and Norm started the business of paying while she picked up her jacket and hat and purse and a bag containing something she had bought at the last minutes at the airport. She couldn't remember what it was. Spending her last foreign coins because the U.S. banks wouldn't take them and she didn't expect to return. When she climbed out of the taxi, she was stiff from the long plane ride and then the even longer taxi ride, and tired, though she had done almost nothing all day except sit in one place and then another.

Norm and the driver had most of the luggage out of the trunk already. "Here, you take this, Birdie."

She accepted her carry-on and another purchase. It was very, very nice to have a man to take command. It had been wonderful all through Honduras. Had even begun to feel normal, till she had reminded herself of how many years she had been lugging her own suitcases and arguing with taxi drivers and facing down repairmen.

"I gave him a seven dollar tip," Norm mused, thinking over the expenditure carefully, and Bridget thought it wasn't enough, but knew better than to give an opinion on that subject.

They trundled rather slowly to the front door. Norm's suitcase was on the small side, but he had also Bridget's second case. Hers was as large as an international flight would allow, and didn't roll very well because it was overpacked. At the last minute she had forced into it a plaster Mayan god which she hadn't been able to resist. In order to get it in, she had left behind in the hotel room several new outfits which she had brought with her. It was too bad but probably the maids would take them home or sell them in the market. Most of them had hardly been unpacked; while Jessie traveled up river, she had had to leave in Tegucicalupa all but some wash pants and T-shirts. Probably she should have left the god in the hotel as a goodwill gift to Honduras but Norm had talked her into bringing it home.

"Birdie, next time…"

"I know. I'll pack better."

Just before they go closer to the house, onto the porch and under the overhang, Bridget stopped and looked up again. No, the house was the same. It was her eyes which had changed, looking at an entirely different kind of buildings, till they were stretched the wrong way and California houses looked all wrong. That was one of the unfortunate facts about travel, wasn't it? It made everything familiar look strange.

Norm held out his hand, wordlessly, and Bridget handed him the door key. They had gotten rather good at silent communications. Norm hated wasting words on the small necessities of day-to-day living, and she found she liked that. Words were for creative and intellectual thoughts.

Inside, it smelled a little musty but also familiarly of coffee and lemon oil furniture polish. Bridget dropped her packages gratefully, thinking the stairs looked too steep right now. Norm headed straight for his room.

"Do you want some coffee?" she asked, because the tiny trace of it had smelled so good, the Peet's which she always bought.

"No. A lot of water and then maybe a small red wine."

"Okay." She debated carrying her things upstairs to her room first but if she waited, perhaps Norm would do it. Then she thought, inevitably, about Norm coming up to her room at bedtime. For, yes, it had happened in Honduras. There they were in bed together just as Bridget had promised herself they wouldn't be. And it had all come about so easily that she saw no point at which she could stop it. If she had even wanted to.

Was that going to continue? Or had it just been part of the strangeness of being in a foreign land, of struggling with the language, and wondering if they could trust the guide who had been recommended, and whether he really knew the area where they were going or whether he had said he did just to get the job.

She went into the kitchen, shadowed by the magnolia outside and spotlessly clean because Maria Theresa had come in while they were gone. She turned on the overhead light and opened the refrigerator to see what was there. Probably she had lost weight on the trip because there had been so much walking. Her clothes certainly fit more loosely. But she wasn't going to get on a scale till tomorrow when she would officially be home. Right now, while she didn't have to count every calorie, she would like to have a guiltless meal.

Except that there wasn't much in the refrigerator! Of course. She had told Maria Theresa to take everything home that might spoil.

She took some lamb chops out of the freezer and was contemplating them when Norm walked in. He had changed his shirt and put on sandals. Examining him, she thought how good he looked. His grey look and slight frown had changed during the trip. She could see no other signs of illness. There was a line of sunburn on his cheeks where the protection of his hat had stopped. All that sun, and maybe also the evenings where they debated everything under the stars almost as they had years ago, had made a difference. She reminded herself that cancer was silent, painless for a long time while it grew in stealth.

"Are you tired?"

"Not at all. Are you going to eat those? Do you have any merlot?"

She opened the door of the cabinet which was her temperature-controlled wine cellar and gestured to him. "Look and see what you want. I don't think I'm really that hungry. Maybe I'll just have a biscuit or a piece of fruit. Except that there isn't any fruit because we got rid of it all. Would you eat some biscuits?"

Norm found the bottle he wanted and opened the wrong drawer searching for the cork screw. "I don't think so. Maybe."

Bridget pointed to the right drawer and let him wrestle with the cork. She had put the lamb chops back in the freezer.

They settled at the kitchen table with small glasses of wine and a tin of tea biscuits. Bridget thought the kitchen was different too. The cabinets seemed so far apart. It was huge by comparison with her memory of it. Maybe huge with possibility.

"It was a good trip, wasn't it? In spite of everything we found the schools and they were happy to get all the supplies. I hope Graciela likes the pictures."

"She should."

"They are terrific pictures. You did a great job."

They were silent for a minute, then Bridget said: "They were such nice kids. And bright too, in spite of a school with no supplies."

"It's a hard life. Maybe hunger keeps them alert."

She tried to make sense of that but couldn't. "I keep thinking I'd like to do something else for them."

"I keep thinking what a computer would do for that school."

"A computer? But they hardly have electricity…every third day or so."

"I know but people are doing that all over the world…working out ways to get computers going in remote spots. I've talked to a couple of guys…"

Bridget got up and put away the biscuits and rinsed out their glasses. Sometimes she hated it when he got off on these tangents when she wanted to talk about something they had shared.

After a while, Norm came back from his reverie. "Birdie, I have to hand it to you. You kept your cool remarkably. You held up through all the craziness of loading and unloading all those boxes every night and stowing them beside our bed. You never once got mad at me when I made a mistake."

She grinned. "I know. I was terrific. Better than I expected to be. But you were too, Norm. For someone who didn't particularly want to be there, you were very good-tempered. You've improved over the years."

He nodded acceptance. "Oh, but you know, the harder a task is, the better I like it. I feel much more like myself if I'm slaying dragons."

"I remember that."

"You must be one of the few people around who knows what I'm really like."

"The marriage was spoiled by success," she said softly.

He nodded. "I know. First, by my not being around most of the time, and then by all the money and not knowing what to do with it."

"There was also a certain stewardess…"

He looked embarrassed. "I'm sorry about that. We only stayed together for a year. She was impossible to live with."

Bridget nodded peaceably, thinking that she had put this hurt away years ago. They sat and looked at each other for long minutes. After a while, they recorked the wine and went up to bed, even though it was still only eight thirty.

Next morning, Norm was out of bed before she woke up. She heard him running down the stairs, whistling to himself. But once she was down stairs, she scarcely saw him. He spent the day between his phone and his computer, and Bridget had to laugh at her reaction, and how familiar it all was.

At one point, he walked out into the living room where Bridget was watering the plants and said, "Everybody says it's easier than you think." Without waiting for a reply, he went back into his room.

Bridget had to admit, however, that it wasn't unpleasant to have him happily pre-occupied so that she was free to get some other things done. She went to see Graciela and tell her about the trip and promised her the photos they had taken. Then she dropped in to see Phyllis who was settled down with Don as a housemate. Now, wasn't that interesting?

Finally, she did a grocery shopping and stopped to drop off some shoes to be repaired. All of this was accomplished with the thought that Norm would be there when she got back.

No, it was not at all unpleasant.

Chapter Twenty-Eight

Bridget caught Jessie just as she was parking in her driveway, looking years older than she had looked two weeks ago, and not well.

"You look wonderful," Bridget said. "I'm so glad to see you." Impulsively, she kissed her to make up for the lie.

Jessie accepted the kiss willingly enough but seemed too distracted to return it. "What was the trip like?"

"Well, I couldn't say it was wonderful, a lot of wading up and down muddy river banks, and lots of confusion because we couldn't understand half their Spanish, even with a phrase book. But it was interesting."

"Aren't most trips like that?"

"I've been worried about you. How have you been?"

"Oh, fine. No problems." But Jessie's appearance belied this. Her clothes hung on her as if she had lost a lot of weight, and her complexion was pale.

They went inside. Bridget sat down at the table while Jessie took out the coffeepot.

"I have to tell you...." she started. Then she stopped because it didn't seem right to talk about Norm. Jessie had opened the freezer and was taking the coffee out and paid no attention to the words.

"I need to go to the store," Jessie said, shaking out the last of the coffee from the can. "Maybe I'll go this afternoon while I'm in town having my hair done."

"I'm going into town. I can go for you if you want."

But Jessie seemed not to have heard. When the coffee was done and poured, and Jessie finally brought two orange Fiesta Ware cups to the table and sat down opposite Bridget, it seemed for the moment to be like old times. Bridget reached over and touched her hand. "You don't look very well," she said softly.

Jessie raised pink-lidded eyes to her friend; the whites of her pale blue eyes were also shot with pink. She was silent for a moment as if not knowing how to respond. "I'm fine," she said. "He came by!"

"JR did? You've seen him?"

"Yes. But that's all in the past. Other things are happening."

Bridget was afraid if she spoke, Jessie would stop. She spoke anyway.

"He came here?"

"Yes, by taxi. And he was very bad. So weak. And he said it was for the last time."

Bridget stirred her coffee round and round though there was nothing she was stirring into it. "Why?"

Jessie's tears had started and were running down her face unchecked. "I can't talk about it."

"He didn't give you a reason why it was the last time. Isn't that just like a man?" Bridget sat and stared at her cup. Love should have held them together, and hadn't. Why was that? It was hard to accept. Maybe everything changed when you got old.

She reached out and took Jessie's hand in hers and held it. Slowly Jessie stopped crying. She took her hand loose gently and reached over to the counter and pulled a tissue from the box there.

"Anyway, it's all right. I've met someone new."

"New? Already?" Bridget shook her head to clear it.

"We've been talking on the phone. He's coming tonight for the first time. He's a retired developer who keeps a boat in Sausalito and loves dogs."

"Jessie, you only just saw JR."

"For the last time. He made that clear."

"But even so."

"Oh, you can say that! You can say anything because it's not you who's lost him." Jessie mopped her eyes and blew her nose, trying to end her crying. "Didn't you tell me to find someone else?"

"Well, yes, but…I loved JR."

"No, you didn't. You just love enjoying someone else's life. You go around from house to house and gather all these stories, and tell them to your other friends. You're nothing but a gossip." Jessie stood up from the table.

Bridget blinked at the attack. She felt burned by Jessie's hot eyes, as well as her words. Surely she hadn't meant it!

But Jessie turned away from the table, as if the visit had ended. Bridget stood up and crossed the room reluctantly, waiting for Jessie to stop her, thinking she would say something that would keep her there.

At the door, she paused. "Do you really mean that? Haven't we been friends?"

When there was no answer, she added: "Are you sure you want me to go?"

"Yes, go," came the angry voice.

Outside the screen door, Bridget paused again. "I'll come back another time…"

But the kitchen door was closed in her face. Jessie had turned her out. Scarcely able to drive, Bridget went home and sought solace in her own patio.

*   *   *

Every day she had thought she would call Jessie. But when she started to pick up the phone, she was still too hurt. Several days after this scene, Bridget took the books she had borrowed on Honduras back to the library. She wandered on through the library and turned a corner around ceiling-high shelves and there, slamming books into their proper places with gusto, was someone who seemed vaguely familiar.

The woman was thin and her hair was a flaming purple-red, cut very short. Not a color Bridget had seen in hair before. Below the red hair were huge, long, clacking earrings and the sharpened profile had a look of fierce concentration.

Marion Frewalter.

"Marion…" Bridget squeeked too loud.

Marion turned reluctantly away from her work, glaring, but then when she saw who it was, responded, "Hello there. How are you?"

"Great."

"I heard you've been away?"

Bridget lowered her voice to Marion's whispered level. "Just for a few days. What are you doing here?"

"South America, was it? How'd you happen to do that?"

Bridget looked around but no one seemed near enough to be disturbed by their chat. "No, Central America. Are you working or volunteering?"

Marion nodded with satisfaction. "It's a change, isn't it? I had to return some books we had taken out on Alaska. Way overdue. There was a sign up for Help Wanted. I used to do this in college so I talked to Colin, you know, the head librarian and he offered me the job."

"That's wonderful."

"It's only part-time but gets me out of the house. If I take a course, they'll hire me fulltime."

Marion stood still, her head cocked, examining Bridget rather than continuing her work.

All the animosity of a few months ago seemed to have dispersed. Bridget wondered if she should apologize for anything. Jessie's words still rang in her head. She thought she had cared about Marion also. Or was she just a gossip?

"How long has it been?"

Marion considered. "Jeb died in May so it has been a few months. Listen, I need to keep working but I get loose in an hour. Do you want to have lunch?"

"Of course."

They met across the street at the bakery, which sold bagels and buns with cheese baked inside, as well as coffee and sodas. Marion seemed well-acquainted with the place and got them a space on the bench out front where they spread out their buns, drinks and purses. "This is fine in good weather. Don't know what I'll do when the rains start."

Bridget was still marveling at the change in Marion. She must have lost weight because she looked fashionably bony and her jaw jutted out in a new way. Her bright red blouse and long purple skirt with a zigzag hem were something Bridget hadn't seen before and she did a lot of clothes-shopping. "Has your daughter been to visit you?"

"Yes, she came for a week. She is such good company, even took me shopping. Do you like the skirt?'

"It's beautiful."

"And got me to join a salsa dancing group."

Bridget decided that, with the skirt, she could maybe just see Marion salsa dancing though she never would have thought that in the past.

"Do you want to work full time?"

"Oh, I think so. The work is really easy. And everyone in town comes in to the library sooner or later. I'm always bumping into people I haven't seen for years. The money would be nice too." Marion looked around her with a satisfied air.

"How long had it been since you worked?"

"Not since the first year after college. Jeb never wanted me to. But I always did spend a lot of time reading. He used to make fun of me always trundling off to the library for my next load of books."

Bridget almost said, "Well Jeb isn't here now so do what you like," but instead Marion said, "He isn't here now so I can do what I like."

Wonder of wonders. Bridget was afraid to make any comment on that.

"I'm glad for you. Don't let me keep you too long."

Marion nodded with satisfaction, working her way through the ham bun rapidly. "I hear you've got a man living at your house."

This had been said several times in the last week and Bridget still blushed as if she was fifteen and being accused of hanky panky. "One of my ex-husbands is staying with me while a contractor is working on his house in Palm Dessert."

"One of your ex-husbands? How many do you have?"

Bridget always hated to be asked. "Three."

Marion examined Bridget's face while she chewed on her bun. "What an interesting life you've led. All I did was marry once and raise three children. Oh, I remember now. That thin fellow who is always fussing about the street trees dropping leaves on his patio, he was one of them, wasn't he? Phyllis told me that. What's his name?"

"Edgar."

"Yes. Someone told me you had been married to him and didn't know he was here till you moved in. Is that right?"

"Yes. But we've stayed on good terms."

"And he used to go out with that friend of yours who always looks like a magazine cover."

"Yes. Jessie. He was my first husband."

Marion nodded and reflected. "And the one who's staying with you?"

"Is Norm, my second husband." But really, why did she always have to tell the truth. Why couldn't she make up some of it?

Marion looked again at Bridget as if trying to dig out the secrets of her past. Was she thinking that Bridget didn't look as if she had enough allure for three husbands?

Instead of commenting, Marion popped the last of the bun in her mouth and dusted off her hands. "And how many children did you have?"

"Three."

Marion's face, which a minute ago seemed to have no soft expressions, now softened. "I guess it couldn't have all been easy. That's what I'm beginning to see. No one really gets off easy. Have you seen that…looking around?"

"I agree. Do you see a lot of Phyllis?"

"Not as much as I used to. Now she's got a live-in too and that takes up her time. Don't know that I'd care for him but he seems to make her happy."

Bridget nodded. It was hard to catch Phyllis for a comfortable chat now that Don was living there.

"Marion, I'm so glad to see your life working out all right. I'm sorry if I was hard on you."

Marion wadded up her napkin and stood up. She sounded almost embarrassed. "You were. But thank you. No one else tried to help the way you did. I did sell the Navigator. Got what we asked for, and the money sure made a difference."

"I'm glad I did something that worked."

They got busy simultaneously, gathering up their paper cups and trash, and picking up their purses. "Oh, the one who looks like a magazine cover…"

"Jessie?"

"That's her. Do you know she's got a new boyfriend."

"Already?" That couldn't be true, could it?

"I ran into her at the market yesterday and she told me all about him. "He's a retired developer, keeps a boat in Sausalito and loves her dogs. I don't believe anyone could love those dogs but that's what she said. She says he is looking around for one just like those two for himself. Must be crazy, if you ask me."

The retired developer had worked out, at least well enough to do things with. What a marvel Jessie was! Wasn't that like her – the woman who had developed a prosperous career with only a high school diploma and, when her husband turned out to be a dud, had made him over into something nearly satisfactory? Just when it seemed as if her life was over because JR was gone, she had somehow worked some magic and acquired a new man.

Driving away, Bridget was filled with a sense of how rich with possibilities the world was. If Marion could start a new life, and Jessie also, then anything could happen.

After lunch, Bridget went on to do her marketing and ran into Phyllis. Before Bridget could say a word, Phyllis told the same story.

"Jessie must have been trolling in the Personals again. She has a new man."

"That's what Marion said."

Phyllis shook her head hard, making her new small curls bounce around. "I never see Jessie much but Don and I were walking past yesterday and there she was with this new one, and they were putting the dogs in his car to take them for a run. He has a red Chrysler, one of those classic cars, I think."

"What's he like? Was he nice to you?"

"Nice as anything. Beautiful manners. His name is Cedric. He's a retired developer, keeps a boat in Sausalito and loves her dogs."

This seemed to be the party line on Cedric. Was this a bio that Jessie had created?

"She only met him this week. I know that. I was there."

Phyllis frowned but she was on another track. "I don't believe anyone could love those dogs but that's what she said and then he agreed. He wants to get one of the same breed as those two. Isn't that the craziest thing you ever heard of? He was saying that while right beside us those two giant dogs were slavering over all the windows and bouncing around so much in his big car that it was shaking. Who would want that?"

"How did she seem? Was she happy?"

"Seemed like it. She started gushing over Cedric with him standing right there. It was all a little crazy."

Bridget went home, unloaded her groceries and went up to her bed and cried. Why was she crying? Crying for JR who had fallen out of Jessie's life and had now been replaced by Cedric. She remembered the delight the three of them had had when they closed themselves into a charmed circle over a bottle of wine. She was crying, probably more for the friendship and the quarrel. It prevented Bridget from going to Jessie and finding out if she was really all right. Maybe this was only window-dressing at which Jessie was so good. Finally Bridget admitted she was also crying for herself because she had loved Jessie as she had very few other women, had laughed with her and ached with her when JR was spirited away by Dorothy.

When Norm returned at five o'clock, he found her still in bed, her face puffy with crying and the dinner not started. Surprised, he treated her gently, didn't ask for the cause of the tears but brought her a cup of tea in bed and suggested they go out for dinner.

After hearing the story, Norm was of the opinion that Bridget might call Jessie up tomorrow and test the water, see if she was still angry. That was less provocative than appearing at her door, and would allow Jessie to say how she felt, while Bridget could hang up if it got nasty.

"Men don't know anything about friendship," Bridget thought but didn't say.

That evening, after returning from the restaurant, she took her courage in hand, sat down at the kitchen table with a cup of tea and made the call right then. She was prepared to apologize, however much it took, but what she really wanted was to know if Jessie was really happy. If she was, then Bridget could stop worrying about her.

Good in plan, but the phone was not answered. After a while, the message came on but Bridget hung up rather than leave word.

Chapter Twenty-Nine

The next day Bridget dressed in the morning with the knowledge that she was going to go to Jessie's and take her chances. Had Jessie really been her friend or had Bridget imagined the whole relationship? After breakfast, she drove immediately the three blocks to Jessie's house and knocked hard. She was trembling a little.

The gate to the patio was open as it often was. This was not the garden patio where the dogs spent most of their days but a smaller one on the street side, with a hedge of spirea bushes and the five tubs which held tall, staked tomato bushes. The exterior of Jessie's house was not as well-kept as it had been when JR was around. The smoke grey of the kitchen door was scuffed, and the small pane of glass at face height was cloudy.

Jessie's face appeared in the small glass and she quickly opened the door looking better than she had just a few days ago.

She frowned at Bridget. Then she stepped back and gestured her to come in.

"Hi."

"Hi."

Jessie's neck looked very thin and extra skin was beginning to sag below her chin. In spite of this, she looked ready for an event, a celebration - her hair had just been done and she was wearing a new outfit of matching culottes and shirt in peacock blue.

"Jessie, don't be angry with me."

"All right. I don't want to fight. But we won't talk about JR. I can't do that."

"Okay. I'm sorry if I said anything wrong."

"Well, we'll forget about it."

Bridget opened the screen, and Jessie stepped back and allowed Bridget into the bright room. It was hard to know what to say next. All the things Bridget wanted to say in her concern for Jessie were probably off limits.

When Jessie closed the door behind her but said nothing, Bridget cleared her throat. "Tell me about Cedric. Both Marion and Phyllis were raving about him."

Jessie nodded with a triumphant smile. "He's a …."

"I know. A retired developer, keeps a boat in Sausalito, etc. Do you really like him?"

"Of course. He's so handsome."

"I've heard that too. You found a man you liked in – what was it? – four days? You are a marvel. How did you do that?"

"I don't have any time to waste. Sit down." The house looked to be in good order but Bridget was surprised to see a bottle of pinot noir out and a glass half full though it was only ten o'clock. Jessie had always been firm about the no alcohol till five o'clock. Wine time, as JR had called it.

"Would you like a drink?"

"Too early for me. Tell me about Cedric." They walked through the dining room and into the living room, not quite at ease.

"He loves the dogs, and he's so good with them."

"I think I've heard that before."

Jessie nodded with satisfaction. "He even takes them out without me. JR would never do that. Cedric is taller than JR and he has much better manners."

"That's wonderful. Where did you meet him?"

Jessie smiled, pleased, but was not going to say. "We know loads of people in common. I sold a house for his next door neighbor."

"So you've gone back to work?"

"Oh, this was years ago. He lives in Sausalito; that was when I was selling down there. He's so sweet. He brought me one red rose and a box of Godiva chocolates on the first date and said he wanted to go dancing but it was during the week and there's no place to dance except on weekends. He's such a gentleman."

Bridget had been worried that when she saw Jessie, she might talk too much about Norm. She could stop worrying. She couldn't get a sentence in about Norm in the torrent of words about Cedric. He had plenty of money and wasn't tight the way JR had been.

Jessie's posture, her voice, the tilt of her head, all breathed Triumph. She had won. She had won. If it had cost a little wear and tear, if she had lost more weight and was drinking in the daytime, what did those things matter? Cedric was what counted.

"JR wasn't tight. He wanted you to go to Europe on his money, remember?"

A shadow passed over Jessie's face but she put up a hand and brushed it away. They had seated themselves on opposite sides of the coffee table as if at a conference.

"Did you hear from JR again?"

"Remember, we're not going to talk about him."

"I'm sorry."

"No. Not after the time he came. He might at least have called me, but he never did. He turned himself over to her." The 'her' was spat out like a bad word.

Bridget nodded pacifically.

Jessie threw back her head and picked up her theme again. "If you see a 1960 red Chrysler outside; that's Cedric's car. He also has a dark blue Jaguar and he loves eating at Avignon even though it's so expensive."

Bridget contemplated all this, not sure whether she was happy or sad. Jessie had not been interested in the make of JR's car or where he took her for dinner. Only in him. If she really cared for Cedric, did the Jaguar matter?

But if it made her happy, that was enough, wasn't it? Maybe this was not a story about love as the story of Jessie and JR had been. Cedric might be good for her anyway. She was clearly happy. Maybe she needed the companionship, the activity, the distraction. Bridget felt a small stab of anger on JR's account, for being so easily replaced.

"We're going to take one of those sunset cruises on the Bay where you can dance and eat dinner."

No word about Bridget joining them for a glass of wine. But of course, now she wouldn't have a drink with Jessie and Cedric without Norm. And she wasn't sure how Norm would take to Jessie. Or how they would both take to Cedric, the paragon. Norm, truth to tell, was not as interested in people as he was in puzzles, molecules, challenges and stories about people making their first million.

"When do I get to meet him?"

There was no immediate answer to this but later, when Bridget left, finally, to do her marketing, kissing Jessie goodby, Jessie promised: "We'll get together soon."

Somehow Bridget was not as happy as she had expected to be. The quarrel appeared to be over but there was something not quite right with Jessie's manner. Be fair, remember how miserable she had been only a short time ago! Wasn't this much better?

Phyllis called Bridget that night to get her reaction to Cedric. "All right, you tell me what you think."

"Well, I don't think anything because I haven't met him yet."

"I think it's all a put-up job."

Bridget had to laugh. "Phyllis, you're so easily critical. What if someone said that about Don?"

"Oh, Don's the salt of the earth. No one would say he was a put-up job. There was something I forgot to tell you about Jessie. You tell me what you think! This is what she said to me: He took her dancing in the city and while they were there a woman came up to her and said: 'The man you're with is so good looking. If you decide you're not really interested in him, let me know. And she gave Jessie her card so she could contact her. Do you believe that?"

Bridget shook her head, then laughed, realizing the head shaking was wasted on a phone call. "Have I ever known anyone to say something like that? No. Would I or anyone I know go up to a stranger and say something like that? No. On the other hand, I've never known Jessie to lie either. What do you think?"

Phyllis made a doubtful sound. "I don't believe it. I don't think he's that good looking – besides 'beauty is as beauty does' and a man is not supposed to be all that good looking anyway."

"If it makes her happy, it's all right. Whatever we think!"

"I'm waiting for my invitation."

Bridget thought it doubtful that Jessie would invite Phyllis into her life. Especially as she had not even invited Bridget to meet Cedric.

*   *   *   *   *

Jessie did not call Bridget that week with an invitation to meet the paragon but Bridget scarcely thought about Cedric; she was busy enough with Norm as they slowly built their new relationship. And almost happy, she realized. There was a contentment spreading in her heart. When she woke in the morning, even if they had quarreled the day before as sometimes happened, she looked forward eagerly to the day ahead. Norm had such a lively mind, no one who followed his thoughts could be bored. There was also the complex enterprise of fitting their lives together. We're both different now, Bridget thought. We're more complicated than we were when we were married. Or at least I am.

Then, one day, she was coming back from the market and realized how long it had been and, abruptly, she turned the other way and stopped at Jessie's house.

Today the screen was closed but behind it the grey door with its square of glass was standing open, and Jessie was not far inside.

She came out of the shadow, welcoming Bridget. "I've been hoping you would stop by."

Bridget kissed her, relieved that the quarrel seemed to be over. What had the quarrel been about? Had they quarreled over JR? Surely not. She stepped back to look at Jessie and found her not as triumphant as she had been, but rather watchful, anxious, gaunt. "Then everything is all right? You could always call me, you know."

"True. I've hardly had a moment to myself. Cedric bought a house here and that has kept us busy. You know he's been coming up from Sausalito each time we want to see each other. But once he's moved here, he'll be able to run the dogs every day, morning and evening. Escrow closes in just one week."

"You sold him a house?"

"Yes, of course. I wouldn't trust him to any of those other women in the office. He's so kind-hearted they could sell him anything."

Plus, she would make at least one third of the money she needed for the year, and Cedric would be here to run the dogs twice a day.

Bridget thought that over; would she have felt guilty at such successful opportunism? Practiced on someone she thought she loved?

"I have to meet this gentleman wonder."

"Of course. I'll have you to dinner one of these days."

Bridget felt put off. She remembered how quickly she had been invited to meet JR. Was there something wrong with Cedric?

"Why don't both of you come to my house for a glass of wine tomorrow. There's also someone I'd like you to meet."

Jessie blinked. "I don't know if he's going to be here. I'll find out and let you know."

"Well, if not tomorrow, then Thursday is fine."

Cornered, Jessie said: yes, they could come Thursday. She didn't look happy at this and Bridget regretted her insistence. What difference did it make if she approved of Jessie's new man?

"Jessie, if you don't want to, it's all right. We can do it another time."

Jessie had walked with her out to her car while they debated their next meeting. They were both standing at the edge of Jessie's sidewalk, outside the back gate where the dogs could be heard, moaning quietly for attention. It was a grey day, most unusual but it was autumn now and sooner or later the rains would come, the lawn furniture would have to be put away and the people of Shady Acres would retreat indoors. Then, after eight months of sunshine, everyone would complain bitterly about the terrible weather and do their visiting either by telephone or when they met at the market and stood under the overhang, listening to the dripping eaves and lamenting over clogged gutters and darkness arriving at five o'clock.

Jessie stood silently beside Bridget while she looked up and down the street though there was nothing new to see there. She was wearing a bright yellow cotton pantsuit, new and fashionable, but how different she looked than she had a few months ago. She was no longer slender, but bony. There were lines down beside her nose and mouth, and her once-proud posture had disappeared. When she stood, she leaned forward and slightly to one side, jutting her elbows out as if for balance.

"The only thing that is important is that you like him. That you're happy with him. You are, aren't you?"

"Absolutely. He's wonderful. He's madly in love with me and keeps telling me he wants to marry me. He doesn't seem to wait for anything."

"Then that's wonderful."

Norm was not thrilled that Jessie and Cedric were coming for drinks. "Can we put them off a month or two?"

"No," Bridget said, patting him to make him agreeable. "This is my good friend and her new beau. If you don't enjoy them, you can make some excuse and leave after fifteen minutes."

"All right, that will work."

Chapter Thirty

Jessie and Cedric arrived at Bridget's house twenty minutes late. Bridget had been watching from her kitchen window, wondering if Jessie had decided not to come, when she saw the huge, bright red vintage Chrysler park at the street. Then a tall man got out and stood for a moment looking critically at the car as if for new damage. Bridget had a flare of hope. Maybe everything really was okay – Cedric was as advertised and would make Jessie happy.

"Norm, they're here."

"Okay. In a minute."

Would she have to go to his workroom and drag him out? Instead she went to the front door, and in a minute he joined her there, grinning at her surprise. Bridget opened the door just as the bell pealed.

Jessie jumped a little at the door opening so suddenly, but she was smiling widely. Her hair was done in an upsweep, something very new, and she was wearing a ton of perfume.

"Bridget, this is my friend, Cedric. Cedric, Bridget has held my hand through all sorts of crises. She really is…"

Bridget stepped back so they could enter and held out her hand to Cedric.

"Delighted. How nice to meet…" Bridget felt the warmth of his hand and looked up at him. He really was very good looking, with his triangular nose and thick salt and pepper hair, and he was something over six feet tall. He had taken her hand in both of his and held it for a minute. However attractive he was, she felt something tentative there. Then she turned to introduce Jessie and Cedric to Norm. The men shook hands while Jessie appraised Norm, and then she was kissing Bridget with something like delight, and Bridget was relieved.

"So nice of you to have us."

"Of course. Glad you came."

When Bridget had moved them all to the living room, she excused herself and went to the kitchen to get the tray of glasses and wine. Norm was playing host with a charming manner, and she thought for the first time that he was happy being in her house and with her. Why had she doubted him?

"What a nice room you have here." "Heard so much about you..." "Pleasure to meet you..." "Bridget has told us..."

When Bridget returned from the kitchen, she was much reassured by all these bits of conversation. This promised to be a happy occasion, maybe as good as those they had had with JR. She wanted to say that but knew she couldn't. And now there was also Norm to share it with. "Norm, there's another tray out there. Could you get it?"

Cedric had taken a seat on the couch beside Jessie. He touched her gently, quickly on the arm, and Bridget wondered, was he reassuring her? Because Cedric might look attentive and pleased, but Jessie was sitting awkwardly askew on the couch.

Norm returned from the kitchen with the tray of cheese and crackers and set it on the coffee table. Bridget turned to Jessie to chase away her unease, and Norm sat down across from Cedric.

"Cedric, have you been involved in the high tech world?"

"No. I've been in real estate and development..."

Norm had probably been hoping for a fellow techie. The Silicon Valley bug had bitten him early, and there were few men in his life who were not equally absorbed. He began sounding Cedric out gently on his background and other interests, but Cedric didn't seem to fit into any of Norm's prescriptions.

That was all right. She and Jessie could have a happy friendship without the men being fast friends. She poured out the wine and handed glasses around.

"Did you go to work today?" Bridget asked Jessie, but Jessie was listening to Cedric and Norm's conversation.

Cedric was cooperating in Norm's quest. He had gone to USC, started out in pre-med but didn't take to it, switched to pre-law but didn't like that either. Ended up working in the shipping business for several years until he joined his father in a development company and they built shopping centers in the Central Valley.

"That sounds profitable," Norm responded happily. The subject of making money was always interesting to him.

Jessie was still turned away from Bridget and toward the men. Bridget was disappointed but sipped her wine in peace.

"No, I never paid any attention to that…" Cedric was saying.

Was that why Jessie seemed anxious, wanting the two men to like each other? She might guess that Norm was not very patient with people he didn't enjoy, especially when he had a project he wanted to get back to. If the two men got along, they might find some event that all four of them liked.

"Shopping centers sounds interesting, doesn't it, Norm?" Bridget tried.

"Concrete blocks, blacktop and leases," Cedric disparaged his former occupation.

Bridget gave it up and poured more wine. "What did you do about the tomato plants?" she asked Jessie.

"Oh, they're long dead and all pulled out. After I picked off the tomatoes, still green. I made some relish, but it wasn't too successful. I'm not going to plant them next year. Wasn't it incredible how enormous the plants got? They were so big, I couldn't pull them out of the pots. I had about given up when Cedric came along and offered to do it for me." She patted his knee. "He's so efficient."

"What did I do?"

"You remember, you took out all those old dead tomato plants for me!"

"I did?"

Jessie's eyes flashed suddenly. "Yes, you did. And you did a great job."

Bridget looked at Cedric and saw on his face a look of doubt and confusion that erased the gracious man he had been a minute before. Something was wrong here.

"What a job!" Bridget said to keep the conversation going. She remembered those five foot plants with stems two inches thick.

But Jessie had caught Bridget's look of surprise and flushed with anger.

"You needn't be so superior!"

"What do you mean superior? What did I do? I'm not superior."

Cedric looked stricken. "Did I do something wrong? I'm so sorry, Jessie."

"Don't start apologizing!" Jessie stood up suddenly. "We're leaving. Bridget, you have to learn not to do this to me!"

Bridget was at a loss. "Me? What did I do?"

Now Cedric stood up because Jessie was standing. "Please. I'm so sorry. You know I didn't mean to do it." His face crumpled into a child's consternation and confusion. "Don't be angry."

Still confused, Bridget stood up because the other two had. What had happened? Then Norm stood up politely also, looking blank because the whole drama had gone too fast for him, and he was trying to replay it in his head.

Only Jessie seemed to know what was happening and was determined on a course of action. Purse in hand, she whirled around Cedric and past the coffee table, and a tall, fragile, stemmed glass of wine somehow overturned onto the table and then rolled off and onto the white carpet below.

The bouncing glass was followed almost instantly by the wine which had poured onto the table first, and then spilled eagerly from the table edge into a widening pool of red on the velvety white of the carpet. Jessie's head turned back to see what had happened and when she saw the widening stain, her face contorted. She shook her head in consternation, and her upswept hair began to come loose from its pins and fall to her shoulders.

"Oh, my God! Red wine," cried Bridget unnecessarily. She usually served only white wine for just this reason.

"I didn't do anything!" Jessie proclaimed loudly, but she stepped as far away from the spill as she could without backing into a chair.

Bridget ran toward the kitchen for a cloth.

Behind her, Norm yelled out: "Get salt. Salt takes away the red stain."

"NO. NO." Jessie said, "Baking powder! Get baking powder."

Bridget stopped in the kitchen. She thought salt was probably useless and she hadn't used any baking powder for a long time and doubted if she had any. She grabbed a dish towel and soaked it in cold water.

When she returned to the living room, Cedric was begging Jessie: "Please, please tell me what I did wrong."

If anything, Jessie was angrier than she had been a few minutes ago. "You never know, do you? Or you act as if you don't know. I'm so sick of this."

Cedric was crying, there were tears all over his face. In his hand, he held a large, elegant white handkerchief. "Let me do this...."

He dropped to his knees and began to wipe at the bright red stain with the white handkerchief. Which only served to soak the handkerchief and spread the color further across the white carpet.

"Say, Man," Norm protested. "I think you..."

"I know how to do this. I've wiped up lots of stains..."

"Get out of my way," Bridget said. Her own dish towel at the ready, she got down on her knees and quietly butted at the large man between her and the spill.

"It's all right. I'll do it," Cedric cried out.

Bridget had tears on her face. She had only bought red wine because she knew Jessie preferred it. The stain might never come out. After this, she would serve nothing but white. The burgundy had an amazing amount of color to it. It now stained both Cedric's handkerchief and Bridget's towel without diminishing the color on the carpet.

Norm tapped Cedric on the shoulder. "Let me help you up, Man. She'll get it."

Cedric sat back on his heels and raised the red handkerchief to his face to mop it. When he rubbed the handkerchief across his face, he left a long smear of red wine from eyes to chin. "I'm so sorry. I didn't mean to do it."

Jessie erupted. "YOU DIDN'T DO IT. I DID. Come on. Let's go. You've done enough damage for one evening."

"Jessie," Norm said. "It really is all right. We'll get the carpet cleaning company in here tomorrow. They live for this kind of job."

Cedric had responded to Norm's urging and stood up beside him. "I do everything wrong. I didn't used to be like this. My apologies."

Bridget was still on her knees but sat back, admitting that nothing she was doing was helping.

Norm took Cedric's hand. "Don't worry about it. I'm sorry you can't stay longer. Good meeting you. We'll have our next get-together outdoors and laugh about this."

Jessie had continued to the front hall and was almost at the door. Cedric hurried along behind her as if afraid of being left behind.

Norm followed them trying to be a host "Wait Jessie!"

Now Jessie had her hand on the door knob. Norm was close behind her. "Bridget! Your guests are leaving."

This was unnecessary. Bridget had already dropped the towel and given up on the carpet. She got to her feet and hurried to the front door. "I hate for you to go so soon. Jessie, all the times we've drunk wine together this has never happened. It must be a full moon coming on. We'll have better luck the next time."

"You don't have to say that! I know it's never happened before. Cedric, say goodnight."

Cedric did so with a hopeless air, the splash of wine still smeared across his face while the red-stained handkerchief was neatly folded and tucked in his breast pocket.

Norm had given up trying to be gracious and instead stood back and watched them all with a bemused look.

When they had left, Bridget threw herself into a chair far away from the stained carpet and let her head rest on the back.

"What was that all about? I don't even know what happened."

"Her boyfriend has a problem, that's all."

"What do you mean a problem? What kind of problem?"

"That's what she doesn't want you to know. Poor lady! And we wouldn't have tumbled if she hadn't gotten in a stew over it all by herself."

"You mean because he couldn't remember he pulled out the tomato bushes…?"

"Exactly. But who would have noticed if she hadn't gotten into a stir and insisted on leaving? Poor guy. She didn't leave him any place to turn."

"But that doesn't mean anything, does it?"

"Think about it. Think what you lose when you lose your memory!" And he went off to his workroom, formerly Bridget's guest room, where he had now established his several computers and other gadgets and from which it was often difficult to coax him.

Bridget's first reaction was anger, her hospitality had been thrown back in her face, her friendship with Jessie was definitely over this time. But the anger was quickly drowned in anxiety.

The next day, immediately after breakfast, Bridget got in her car and drove to Jessie's house. She stood in front of the smoke grey door not knowing what she would say. But it was opened quickly and Jessie was revealed, still in her robe, as if she had been waiting there for hours.

"I'm sorry about last night," Jessie said quickly, guiltily, waving her hand for Bridget to come in. "We were very rude."

Bridget nodded, somehow justified, and sat down at the dining room table, waiting for more of an explanation. None came immediately.

"What happened? One moment everything was fine, then…"

"Nothing really. He's a lovely man, isn't he?"

"Yes, he is." Bridget waited. "But what was it?"

Jessie's face had a raw, unfinished look; she hadn't applied foundation or powder yet, or rouge, or eyelashes. She spoke rapidly as if to make up for this. "Sometimes his short-term memory is very bad. He's very sensitive about it."

Her eyes left Bridget's face and sought, through her window, her neighbor's fence and high box hedge. "It was all my fault. If I hadn't gotten on the subject of those tomato plants, nothing would have gone wrong."

"What doesn't he remember?"

"He's so sweet. Don't you agree?"

"Of course. Yes, he seems very nice. But what doesn't he remember?"

"It comes and it goes."

Inside, Bridget was saying, damn, damn. This was not the triumph Jessie had presented! She remembered the look of doubt and confusion on his face. Cedric was too easily reduced to a shell.

"Is this really what you want?"

Jessie colored a little. "Don't you think I'm lucky? I care about him so much. We're going to build a house."

"I thought he just bought a house from you."

"Well, he did. That's a house just for now so we'll be close. But then we're going to build another one."

"That's wonderful. But why don't you just concentrate on enjoying each other? Go dancing. All that."

Now Jessie was angry. "You don't have to treat me like a child! I know what I'm doing."

"Of course you do. And he's a very nice man. But he's not JR."

Jessie stood up. "I think we should quit here."

Bridget felt her scalp crawl, her eye shadow melt, her clothes wilt around her. Almost without realizing it, she had broached the forbidden subject. She couldn't seem to help it. The memory of JR and of JR and Jessie together was still too strong. "Please don't be mad at me."

Suddenly Jessie was standing. "Well, I am. You have no right to talk about JR. It's time for you to leave."

"Jessie..."

It was not that Jessie really pushed her toward the door. It was that Jessie marched there and Bridget went with her as if she were being pulled. "Please, Jessie."

Jessie opened the door, and Bridget went through it and was outside, and it was closed behind her.

There was no going back after this.

Chapter Thirty-One

Bridget now got all her information about Jessie and Cedric from Phyllis.

"Who would have thought I would be the one to tell you this?" Phyllis said with satisfaction.

Phyllis had become good friends, not with Jessie, but with Jessie's next door neighbor, Mimi, who kept track of everything that went on in the corner house, and was sufficiently aghast at all these goings on to talk and talk:…'what is a woman her age doing with all these boyfriends? And overnight. It's disgraceful.'

Phyllis would *tsk-tsk* properly and be rewarded with the day's news.

"Cedric did get a dog, another Afghan, just like Jessie's two," she related to Bridget. "Only this one's young and hasn't been trained so it's always running away."

"Just what they need," Bridget said.

"And, of course, it's not Jessie who is running after him. Mostly she stays home and looks mad. It's Cedric. That man has clearly never smoked because he runs like the wind, but of course he can't catch that dog till the dog wants to be caught. I was standing on the corner of Shady and Alice, and here comes this huge dog at a run. He would have knocked me over if I hadn't moved out of the way…fast. Then, on the count of three, just like in a movie, here comes Cedric around the same corner, puffing and panting.

"Which way did he go?"

"I pointed, and he was off again. What a sight! Don't know what that dog is going to do to that man. He could have a heart attack that way."

Bridget went home and told all this to Norm who, truthfully, wasn't that interested but listened politely.

"I should go talk to her. She needs me," Bridget said.

Norm shook his head. "Don't do that. She's thrown you out a couple of times. Wait and see if she gets over it and calls you."

The next time they met, Phyllis had another story. Bridget wanted to hear about Jessie...did she look as if she was well?...but Phyllis was talking about Cedric and the dog. The dog had come around a corner at a good clip and knocked over Suzie Altman who was eighty five if she was a day, and in very good health but tiny, must not weigh over ninety pounds.

"Was she hurt?" Bridget asked.

"You bet she was hurt. Got a broken arm, putting it out to catch her fall. Her doctor told her to sue."

"But what is he doing in this neighborhood all the time? Don't tell me he's living with Jessie."

"No, no, he's moved into that house she bought him. Or the house she got him to buy. That nice green house on Spruce Street that has all the marguerite bushes in front."

Well, at least one part of Jessie's plan had come about.

"You spend more time worrying about that woman than you do about me," Norm accused when Bridget relayed this news. and he made a little pout so that Bridget kissed him reassuringly. In addition, she cooked a dinner of risotto and veal which he liked and refrained from talking about Jessie.

Why did she care so much? Her time in Jessie's life was over, and Jessie was off on a new chapter. Still, Bridget woke in the night in pain because she had dreamed that Jessie was in tears.

"You have to hear the latest!" Phyllis said a few days later.

They were at Phyllis's house, and when Don heard her tone of voice, he stood up and picked up his newspaper and went outside.

Bridget crossed her fingers and hoped it was good news. "All right, what is it?"

"Suzie Altman didn't want to file a lawsuit, but someone sent the police down to interview her anyway, and she told them how she got knocked over, so the animal control people went to Cedric's house and picked up the dog. He's being held as a dangerous animal."

"Was Cedric upset?"

"Oh, he was upset all right. He called an attorney to spring that stupid dog out of lockup but that failed. Don't you think he should be glad?"

Phyllis paused to think this over. "I was glad when I had to give Pudgie back to Animal Rescue. It was either him or Don. All right, I admit I was also sad." She shook her head in mystification. "Animals are not people. We shouldn't value them more than people."

"And they have the other two." Bridget nodded, remembering, almost affectionately, Tibby and Belvy with their heads sweeping along her coffee table. "They don't need a third one."

A couple of days later, Phyllis was able to add to the story.

"You'll never guess…"

"Okay, tell me."

"They won't let him have that dog. It's probably going to be put down. Cedric's all broken up about it. Jessie gets mad and yells at him, but he goes down to the pound every evening at dinner time and takes his own dinner and sits by the dog cage and cries while they have dinner side by side. Now did you ever hear of anything like that?"

"No." Bridget said.

Chapter Thirty-Two

"Bridget, she died," Phyllis said over the phone, her voice stunned.

"Who?" But Bridget's insides told her, her heart, her breath, her stomach, all stopped for a moment.

"This is what I heard. The medics came in the middle of the night. She must have called them herself because Cedric wasn't there. They took her out leaving the doors open and the lights on so Mimi went over to turn them off. And Mimi called Cedric but by the time he got to the hospital, Jessie was dead.

Bridget said nothing because she was crying. She remembered their race to the hospital to follow JR. But this time no one had been with Jessie when she needed someone. Cedric had been no help. Probably he had been the cause.

"I can't talk now. I'll have to call you later," she said.

All traces of Phyllis's delight at Jessie's problems were gone; she sounded close to tears herself. "I know, I know. Do you want me to come over there."

"Maybe. I don't know yet."

*   *   *

Bridget went with Marion to Jessie's funeral. Norm had a meeting in Boston with someone who was interested in a new idea of his and he had the tickets already.

"I'm sorry," he said. "I know she meant a lot to you, but I've put this guy off once before. I can't do it again."

"It's all right," Bridget nodded.

She didn't really want him to go with her. Norm hated funerals, always had. Plus his feeling about Jessie had not been particularly warm. He might say something slightly caustic that would make her feel worse.

Still she wanted to collect something for his absence. "You know, I'm interested in your new idea too. You need to make a place for me in this new company."

"I didn't know that." He looked flustered, but also interested. "You're right. We don't want to do what we did the last time."

"Exactly."

He came across the room to kiss and hold her. "Okay. What position do you want?"

"Really?"

"Yes. Think it over, and we'll talk about it when I get back."

Wasn't life amazing? To think she might have said this years ago, and everything would have been different. Or would it?

Jessie's funeral. The simple idea of it spread a throbbing pain in Bridget's head that no aspirin could touch. While she didn't want Norm, at the same time she wanted someone with her. She tried Phyllis, but Phyllis wasn't planning to go.

"I just hated the way she treated you. How could she do that after you were so good to her?"

"Was I?" Bridget wondered. She couldn't remember if she had treated Jessie any special way, only her own feelings - that Jessie had been someone so special that Bridget had been excited to be her friend. She had felt happy every time she was on her way to Jessie's house. And then, the times spent with Jessie and JR and their blossoming love were even better, the warmth of them, the delight of their laughter. Why was all that special to her? Was it just because she hadn't been in love herself for so long that simply being near it rewarded her?

"You have to go," she told Phyllis, "Not that many people will. You go with Don and I'll go with Marion."

That much she could do for Jessie, see that at least that a few people came to the funeral. Not let their quarrel be a blight on this last event.

"Please go with me to Jessie's funeral," Bridget said by phone to Marion.

"I was wondering if I should, if you were going. She wasn't very nice to you."

"Oh, that was long ago," Bridget said about the quarrel, amazed that even Marion had sided with her. Of course it wasn't nothing. It still hurt like a knife, but she could forgive that, remembering how desperately Jessie had been hurt at the loss of JR.

Marion came from work and picked Bridget up. She wore a black blouse with her purple skirt. "Do you think this is all right? I didn't have another thing black that would fit me."

Since their meeting in the library, they had become friends again, however unlikely that had seemed right after Jeb's death. But now Marion was an eager mind, interested in everything, curious, willing to try all sorts of things. She was taking the recommended short library course and would soon work full-time. She was also reading *The Atlantic Monthly*, *The New Yorker* and *The Nation* and was constantly astounded at inquiries into subjects she had never considered. She often debated these with Bridget who was now doing more reading while Norm puttered on his projects. It was fun to debate these subjects with Marion who was thinking that sometime in the future, she might like to be the book buyer, choosing new books for the library.

"It's too bad I wasn't reading these things when my children were in high school," she confided to Bridget. "I might have interested them in going on to college or trying something other than dead-end jobs."

Bridget thought that, luckily, her children had done their own inquiring. She had to admit that she had been lucky in her children. Probably not due to any special efforts of her own.

"You look fine," said Bridget, who was wearing navy blue because she didn't have anything black that fit. Her pocket was stuffed with tissues, just in case, and she wondered if she could possibly get through the ceremony without breaking down. She hoped JR would come. As far as she knew, nothing had been heard from him since he left Jessie's house in a taxi. So probably not. His daughter had succeeded in cutting him off from all these people who might have become his friends. Or, perhaps he had died.

"Who arranged the funeral?" Bridget asked, because Marion had been talking to the neighbors.

"Her daughter came back from Africa just that day she died, expecting to see her mother and never saw her alive. Isn't that a pity? And she brought an Englishman with her. Says he's her fiancé'. They're staying in Jessie's house. So you didn't see her at all these last months?"

"She didn't want to. She thought I had criticized her boyfriend."

"I thought you liked him so much."

"No, this was her last boyfriend. A man named Cedric."

"Yes, I heard about him. He's very broken up they say. Did you criticize him?"

"I guess I did, in a way."

And there Cedric was, standing just outside the door to the church, attired in a perfectly beautiful black suit, his distinguished head above the crowds, his face covered with tears.

At least she could do this much. Bridget went up to him immediately. "I'm so sorry," she said, taking his hand.

She meant sorry for both things - that when he came to her house, things had not gone well, and then that Jessie had died. She wanted to explain but knew she couldn't without bursting into tears.

He turned his handsome eyes on her and did not recognize her.

"I'm Bridget," she said. "Jessie's friend. You came to my house."

He continued to cry. Bridget stood there in front of him, wanting to offer some peace, some help, but not knowing how. That he did not recognize her indicated all her doubts about him as a solace for Jessie had been right. She felt frozen by the predicament. Marion stood helplessly by her side.

"Hey, come on, Dad," a young man in his early thirties, equally handsome, came up and took Cedric's arm and led him inside.

"That's him, isn't it? The last boyfriend, the one with the dog." Marion whispered. "The developer..."

"Yes, Cedric." Probably responsible for her death, Bridget thought angrily. Oh, I am going to cry! She was determined to put it off as long as possible.

"He looks a little gaga. What did she want with him?"

"It's a long story."

Side by side, they went into the big, formal Presbyterian Church which offered little in association with Jessie. Bridget couldn't remember Jessie ever talking about churches. This must be the choice of the daughter, or maybe of the Englishman.

The coffin in front of the altar was closed.

"What do you think she's wearing?" Marion asked.

Bridget shushed her, afraid someone might hear this. Then she began to wonder also. Jessie had such beautiful clothes.

"Maybe the grey Armani suit," she whispered finally and felt her eyelids begin to prickle. The thought of the suit brought a fresh image of Jessie, of her beautiful mouth puffed out when she was about to make a joke, her graceful hands, the way she stood, her eyelids (usually green), her perfect hair. Her throaty voice. All that gone away. Dear God! How terrible!

Clustered near the front, about forty people – many more than Bridget had expected - sat quietly, some fanning themselves though the day was cool. Sitting alone up front was a thin, blonde young woman in rumpled clothing. That must be the daughter, looking awkward and impatient, with none of Jessie's style. And where was the Englishman?

There were some mourners obviously from Shady Acres, in Dacron slacks and blouses worn over the waistline. She saw Mimi and one she thought was named Francine, the rest she didn't know. Then there was a small group of men and women sitting tightly together, carefully dressed for business, in dark colors for the funeral. Those would be from her office, realtors planning to go back to work.

She hadn't thought about Jessie's office, that there were those people who saw her nearly daily, maybe over years. And what did they think of her?

There were other people not easily placed. Maybe trades people or her housekeeper. Had her ex-husband come? But surely he would sit up front with the daughter? Did Jessie have other relatives? Or were they people who had bought houses from her?

There were pots of white chrysanthemums placed across the front; a few candles were lighted, and the coffin was there on a stand in the center.

Tears came to Bridget's eyes. Not now. Not now. She remembered how Jessie had looked in the parking lot, trying to hold onto JR's hand. Trying to hold onto happiness. Oh, this was too much.

"Aren't you going to speak?" someone whispered.

And there was Phyllis, almost fashionable in a black cotton dress, along with Don wearing a plaid sports jacket and a string tie. The jacket was too big for him, perhaps borrowed from his son.

Bridget whispered. "I'm glad you came. Sit down."

"Oh, I thought I should," Phyllis said. "It's just I didn't like the way she treated you."

Bridget nodded acceptance of Phyllis as she was. "Well, it's too late to let her know."

She and Marion moved in two seats and let Phyllis and Don sit next to the aisle.

Bridget watched those two glance at each other, a glance full of meanings only they knew, as they settled in their seats. She thought for the first time that Phyllis looked very different than she had six months ago. Of course. She was in love. This was love that worked, that satisfied, as it had between Jessie and JR. As it was working between Norm and her. Wasn't that wonderful? Cedric had only proved that there was no substitute.

But that was the proof - Jessie's overwhelming desire to replace JR and have it all again – that showed how remarkable love was. Even if it came very late in life, there was nothing else like it. It made all life worthwhile.

The minister came out in his black suit and stood beside the coffin. Bridget took the hands of both Marion and Phyllis, thought about Norm, and held back her tears.

The service began.

##

Printed in the United States
141792LV00004B/2/P